Praise for the novels of Jackie Lau

"Heartfelt and hilarious . . . Lau brings the goods."
—*Publishers Weekly* (starred review)

"Lau's books have some of the best effort-to-emotional-payoff ratios in romance."
—*The New York Times Book Review*

"Masterful, inspiring, and full of heart!"
—Ali Hazelwood, *New York Times* bestselling author of *The Love Hypothesis*

"Anyone who loves baking and rom-coms will breeze through this flavorful read."
—*USA Today*

"The perfect proportions of emotion, heat, family ties, and romance to make one absolutely delicious treat."
—Courtney Milan, *New York Times* bestselling author of *The Earl Who Isn't*

"A quintessential comfort read, full of good, well-intentioned people attempting to navigate complicated family relationships, careers, friendships, and grief."
—Olivia Dade, national bestselling author of *Spoiler Alert*

"The perfect fake dating romance! Full of banter and sexual tension, Jackie Lau's books feature richly drawn characters who completely captivate me."
—Falon Ballard, author of *Right on Cue*

"Jackie Lau's deft touch weaves together heart and charm . . . filled with appealing (and hilarious) side characters, emotional complexity, and Lau's trademark humor, resulting in an enchanting and satisfying read."
—Lily Chu, author of *The Stand-In*

"Fun, funny, and nuanced."
—Cathy Yardley, auth

T0349077

Time Loops & Meet Cutes

a novel

JACKIE LAU

EMILY BESTLER BOOKS

ATRIA

New York Amsterdam/Antwerp London
Toronto Sydney/Melbourne New Delhi

EMILY
BESTLER
BOOKS

ATRIA

An Imprint of Simon & Schuster, LLC
1230 Avenue of the Americas
New York, NY 10020

For Dad

part one

Girl Meets Boy

1

Noelle

Sometimes I feel like a poorly planned design project, the sort cobbled together by engineering students pulling an all-nighter, possibly held in place by the miracle of duct tape. It might work under very specific conditions, but it could be knocked over by a stiff breeze.

Except in my case, I'm held together by routine and caffeine. Although I might seem calm on the outside, I have a sneaking suspicion that I can't deal with anything approaching an emergency, or even a minor surprise.

I take another sip of my tea and stare at the computer. I should do some work so I can get out of the office at a half-decent time, rather than ruminating on the state of my life.

"Last one here again?" Fernando asks as he heads to the door at six.

I paste on a smile. "Yep. Just want to get this proposal finished." Then I'll read through it over the weekend, and it'll be ready to go out on Monday.

"Don't stay too late. It's Friday, after all."

"I'll be done soon."

That's a lie. I've got at least another hour of work to do on this proposal, since Tyler did a piss-poor job. That man is the bane of my existence. I was supposed to just look over his work, but I've had to rewrite much of what I've read so far. As usual.

I reach the "Cost" section and find only blank space under the heading. Since I'm alone in the office, I release a little howl of frustration, then get on with what I do best: keeping my head down and doing the work. It'll pay off eventually.

Tyler waltzed out of here at four thirty, but I don't leave Woods & Olson Engineering until after seven. As I pack up my laptop and lock the door behind me, I realize I haven't eaten since lunch. I stuff my hand into my bag and come up with two mints and a granola bar wrapper that I forgot to throw in the trash. Hmph. The Jamaican patty place near the office is closed, and I don't feel like delaying my trip home any longer—I want to put on my pajamas and turn on the TV—so I head to the nearest TTC station and get on the subway.

My stomach, however, keeps growling, which I don't understand. It's used to me forgetting to eat, and it's usually better behaved than this. But today, I'm so hungry I can barely pay attention to a podcast. I take out my earbuds with a sigh. My usual routine is to go right home after work, but maybe I can do something different for once. There's a night market this weekend, not far from the station before mine—I saw signs for it earlier. Yes, I'll do something fun on a Friday for once. By myself, but still.

Unfortunately, the thought of what food I might find there makes my stomach growl even louder, but at least I have a plan.

My friend Veronica—I really should text her—used to talk about the night markets she'd visited on her trips to Seoul and Singapore, but I've never left North America. This market in the north part of Toronto won't be like those, but surely they'll have something good.

When I get to Mel Lastman Square, the place is crowded

with booths and people and mouthwatering fragrances. The first booth I examine is selling upscale bánh mì for prices that make me clutch my wallet. The second has a selection of ube treats, the purple hue particularly tempting, but I need something other than sugar. I get jostled while trying to read the menu for the third booth, which has a long line—too long for my hungry stomach.

Before I turn up the next row, I see someone wearing a Pocky box costume, then a young man and woman feeding each other satay sticks. She holds one up to his mouth, and he nibbles off a piece of meat before she tries it herself. A young kid bumps into her, but she doesn't notice. They're off in their little love bubble.

I roll my eyes and continue. I see booths selling noodles, samosas, mochi . . . all with several people out front. Then I come to a booth that has no customers and no sign. There's only one woman working here, and she looks old enough to be my grandmother. On a piece of white printer paper, a menu is scribbled in blue ballpoint pen.

Dumplings: $5

No explanation of what kind of dumplings are on offer. It doesn't fit with the rest of the businesses here, which all have nice, clear signage. But dumplings do sound good, there's no line, and it's not expensive, though how many I'll get for the price, I don't know. I step closer to the booth, and the woman says something to me in Mandarin, I think.

Before I can explain that I don't speak it, she switches to English. "You want dumplings? They give you what you need most."

Well, what I need most is food to ease my hunger, so yes, they should do the trick.

"What kind?" I ask.

"Anything you don't eat?"

I shake my head.

"I choose for you." She taps her temple before pointing to a sheet of paper that says "Cash Only."

That's probably another reason the booth isn't busy: a lot of people don't carry cash anymore, but I always do. I pull out some money and hand it over.

"You come back in fifteen minutes, yes?"

My eyes widen. Fifteen minutes might as well be an hour to my stomach. There are boiled dumplings in a metal tray—why can't I have some of those?

"You don't need to cook them fresh," I say.

She clucks her tongue. "Trust me. Better this way."

Since she seems so insistent, I nod.

I walk around the rest of the night market, in a bit of a daze because I'm so ravenous. I'm also thirsty, so I buy some calamansi iced tea. I've drunk most of it by the time I return to the dumpling booth, which is still empty. The elderly woman is bent over, scooping some pan-fried dumplings into a paper food tray. Her hand shakes slightly. After giving me the food, she gestures to the soy sauce and vinegar jars. I help myself and grab some chopsticks.

"Thank you," I say.

I swear I can feel her watching me as I seek out a place to eat. Since the nearby benches are full, I simply stand at the end of a row of booths.

At the first bite of dumpling, I groan. Oh my god, that was definitely worth the wait. Juicy pork and vegetables . . . and something else that I can't pinpoint. It's a little different from any dumpling I've had before—and I've had a lot of dumplings. If I weren't so hungry, I'd try to figure it out.

I pick up the second dumpling with my chopsticks, and it's

somehow even better than the first. Or maybe I'm just better able to appreciate it because I'm not quite as famished now.

By the time I get to the sixth dumpling, my pace has slowed, and I'm taking my time to appreciate how good these dumplings are. I'm also eyeing the food that the other market-goers are carrying. I see ice cream, donuts . . . and that same young couple again, sharing a cup with alternating white and green layers. Matcha tiramisu?

After finishing my dumplings, I discard the tray in the overflowing trash bin and continue walking around the market. I'm feeling too stingy for some picture-perfect cupcakes, but I happen upon a small stall selling flavored pandesal and decide one of those would be an appropriate, not-too-extravagant treat. I also happen upon, miracle of miracles, a half-empty bench. A man and a toddler are sitting on one end, but the other half is open.

After taking a seat, I bite into my ube halaya pandesal. It's fluffy and buttery and even better than I expected. I close my eyes and savor it, then debate whether to get another one for breakfast tomorrow, eventually deciding that I should. I wince a little as I hand over some coins in exchange for a second pandesal, but it smells heavenly. I pack the bag into my purse, careful not to crush it.

Today is the longest day of the year, the summer solstice, and as dusk finally falls on the market, there's an almost magical quality to it. The lights, the faint music, the crowds enjoying their food. The scent of grilled meat and fried food is nearly enough to make me hungry again, even if my stomach is pleasantly full. As I wind my way to the subway station, I pass the dumpling lady. She smiles at me and I smile back. Still no customers at the booth, which is curious, even if it's cash only and the signage leaves a little to be desired.

By the time I get off the bus, it's almost ten. I begin the short walk home, and when I see a car whose bumper is precariously held together by duct tape, I chuckle. I wonder how long that will last.

Back at my apartment, I pack the pandesal into a container, take off my work clothes, have a shower, and flop into bed. Another long day at the office, though at least I did something to celebrate the fact that it's Friday, and tomorrow, I can sleep in. Then I'll spend a couple of hours on that proposal, buy some groceries, call my parents . . .

My list of things to do running through my head, I fall asleep.

June

Cam

I'm in the kitchen, leaning against the counter and having a midnight snack—the ube cheesecake that I bought at the market—when Justin returns. We've been roommates for years now, and while having a roommate and living in an old high-rise is not where I thought I'd be in my thirties, I don't mind. It's nice to have someone else around.

"Hey. How was your date?" I ask before sliding another bite into my mouth. I'm eating out of the cardboard box because I'm classy like that.

"Good," Justin says as he pours himself some water. "Really, really good."

"Two 'reallys,' eh?"

Justin looks like he's fighting a goofy smile. I don't know why he's bothering to fight it; I certainly wouldn't if I were in his position, but he's a little more cautious than me when it comes to these things.

"What about your evening?" he asks. "Your meeting went well?"

"Sure." If Justin doesn't want to talk about his first date, I'll let him off the hook . . . for now. "They've got a couple of weekends in August that'll work. I'll add it to the schedule tomorrow."

I went to the night market to talk to someone about bringing their food truck to the brewery later this summer. I also sampled some of their bao and got bulgogi poutine from another vendor before buying a slice of cheesecake to take home with me. The vibe of the market was really cool, especially as it got dark. I love how food and drink bring people together. That's part of what drew me to the industry.

I also loved the red Pocky box costume that I saw someone wearing. When I arrived home, I tried to find a place to buy it online, but nothing immediately came up. Maybe I'll have to make one myself. It would be awesome for Halloween. I've worn my inflatable unicorn costume for a few years now, and I need something new.

Justin and I talk for a few more minutes—he still doesn't let any details slip about his mystery man—before he turns in for the night. I do too. I'm not tired, but I should sleep because tomorrow is a busy day. Every day is a little different at the brewery that I started with Justin and Darrell, and I like it that way. I used to have a job where all my days were so similar, and they seemed to bleed into one another. It's not like that now. Of course there are some terrible days—Tuesday, for example, was one crisis after another—but we get through them.

As I roll onto my side and try to get some shut-eye, my mind flits back to the market. I wish I could have tried all the food there, but alas, my stomach is only so big, and I won't have time to go back tomorrow. For example, there were some satay sticks with peanut sauce that looked delicious. I saw a young couple eating those, and they looked like they were really enjoying them—or maybe they were more enjoying each other. I felt a sliver of envy before I shrugged and moved on.

Ah, well. So it goes.

I wonder how long it'll take me to make that Pocky costume.

2

Noelle

Beep! Beep! Beep!

Why do I hear my alarm? It's Saturday.

Annoyed, I turn it off and curl up under the covers, but half an hour later, I'm still awake. I climb out of bed with a sigh, put on some clothes, and turn on the coffeemaker. As I'm waiting for my caffeine, I pick up my phone and pull up Wordle. I use my usual starting word—I'm a creature of habit—and just like yesterday, I get one green letter and one yellow. I do the same second word.

Huh, that's odd.

For my third word, I do "campy," like I did yesterday. Three green letters. Again. Could it be . . . ?

I type *h-a-p-p-y*, and sure enough, it's the word.

Hmm. The site must be broken, but just to be sure, I look at the calendar on my phone.

June 20.

What?

How is it June 20? That was yesterday. Something must be wrong with my phone. The date got messed up, and that's why Wordle loaded the wrong word. Hurriedly, I turn on my work laptop at the kitchen table. I type in my PIN and look at the date in the bottom right-hand corner of the screen.

June 20.

Is someone playing a trick on me?

I open up the proposal, and it quickly becomes apparent that something is wrong here too. I know I have the latest version on my laptop, yet all the changes that Tyler and I made yesterday? They've vanished.

No, no, no.

I'll have to redo it all.

I go to my inbox. The email I got early yesterday morning isn't . . .

Oh. There it is. It just came in.

I pour myself a mug of coffee. At least my coffeemaker is still working properly, and I have that delicious pandesal for breakfast. I remember setting it on the counter, right next to the fruit bowl. Except the fruit bowl contains three oranges when it should only have two, and the pandesal is nowhere to be found.

And that does it.

"Fuck!" I cry.

What the hell is going on? Nothing makes sense.

I call my parents.

"Noelle?" Mom says. "Is something wrong? It's seven thirty in the morning."

I ignore her question. "What day is it?"

"June twentieth."

"Are you sure?"

"Yes, I'm sure. Is—"

"Sorry, got to go."

I end the call and cover my face with my hands. All the evidence points toward it being June 20 again, but how could that be possible? Am I losing it?

No. There must be an explanation. Maybe I just had a very vivid dream last night. I dreamed June 20 before it happened . . .

and somehow, my subconscious even knew the answer to today's Wordle.

Yes, that must be it. It was simply a vivid dream and an unlikely coincidence.

And since it's actually Friday, I have to go to work.

I finish my coffee and cereal, then get changed and head to the office, where I have a sense of déjà vu all day. For example, I know at four twenty that Tyler is about to come over to my desk and tell me that the proposal is ready. Even before I read it, I know exactly what mistakes he's made. And I know what Fernando will say as he heads to the door at six o'clock, while I'm furiously typing.

"Last one here again?"

"Just want to get this proposal finished," I say.

"Don't stay too late. It's Friday, after all."

It's like my dream is becoming reality . . . or was it already reality?

"What day was yesterday?" I ask Fernando. I try to sound composed, even though I'm freaking out internally.

He tilts his head and gives me an odd look. I can't blame him.

"Thursday," he replies.

"The nineteenth?"

"Yes, Thursday, the nineteenth. Why?"

"Oh, the date on my calendar is messed up. Just wanted to check. Thanks."

I finish the proposal and head out just after seven. I debate whether to go to the night market, eventually deciding that I should. I'm starving, and it's on the way home.

The market is exactly as I remember. The crowds, the person in a Pocky box costume, the young couple with their satay sticks.

Goose bumps break out on my skin, despite the warm night. This is wrong. I seem to be reliving the same day, but nobody else thinks anything's amiss. They're all going on with their lives as though this is perfectly normal.

But one thing is different: the dumpling booth is nowhere to be found.

"Excuse me," I say to the man at the next booth. "Was there a woman selling dumplings here earlier?"

"There's a dumpling stand over there." He points to the left.

"No, no. Was there one *here*? With an older woman?"

"Uh, no. I'm the last one in this row."

"But—"

I snap my mouth shut before I sound even more ridiculous, then open it again to order some noodles. I eat them standing up and consider the situation.

It must have something to do with those sketchy dumplings. They didn't *taste* sketchy, and my stomach didn't complain afterward. But the booth had no name, and there were no other customers.

Those dumplings must have had the power to send me back in time.

Don't be silly, Noelle. That's impossible.

I try to calm myself down by perusing the other offerings at the market. The pandesal was good, though, so I return to that booth and buy two. I sit down at the same bench as before, near the man and his son, and bite into my food. It's just as delicious as it was the first time. Once I've finished, I consider eating the other one. After all, there's no guarantee I'll actually get to eat it if I bring it home. Because what if this happens again, and when I wake up tomorrow, all evidence of today has been removed?

At the thought of having to fix the proposal yet again, I feel exhausted to the bone. What the hell is happening? I don't want to live this day again. I don't want to stay late at the office again. I just *can't*.

My hand clenches around a paper napkin. Around me, people are laughing, smiling, enjoying some food on a warm summer's night. I feel removed from it all, sitting here alone and freaking out. It's ironic, perhaps, that repeating the day is disrupting my routine, but there it is.

A tear leaks out of my eye, and I wipe it away.

"Hey."

I look up. There's an East Asian man crouched on the ground, about a meter away from me. He has a concerned smile on his face and a tray of food in his hand.

"Are you okay?" he asks.

I nod, because *I think I'm trapped in a time loop* isn't the sort of thing you can say to a stranger. At least, not without them concluding you're in even worse shape than they initially feared.

The stranger is about my age. He's dressed in jeans and a T-shirt. He doesn't look as if the duct tape holding him together has been ripped off; he doesn't look as if he's freaking out because the day is repeating itself. I seem to be the only one with that problem.

Though since I didn't eat the dumplings today, maybe tomorrow actually will be June 21. The fact that the booth isn't here suggests that the dumplings did, indeed, have something to do with my weird predicament. It seems like the most logical conclusion, even if it's utterly preposterous.

I imagine how I must look to him. Dark brown hair that reaches below my shoulders. Ambiguously Asian features—I have been mistaken for a wide variety of ethnicities over the years. Slightly red eyes, thanks to the crying. An unremarkable thirty-two-year-old woman, despite the remarkable, terrifying thing that seems to be happening to me.

"Is there anything I can get for you?" he asks.

I shake my head, and he hesitates before standing up and walking away.

When I get home, I put the ube halaya pandesal in a container, make sure my alarm isn't on, and change into my blue plaid pajama shorts—the last two nights, I wore my red ones. I'm not sure I'll be able to fall asleep, worried as I am, but eventually, I do.

Once again, I wake up to my alarm.

And once again, I'm wearing red plaid shorts.

Shit.

3

Noelle

June 20, Version 3

Wordle taunts me with *h-a-p-p-y*, and all my work on the proposal is gone. I want to tear out my hair in frustration because it feels like nothing I do matters. It'll all be erased tomorrow . . . when I repeat June 20 rather than actually getting to June 21.

I slump in my kitchen chair as I sip my coffee. What's the point in repeating the day if I can't make any progress on that proposal? Why even bother going to the office?

Seriously. Why bother working?

I freeze as a terrible idea overtakes me. In the decade since I started working for Woods & Olson, I've only taken a single sick day. A handful of times when I wasn't feeling well, I worked from home rather than going in. Last time, I remember racing to the washroom to throw up, then returning to my living room fifteen minutes later to review some drawings. I am a dedicated employee. You can count on me to get shit done.

Yet here I am, telling my boss via email that I'm too sick to work.

Though maybe it's not a lie. Being stuck in a single day could be a form of illness. But this isn't all in my mind, right? I mean, Wordle is the same. That's proof. My pajamas. The missing pandesal, which I definitely put on my counter last night. They're all proof.

What exactly is happening?

I'm an engineer. I can figure this out.

My first task is to prove that this is working how I think it is. Test my hypotheses. Scientific method and all that. I start composing a to-do list, which I assume won't exist tomorrow—my first hypothesis.

Write a few sentences in the proposal. Confirm that once again, they're missing tomorrow.

Rewatch a few episodes of *The Office*. Hypothesis: tomorrow, Netflix won't remember where I am in the series.

Text Dalton. Hypothesis: tomorrow, today's text conversation with my brother will have disappeared.

Tell my parents something and see if they remember it tomorrow. Hypothesis: they won't.

Buy something with my credit card. Hypothesis: tomorrow, there will be no record of it.

Speaking of money . . . I open my wallet and check how much cash I have. There's a ten-dollar bill, but I know I used my last ten buying noodles yesterday.

I can buy whatever I want. There are no consequences.

That way of thinking leads to danger. Besides, this is only my third June 20. I have to confirm that if I use my credit card, the transaction will be erased tomorrow. I'm pretty confident in my hypothesis, but I need to be certain.

Plus, focusing on the list will be good for me. It'll give me a purpose and prevent me from freaking out too much.

After a leisurely breakfast, I write a mere three sentences in the proposal before shutting down my laptop. I feel guilty for not doing more work. It's not in my nature to do the bare minimum, but what's the point?

Then I text my brother to ask when I can visit this weekend. Dalton replies that tomorrow afternoon would work. His tomorrow is different from my tomorrow, but regardless, I can test my hypothesis.

Next, I call my parents' landline. My father picks up.

My dad worked as a high school English teacher before retiring a year ago. He was born in the early sixties to poor Chinese immigrants, and people were often surprised that he spoke English "without an accent"—which makes no sense because everyone has some kind of accent—let alone that he loved teaching *Macbeth*. My mother, who's white, is probably more what those people would expect of a high school English teacher, but she used to work at a community center.

My mom and dad were, in many ways, good parents, but they were always trying to help everyone, and they weren't great at budgeting. It was stressful.

"Noelle!" Dad says. "This is a pleasant surprise. Are you at the office?"

"No, I'm sick."

"You're working from home?"

"No, I'm just . . . not working."

I've rendered my father speechless. "Is everything okay?"

Ha! Somehow, I manage not to laugh hysterically.

"Yes." I cough, trying to sell this *I am sick* thing. "I'm fine. I mean, I'm not fine, but nothing you need to worry about. I just figured, well, maybe I would get better more quickly if I actually rested for a day."

"And now you're bored, which is why you called."

I don't contradict him, but in actuality, I'm testing a hypothesis. I've now told my dad that I'm sick. We'll see if he remembers tomorrow.

"I was also wondering," I say, "if you had any reading recommendations. For anything about the meaning of today and tomorrow. The passage of time. Philosophy, perhaps."

Once again, he's speechless.

"Not off the top of my head," he says at last, "but I'll think about it and get back to you. If you need us to bring you anything, just let us know." He pauses. "Have you spoken to your sister recently?"

"No, I haven't talked to Madison in a few weeks."

We talk for a little longer, and then I make myself a cup of tea and watch three hours of *The Office*.

———

By four in the afternoon, I'm practically climbing the walls and wondering how the hell my father copes with retirement. I almost turn on my work laptop because I don't know what to do with myself, but I'm pretty sure any work I do is futile.

I buy a paperback from Amazon, and I can see the purchase pending on my credit card.

Now what?

I've completed my list, though I have to wait until tomorrow to see if my predictions are correct. I'm fairly confident they are, but I don't know *why* this is happening. And why is it happening to *me*? Nobody else seems to have any memory of the previous versions of this day. I'm all alone here.

I still have a weird feeling it has something to do with those dumplings, so I pull up the website for the night market and study the vendor listings. There are two dumpling stands, but neither is the right one.

The market opens at six, so I decide to head over and see if

I can find the old woman and her dumplings. Unfortunately, a security incident on the TTC means that I end up walking more than planned, but eventually I get to the market, and all the same booths are here . . . except hers. Just like last night.

"What the fuck?" I mutter, and the person in the Pocky costume gives me a look.

This time, I get bibimbap for dinner and manage to find a seat. For a split second, I wonder if that means this day isn't exactly like the last one, but then I remember that I'm here earlier than the last two times. Surely if I stay awhile, I'll see the young couple sharing satay sticks, but I don't intend to hang around long.

A woman walks by, carrying three trays of food and a drink, and a toddler whizzes out of nowhere, right into her path. She swerves to avoid him, but she drops her drink. Green liquid— was it a matcha latte?—spills onto the ground. I assume that accident also happened yesterday, before I arrived at the market.

Not sure what else to do with myself, I head home and go to bed early.

The next morning, I wake up to my alarm and check on my experiments.

There's no evidence of the three sentences I wrote in the proposal.

Netflix doesn't remember where I am in *The Office*.

My most recent text to my brother is dated June 17.

There is no record of my Amazon purchase.

The list I made doesn't exist.

There's still one more thing to check. I call my parents' landline, and once again, my dad picks up.

"Noelle! This is a pleasant surprise. Are you at the office?"

"No, I'm sick."

This is apparently a surprise to him.

The conversation continues as it did yesterday, except I don't ask him for any book recommendations. Instead, I blurt out, "Have you ever been stuck in a time loop?"

"Uh . . ."

I'll take that as a "no." I was just wondering if there's a genetic component to this. Like, maybe people in my family are particularly susceptible to being stuck in time loops or . . . something. Yeah, that sounds like a science fiction book I might have read back in the day, but I'm desperate. I don't know what's happening, and I hate the unknown.

"Never mind, never mind. Talk to you later!" I say before ending the call.

I could, of course, try to tell him the truth. I'm not sure what his reaction would be. I'm the organized one. The sensible one. The calm and responsible one. Saying I'm stuck in a time loop would be wildly out of character.

I curl up on the futon and put on *The Office*. Even if Netflix doesn't remember where I am in the show, I do. I select the right episode and press play, but I don't really pay attention to what's on-screen.

Everything feels meaningless.

It's just me in this time loop, from what I can tell. If I told someone about it, even if they believed me, they'd forget again tomorrow, and then I'd have to explain it all over again, and the thought just makes me tired. And lonely. I'm used to spending lots of time by myself, but I'm not used to feeling so alone in the world.

They give you what you need most, the old woman said.

If she really is responsible, what the hell was she trying to accomplish? Is what I need most really to be huddled in front of my TV, mindlessly watching a sitcom on a weekday?

Or maybe she thought I needed to live life as if there are no consequences. I've never done that before. It doesn't make any sense to live that way; there are always consequences.

Spontaneously quit your job? You won't be able to pay your bills.

Eat an entire large meat lover's pizza? You'll feel sick.

Get drunk? You'll be hungover.

Don't do your homework? You'll get a bad mark.

I'm used to looking before I leap. But if I have to be stuck in on June 20, maybe I can afford not to think about the consequences for once, though I can't imagine why this would be a good thing. It reminds me of my uncle, who passed away a couple of years ago. His life was always in shambles due to his terrible decisions.

That evening, while making myself a simple dinner—I don't bother going to the night market again—I accidentally nick my finger. It's not terribly painful, but it's bloody. As I put on a bandage, I realize it's the perfect way to test the time loop further.

Hypothesis: when I wake up tomorrow morning, there will be no dinosaur bandage. (I usually don't buy dinosaur bandages, but they were the cheapest ones the last time I went to the pharmacy.) There will be no mark on my skin either.

Indeed, my hypothesis is confirmed the next morning, and somehow, this is what makes my new reality truly sink in: the lack of consequences, even when it comes to my body.

My life is now a strange, strange place. I no longer feel like Noelle Tom, responsible eldest daughter and engineer. No, I'm . . .

Who *am* I?

4

Noelle

June 20, Version 6

I treat myself to a meal at an upscale sushi restaurant and spend the afternoon wondering if I've completely lost my mind. The day after that is similar, except I eat at a steak house that I've never dared to set foot in before.

The following day, I go to a French bistro.

"The moules-frites, please," I tell the server, "and a glass—no, a bottle of wine."

"Which bottle?" he asks.

I point randomly at the list of whites.

"Will anyone else be joining you?"

"Nope, it's just me," I say brightly.

I feel a bit weird for ordering a bottle of wine for myself at noon on a Friday, but whatever. Everyone—except me—will have forgotten within twelve hours or so.

I've never ordered a bottle of wine at a restaurant before. My ex once suggested that we do so on our anniversary, and I frowned and said, "Why? It's cheaper at the liquor store."

I don't know shit about wine, but I do quite like the one I randomly selected. I sip it as I read a novel. When my food arrives, I slide my e-reader back into my purse and indulge in my mussels in tomato-wine broth, plus perfectly cooked fries with a generous amount of salt. Do they taste better than usual because I'm tipsy?

I don't bother finishing the bottle. Three glasses are enough for me. I wince as I hand over my credit card, then remind myself that it doesn't matter.

A long afternoon without plans stretches out before me. I don't know how to fill it, so I ask myself a question that I've never asked before: What would Madison do?

My sister might get a crazy haircut and quit her job.

A haircut isn't a bad idea. I've always wanted to try a pixie cut, but I don't know if I could pull it off. Now I can give it a spin without any consequences, it seems. I walk to the nearest salon.

"I'd like to make an appointment for a cut," I say to the receptionist.

She looks me up and down. I'm not sure what, exactly, she's assessing.

"Our junior stylist has a bunch of openings for next Wednesday."

"It has to be today," I say.

"Lina did have a cancellation . . ."

The salon is named after Lina, so I suspect she's the most expensive, and I must look like someone who doesn't spend much money on my hair. In fact, I used to do it myself, but the results weren't great. I eventually decided that having someone else cut my hair a few times a year was an acceptable use of money.

"I'll take it," I say. "When—"

"Come back in half an hour."

Unsure what else to do, I head to the bubble tea shop two doors down. I order a milk tea with both tapioca and jellies. Once again, a ridiculous indulgence. As I wait for my order, I pull out my phone and look for a podcast, but there are no new episodes of my favorite one, because of course there aren't. It might never be updated again, which is a sobering thought.

Well, only a little sobering. I'm still feeling those three glasses of wine.

"—Iron Goddess milk tea with pearls," says a voice.

There's something about that voice that makes my head snap up. It's familiar, and I can hear the smile in it.

Sure enough, the new customer is smiling. Everything about him says that he's a guy who's relaxed about life. When he notices me looking in his direction, he gives me a pleasant nod before tapping his credit card to pay for his order.

Ah, that's why he sounds familiar! He's the man who asked if I was okay at the market. Curious that I've now seen him in two different places, but it's not like I've seen him in two places at the same time. Maybe this is just what he does on June 20: he has bubble tea in the early afternoon, then goes to the night market later on. A coincidence, nothing more.

After placing his order, this rather cute guy—fine, yes, I admit he's cute—looks over at me . . . and keeps looking. He tilts his head and his smile disappears. "Have we met before?"

He doesn't remember our encounter at the market, but he seems to have a vague memory of me. Interesting. After all I've been through in the past few days, it's nearly enough to make me throw my arms around him.

But rather than explaining the weirdness that is my life, I shake my head.

———

"Do you like it?" Lina asks as we look in the mirror together.

"I do," I say.

My head feels so much lighter. A new me. Temporarily.

I pay for the haircut and add a generous tip, then head toward the night market. At a booth run by a Singaporean café, I'm tempted by the kopi, even though I don't usually drink coffee after five o'clock. That could have actual consequences: I might not be able to fall sleep.

Though it might be a good idea to stay up later than usual. See how this time loop actually works. Does it reset at midnight? Two in the morning? Whenever I fall asleep? What happens if I don't fall asleep? Will I break the time loop? Will I have to stay up forever?

Just as my thoughts start spiraling, it's my turn to order. I ask for a kopi. It's delicious, and since there's no one else in line, I figure I can indulge myself again.

"Another one," I say.

After my second kopi, I'm wired, to put it mildly. A now-familiar child darts into my path, and I manage to avoid him, as does the woman carrying lots of food. But once again, her drink is a casualty.

Yep, everything is exactly as it was yesterday, down to the missing dumpling booth. But there's a white woman with pink hair standing where the booth should be, and I don't think I've seen her before, though maybe I just wasn't paying attention.

—

I'm not used to staying up late, and I'm not sure how to fill the time. A part of me itches to be productive, so I sit at the desk in my living room, turn on my work computer, and pull up the proposal that Tyler emailed me when he left at four thirty. If I'm able to break the time loop, the work I do won't be in vain.

With a cup of herbal tea to keep me company and my hands shaking slightly—thanks to all the earlier caffeine, I presume—I get to work. I correct Tyler's copious errors. There are four errors in the first sentence alone. Then I start adding all the things that he missed.

I've tried to talk to Tyler about the quality of his work before. I've worked here a lot longer than he has—he only gradu-ated a year ago—and I'm supposed to be a mentor to him. It's not just his writing either; everything he does is sloppy. He just laughs and says he'll do better next time, then never does, leav-ing me to clean it up.

By eleven, I'm relatively pleased with the proposal. I need to read it over again, but it's good for now. I back it up in about six different ways, then turn off my computer, change into my pajamas, and rewatch an episode of *Murdoch Mysteries*. I start a second episode, but I keep looking at my phone. 11:59 . . .

Midnight. Nothing happens.

Well, that was anticlimactic, and I'll have to waste more time, which is something I'm not adept at doing. When the episode ends, I turn off the TV and return to reading the book that I started at the restaurant today.

One o'clock rolls around, and I'm still here in my blue pa-jama shorts.

By two, my eyes are drooping, but I have to stay awake. My phone says it's June 21, and I feel a surge of hope. Maybe if I stay awake for a few more hours, I won't go back in time.

Then I remember that I spent rather a lot of money today—a bottle of wine at lunch, a not-so-cheap haircut—and those charges might not go away if the loop is broken. Should I just try to fall asleep?

No. I've gotten this far. I won't give up. I'm not a quitter. Never have been. Besides, I have the money in my account. I'll be able to save less than usual this month, but that's okay.

I make myself a large cup of coffee and return to the futon. It's getting hard to focus on the book, though it's easier than usual to believe in aliens and spaceships that travel at the speed of light. Anything seems possible right now, perhaps even see-ing the sunrise on June 21.

As it approaches three o'clock, my stomach starts to rumble. By the time it's five minutes to three, I'm getting quite hungry. I pad to the kitchen, open the fridge . . .

The next thing I know, I'm in bed and my alarm is going off. *Fuck.*

5

Noelle

June 20, Version 9

Strangely, I feel like I got six or seven hours of sleep, and I don't notice the effects of the caffeine and booze I consumed yesterday. Or the previous iteration of today, whatever you want to call it.

I check for all the backups of the proposal to confirm that, yes, it did indeed vanish into thin air. There's no record of any of the money I spent. My hair is long again.

I'm stuck, and I feel a desperate need to tell *someone*.

I call my parents. The phone rings and rings . . . and this time my mom picks up. I guess if I call at a slightly different time, I'll get a different parent, depending on who's closest to the phone.

"Noelle?" she says. "Is something wrong? You never call at this time."

"I have a problem."

I picture my mom, her hair a mix of blonde and gray, standing at the phone in the kitchen. She has a notepad and a selection of pens by the phone; like Madison, she sometimes doodles while she talks. She also uses the pens to write her plans on the wall calendar.

"I'm reliving the same day over and over," I say.

"Yes, adulthood can be like that. You go to work, you come home—"

"No, that's not what I mean. I'm literally reliving June twentieth."

"What have you eaten today? Are you doing drugs?"

"No, I'm not doing drugs, Mom. I mean, other than alcohol and caffeine."

"You're drinking before eight in the morning?"

"No, but I drank yesterday. Which was also June twentieth." I let out an unhinged laugh-snort, which probably doesn't help my mother believe that I'm telling the truth. "Wordle has been the same for days."

"Maybe it's a glitch—"

"No, I'm really reliving the same day."

Mom was good with the various problems my siblings flung at her when they were younger. When Dalton got bitten by a raccoon, she handled it and got him a rabies shot. When Madison got attacked by a mini poodle . . .

Okay, yes, my siblings had bad luck with animals, but that wasn't all. Mom dealt with my sister's numerous heartbreaks and music obsessions and anxieties, but she seems to have no idea what to do now. Clearly, she doesn't believe me.

"How about I come over after breakfast?" She's attempting to sound like her usual calm self—I take after her in that respect—but she can't maintain the façade. "You could use some company, and I don't think you should go to the office in this state."

"Don't worry, I'm not. There's no point in working when anything I do is just going to vanish. But you don't need to come over," I add hurriedly.

I suddenly regret telling my mother about this. Why did

I bother? If Mom told me that she was literally repeating the same day over and over, *I* wouldn't believe her.

"Sorry," I say. "I've just been rather unhappy with life lately, that's all, and there's this guy at work . . ."

"Oh?"

"Not like *that*, god no. I keep having to redo his work. Anyway, I'll talk to you later."

I put my head in my hands, feeling guilty that I made my mother worry. On the plus side, she'll forget about it in less than twenty-four hours.

I'm still not used to this no-consequences thing, to this hours-of-free-time thing. My usual routine is gone because everything is pointless now.

I send an email to my boss to let him know that I'm sick—even if it's not strictly necessary, sending that email every day still feels like the right thing to do—then consider what I could clean with all my free time before remembering it doesn't matter. Any cleaning I do will be gone tomorrow.

It really is hard to adjust to living without consequences.

I try to find other people with my problem, but my Google searches are unsuccessful. If only I could find one other person with this issue, I'd feel less alone. Or if I had a close friend, someone who would believe me no matter what . . .

I flop on the futon and look through the contacts on my phone. I debate sending a text to Veronica. If I had to pick a best friend—like, if I were forced at gunpoint—she'd be it. Yes, I know that's a weird thought, but my current circumstances *are* pretty weird. I haven't texted her in months, though, and I haven't seen her in half a year. I feel guilty for neglecting our friendship, but I also feel guilty for thinking of texting her only because I'm lonely in a time loop.

However, it occurs to me that there's one way I can "prove" I'm repeating the day: I just need to show someone that I can predict the future.

I think back to the news I've read. There's the TTC delay that I had the misfortune of experiencing. Also, a Canada goose flies into a power line in Scarborough later today, knocking out power for 7,500 people.

In the end, I don't call or text anyone.

———

The next day, I eat moules-frites for lunch again, just because I can, though I stick to a single glass of wine rather than a whole bottle, hoping to avoid a headache. I don't bother getting another haircut, but I do go to the bubble tea shop, and this time, I order something different. The Iron Goddess milk tea— apparently, it's roasted oolong—with pearls.

It has nothing to do with the cute guy who came in and ordered the same thing the other day (err, the other June 20). Just figure I might as well try everything on the menu if I'm going to come here regularly.

It's not like I care about cute guys, after all. I mean, they can be nice to look at, but that's all they are for me. I've had my heart broken once, which was enough, thank you very much. The problem with love is that it's painfully unpredictable. Emphasis on "painfully."

I don't deal well with strong emotions.

After placing his order, the smiling Asian man looks over at me. "Have we met before?"

It's curious that I seem familiar to him, when nobody else has any recollection of my repeats of June 20. The first time it happened, I wanted to hug him, but now I just feel disconcerted.

I need to get out of this alternate reality. Now.

As I watch him walk out the door, bubble tea in hand, I wonder if a kiss would do it. After all, that sort of thing works in fairy tales. I could be like Sleeping Beauty or Snow White.

Hmm. Perhaps I should start Operation: Get Kissed.

July

Cam

As I'm waiting for my bubble tea, I do Wordle.

It's "attic," and I get it in five, which is longer than it usually takes me. I got it in two yesterday, but that was lucky.

"Here you go." The woman slides my lychee tea across the counter, and I thank her.

This place isn't quite as good as the one near my parents' house. I last went there a couple of weeks ago, after having lunch with my family. This one is more convenient, though, located between my apartment and the brewery.

Since it's a nice day, I amble outside and sit on the patio. It's cooler than it's been for the past week. Our air conditioner has been working overtime, and I'm not looking forward to seeing the bill. Today, finally, there's a break in the heat and humidity, and I lean back in my chair and enjoy it. I hope the weather is like this for Darrell's wedding next month. I'd prefer not to be sweating buckets while I'm wearing a tux.

Once I've finished my drink, I head back to work, stopping to talk to Justin before going to my office. It's a bit of a mess—I need to clean it up—but I know where to find everything I need. I really would prefer to stay outside on a day like today, but alas, that's not an option.

Maybe when I get home tonight, I'll sit on the balcony with a can of our Corktown Hefeweizen.

6

Noelle

June 20, Version 12

The idea that a kiss could get me out of this sounds too off-the-wall, but after another day of getting nowhere with endless Google searches—and even a trip to the library—I decide I shouldn't put it off any longer. It sounds ridiculous, but no more so than my current reality. I have to try *something*. Besides, he thinks I look vaguely familiar. Though he doesn't seem to be in a time loop like me, it could be a sign that he's the key to getting out of this. I hope.

I debate what to wear for my trip to get bubble tea. My wardrobe isn't meant for attracting anyone's attention. I have casual clothes that I wear in my apartment, and simple work pants and blouses that I wear to the office. That's pretty much it. I could, of course, go out and buy something, but I can't order anything because it will never get here.

I feel completely out of my depth. I've only had one boyfriend. Dave and I met in our first year of university, though we didn't get to know each other well until our final year. Then one night, we were studying late together . . .

I wince. Not that the start of our relationship is a bad memory, but when I think of Dave, I always recall how it ended, five years later.

"But why?" I asked him. "We were planning to move in together, and now you're breaking up with me? I feel like I have whiplash."

Once, Dave might have laughed if I made such a comment, but he didn't. He just said, "I'm not in love with you anymore."

"But *why?*" I repeated. I wanted him to point to something in particular; I wanted to know exactly what the problem was so I could fix it. I wished it could be like a difficult question on an exam. If I'd studied hard and prepared for it, I could solve it.

Except people's feelings don't work that way, and my long-term relationship had gone up in smoke, even though, as far as I knew, nothing had started the fire.

He was the only man I'd ever loved, and as I got used to being alone, papering over my injured heart with a bland smile, I resolved to never let myself be so vulnerable again. Seemingly mundane things had taken on extra significance. A funny TV show that I'd first seen with him, for example, was now too sad to watch.

Sure, I'd enjoyed being in a relationship, but it wasn't worth it. I didn't want to curl up on my bed, sobbing my eyes out at ten in the morning on a Saturday, rather than going grocery shopping like I was supposed to, then eating instant noodles from the back of my cupboard because there was nothing else. I didn't want to wrap myself in the hoodie he'd given me and torture myself by thoughts of what he was doing on weekends rather than being with *me*.

Two months later, those thoughts became especially bad when I discovered he had a new girlfriend. I couldn't help wondering whether he'd fallen in love with her before he broke up with me. Perhaps he'd even cheated.

That was when I spiraled.

One night, after finishing a bottle of wine and *The Notebook*, I gave him a call. When he didn't answer, I called him three more times in half an hour—that was what it took for him to pick up.

"Noelle," he said, "what's wrong?"

What's wrong? Was he serious?

"You broke my heart," I said accusingly, and then, through the fog of my tipsiness, I felt horribly embarrassed. Because I realized that, although he once would have been angry at the thought of anyone hurting me, he no longer cared.

He'd changed, he'd moved on, and I . . . hadn't.

I hated the person I'd become after he dumped me. I never wanted to be her again. I would not *let* myself be her again. The breakup had spurred a degree of chaos in my life that had been unmatched until the last several days.

I'd never believed in fairy tales, not really, but my parents—who'd met in a history class in their second year of university—seemed to have a happy enough marriage. I'd thought that might be something I could have too.

But I'd been wrong.

I stuck to my resolution: I haven't dated anyone since Dave. Nobody in six years. But my goal isn't to have a relationship with the man at the bubble tea shop. I just want to kiss him and see if it will get me out of this time loop. You know, perfectly normal stuff.

Frustrated by the lack of options in my closet, I put on a pair of gray work pants, a short-sleeve pink blouse, and some sensible heels, then look at the clock.

Shit! I need to get moving.

I hurry to the tea shop and manage to arrive at exactly the same time as before. I decide to order the Iron Goddess tea again so it'll give me a conversation topic. We're getting the same tea, what a coincidence!

He strolls in a minute later and places his order. Then he turns to me as I'm waiting for my drink and says, "Have we met before?"

"No!" My voice sounds strangely high. I open my mouth to say something else, anything else, but what comes out is, "Dajklsjfja."

He tilts his head, as if waiting for me to clarify.

I run out the door.

———

The next day after lunch, I put on the same outfit as yesterday—it's hanging in my closet, all clean—and head to the bubble tea shop at the appointed hour. I place my order and wait, and he walks in, wearing jeans and a dark T-shirt, as usual.

I'm determined to do better today. To at least say something that isn't gibberish.

"Have we met before?" he asks as we're waiting together.

"I don't think so, but I come here every now and then."

"That's probably it." He smiles at me.

"I'm Noelle."

"Cam."

There we go! I'm having a normal conversation with him. But how do I get from learning his name to getting a kiss so I can possibly break this time-loop curse?

"Doyouwantogoonadate?" I ask.

"I'm sorry, could you repeat that?"

My cheeks flame. "Do you want to go on a date? It needs to be tonight."

"Why is that?"

"Um . . ."

"Number thirty-two?" says the woman behind the counter.

I grab my drink and run out of there as fast as I can.

———

I haven't given up on Operation: Get Kissed. But it hasn't been going well so far, and I figure I should try other things too.

That evening, I return to the night market. I still can't find the dumpling woman. However, since I need something to eat, I go to another dumpling stall.

Hypothesis: perhaps it's not those particular dumplings that sent me into the time loop, but *any* dumplings that are consumed at this market. Maybe if I eat dumplings again, my life will return to normal.

Okay, I don't actually expect this to work, but it's worth a try, right?

The dumplings are good, but not quite as good as at the other place. After I finish them, I get an ube halaya pandesal—re-creating my dinner from the first June 20—and see someone familiar in my peripheral vision. Cam. Since the day hasn't reset, he'll remember who I am.

I duck behind the person in the Pocky box costume, too embarrassed for Cam to see me after our earlier interaction, but I keep an eye on him. When he disappears from view, I exhale and start walking toward the subway station. I look at my phone to check that the security incident is over and—

I bump into someone.

"Sorry," I say. "I was—wait. You have green hair today." It's the white woman I saw the other day, the one with a pink bob.

"And you have long hair." Her eyebrows draw together. "I know this sounds ridiculous, but are you reliving June twentieth over and over?"

7

Noelle

I can't believe it. After thinking I was the only one for so long, it turns out that I have company in the time loop. I nearly cry in relief.

"Yes!" I say. "I am."

"Oh, thank god," she says. "I thought it was just me. I'm Avery, by the way."

"Noelle."

"Did you eat dumplings at the booth next to the noodle place? There's nothing there today, but I swear, on the first June twentieth—"

"Yes, I did."

"It's not on the night market website—"

"That's right!" I say. "I checked. Couldn't find anything."

I shouldn't interrupt Avery, but it's so exciting to find someone who's experiencing the same thing as I am.

Deciding we should discuss this further, we walk a couple of blocks to a coffee shop, where it's a littler quieter. We sit on the patio with our drinks.

Avery is dressed casually, in shorts and a tank top with horizontal stripes, a black bag slung across her body; she didn't remove it when we sat down. Square frames are perched on her nose. I figure she's a few years younger than me.

"I stopped going to work after the first repeat," she says.

"Me too. What's the point? Although I did some work one evening because I wasn't sure what else to do with myself."

"I've dyed my hair three different colors. Pink is my favorite. Blue looked ghastly, but at least it was gone the next day."

"I've never wanted to dye my hair, but I did like trying a new haircut consequence-free. If I ever get out of this, I'll get that haircut for real."

"I assume you've attempted to get out of the loop," she says. "What have you tried?"

"One night, I stayed up as long as I could. It appears the reset time is three in the morning, because all of a sudden, I found myself back in bed, waking up to my alarm. On the twentieth."

"Oh! I never thought to try that. The dumpling lady . . . did she tell you that the dumplings would give you what you needed most?"

"She did," I say. "And I was hungry. I needed food."

Avery laughs. She has a booming laugh.

"Is it your birthday too?" she asks.

"What? No. It's yours?"

She nods. "When I was a kid, I'd have thought reliving my birthday would be great fun, but it's not so fun when your boyfriend forgets about it."

"And now you have to relive him forgetting over and over."

"Exactly. It's awful."

"I can imagine. I wonder if anyone else is stuck in this loop with us?"

"I don't know," she says, "but I'm very glad to have you found you. I couldn't talk to anyone else about it. Even if I got someone to believe me—"

"You'd have to explain it again tomorrow."

"Yeah. Tomorrow. Whatever that even means now."

I can't remember the last time I clicked with someone I just met, but these are unusual circumstances—though aren't friendships often about circumstance? You know, the people who happen to be in your class when you're a kid. As you get older . . .

Well, I've struggled to make friends as an adult. I'm not close with any of my coworkers.

"I still don't understand how we got into this mess," I say. "This woman made magical dumplings that can make you repeat the day you ate them?"

"Or maybe they do different things for different people, and they caused the time loop for us because that's what we need most."

"But why? *Why* would someone need to live the same day over and over?"

"Maybe," she says, "there's something we each have to do that will get us out of the loop, and what each of us needed was another chance at the day."

"It was a pretty ordinary day for me. Stayed at the office late, ate dumplings, went home."

"Well, as I said, it's my birthday. When I reminded Joe— my boyfriend—about it, he sent me an e-card. An e-card! I complained about his lack of effort, and I got a speech about how celebrating your birthday when you're over twenty-five is childish and embarrassing."

"How long have you been together?" I ask.

"Three years."

"Do you live together?"

"Yeah."

This is one thing that Avery and I don't have in common. But as we continue to talk, it becomes clear that there are lots of similarities. We both have steady jobs but don't have much going on in our lives other than our work. We're both the oldest of all our siblings. We both grew up in the Toronto area. We both enjoy reading—at least, I've rediscovered the joy of reading now that I have more free time. It sounds like she's a voracious bookworm.

"I admit I'm a bit of a workaholic," I say. "I don't like doing anything but my best, and sometimes it feels like, because I'm so competent, they just keep piling more stuff on me, knowing I'll get it done. But I've stopped working, and clearly that didn't get me out of this situation."

Avery taps her finger against her chin. "We have to figure out what the dumpling lady would want us to change about our lives."

"Except we don't know her at all, and she doesn't know us."

"Maybe, by some magic, she does?"

"If so," I say, "she might not approve of the fact that I'm single in my thirties. She might think I ought to settle down and get married and have kids. Not that I can do all those things if I'm stuck reliving a single day. But . . ."

"What is it?" Avery leans forward.

"I've been hoping to kiss someone. It ended the sleeping spell for Sleeping Beauty, so maybe it'll end the time loop for me." I can't believe I just said that out loud, but here we are. "Unfortunately, my flirting skills leave a little—a lot—to be desired."

"You have someone particular in mind?"

My cheeks heat as I think of his face. Embarrassed by my physical reaction, I duck my head before saying, "Yes."

Avery grins. "Tell me about this person."

"His name's Cam. That's about all I know. He, uh . . . He's nice." It seems like an empty word, but what more can I say? "He's convenient. I know where to find him. I don't expect anything more to happen, but I figure a kiss is worth a try."

He won't remember my failures, so if I make a fool of myself, it won't matter. Much.

I'll still remember. I remember silly things I did in elementary school, and that was twenty years ago. But to get out of this time loop, I'm going to have to take risks beyond getting a new haircut.

"Kissing Joe hasn't gotten me out of this loop," Avery says.

To be honest, I don't like the sound of Joe very much. I think he—

That's it!

It makes perfect sense, doesn't it? Perhaps we both have to do something about our so-called love lives, but Avery, who seems rather unhappy with the boyfriend who forgot her birthday, has to dump hers, and I have to kiss someone new.

"What about . . . never mind," I mumble.

"Do you have an idea to get me out of this?" she asks. "You have to tell me. There are no silly ideas right now."

I hesitate. Not because I think it's a silly idea, but because I'm unsure how she'll react. "I think you should break up with Joe. Maybe breaking up with him . . . is what you need most," I say, echoing the dumpling lady's words. "My ex—for all his faults— never would have acted like Joe did if he forgot my birthday. I'm sure you can do better. Besides, being alone isn't so bad."

As soon as I say that, there's a painful clench in my chest, but it's not like I need someone else. My life was satisfactory before I started repeating the same day.

I suddenly remember that on the original June 20, I ruminated about being a bad engineering project held together by duct tape. I might be looking at the days when time moved forward with rose-tinted glasses, but at least I wasn't sobbing on my kitchen floor because of a relationship.

"Joe's a decent boyfriend," Avery says.

"Aside from the birthday thing."

"And the fact that he never cleans the washroom or the

kitchen. It's like he just doesn't notice when anything's dirty." She sighs. "But you're right. It's worth a try."

"If we ever get out of this, I'll do something nice for your birthday. I promise. What would you want?"

"I don't even know anymore, but not an e-card."

"Two e-cards, then."

She laughs. "I'll text you after I do it. Let me know how your flirting goes."

"I can't see it going well. I asked if he wanted to go on a date tonight. When he inquired why it had to be tonight, I panicked and ran away. I'm no good at this."

"Maybe you need to do some research."

"Like, Google how to pick up a guy?"

"I was thinking more along the lines of watching movies to get ideas."

I believe this suggestion has merit, and it has the added benefit of giving me a reason not to talk to Cam tomorrow.

"I'll do that," I say.

She takes out her phone. "What's your number?"

"You'll have to memorize it. Your phone won't remember it tomorrow, and even if you write it in pen on your hand, it'll be gone."

"Good call."

We tell each other our numbers and practice reciting them. It reminds me of when I was little and my mom taught me our home number. I'm not used to memorizing phone numbers anymore.

Then we leave the patio and head to the TTC. We're going in different directions, and I wave to her as my train arrives.

I can't help smiling as I step inside. I made a new friend! I can't remember the last time I made one . . . and it only took getting stuck in a time loop for that to happen.

But what if I actually get out of the loop thanks to the dumplings I ate earlier?

Well, I can still text Avery. I know her number, and hopefully she'll be able to receive my texts from the future, and I can tell her how to get out of the loop.

For once, I'm actually looking forward to tomorrow, whatever that happens to be.

8

Noelle

June 20, Version 14

The next morning, I add Avery's number to my contacts.

> ME: I assume you're still stuck on June 20?
> AVERY: I am. Wordle is still happy.
> AVERY: And that terrible take on what's wrong with women these days is still going viral, as is the bizarre baby squirrel video.

It's nice to have someone who actually *remembers*, and once again, I wonder if there are others like us. I've already tried a little internet research on time loops, but I need to expand my efforts.

I create a new anonymous Reddit account and post about our issue in some subreddits. I try a few different social media platforms as well, but the fact that I don't have a big following anywhere makes me worry that my reach is limited. I also comment on an article about the night market. When I see that I've gotten a response to my first post, I tell myself not to get excited.

boba247x: The mods should delete this. What a stupid hoax.

It's in a Toronto subreddit, so I respond by predicting the specific TTC delays that will happen later today, as well as the power outage caused by the Canada goose. I add that a certain celebrity known for being a "wife guy" will be exposed as a cheater.

Then I force myself to put aside my phone and dedicate my time to watching movies.

I figure I'll start my research with Julia Roberts. She has lots of films to choose from. I watch *Pretty Woman*, which, unfortunately, doesn't translate very well to my life. Then I move on to *Runaway Bride*, and it crosses my mind that Cam could be a journalist. It seems marginally more likely than a billionaire, doesn't it? And if he's a journalist, he could write a story about me, the woman stuck in a time loop.

That seems far-fetched, but I'll give it a try.

While eating a late dinner, I pull out my phone and look at the responses I've gotten to the posts I made earlier.

piedpiper16: Holy shit. She was right about the power outage and all the TTC delays.
discogirl_: There are delays every day.
piedpiper16: But she predicted the exact times and locations.

The thread becomes a discussion of whether or not people believe I'm trapped in a time loop. Sadly, no one has any advice or personal experience to offer, and before long, it will all vanish anyway.

"Have we met before?" Cam asks when I see him the next day.

"We have," I say. "Cam, right? Cameron?"

"Actually, it's short for 'Canmore.'"

I've never heard of someone with that name before, but I know it's a town in Alberta. "Did your parents, um, name you after the place where you were conceived?"

I cover my face with my hands after saying that.

You see? This is why I don't try to pick up random guys. I get tongue-tied and end up saying the least appropriate thing.

Cam laughs. "I hope not. They just said they looked at a map of Canada for inspiration." He pauses. "I'm sorry, I don't remember your name."

"Noelle."

"Nice to meet you. Again."

There's an awkward pause, and then I say, "You're a journalist, right?"

"No, you must have me mixed up with someone else."

"Ah, I remember now. Secret billionaire."

"And you're the heiress?" He winks at me.

That wink pins me to the spot. I think he's flirting? What do I say now? I'm so disarmed by that easy smile, the way he's lightly resting his arm against the counter. He's only a few inches taller than me, so when he leans, we're about the same height. That dimple—yes, he has a dimple—is almost right in front of my face.

"Where have we met before?" he asks. "It's strange that I can't remember."

I don't know how to answer. How am I supposed to think straight? I thought he was fairly attractive before, but now, I swear there's a goddamn sparkle in his eyes, and it's bewitched my brain.

"Order thirty-two?"

I grab my drink. "Sorry, got to catch my private jet!"

I run out the door in an undignified manner totally unbefitting of an heiress. (I don't know any heiresses, but I'm making an educated guess here.)

At home, I decide I'm not ready for this flirting business.

I need to do more research.

———

Before continuing with Julia Roberts's catalogue, I read a bunch of articles, none of which I find helpful. *Ticket to Paradise* is similarly useless, seeing as Cam and I weren't previously married.

Notting Hill, however, is quite intriguing. I could play Hugh Grant's part, despite the lack of travel bookshop. I'll just spill bubble tea all over Cam, then invite him to my apartment, where I'll make slightly awkward conversation—I think I have that part down pat—and he'll kiss me.

The "back to my apartment" part is a bit problematic, as I don't live all that close to the bubble tea shop, but it's worth a try, isn't it? Some more movie research suggests that a little physical altercation isn't uncommon.

I text Avery.

ME: Have you dumped Joe?
AVERY: Not yet. I'd rather dye my hair purple, but I should
       try doing it. I know it might not be permanent, but
       if it's the thing that gets me out of the loop, it WILL
       be permanent, and that's scary.
ME: You deserve better than him. Are you concerned about
    your living situation? Is that what's stopping you?
AVERY: Yeah, if I get out of this relationship and June 20, I
       have no family to stay with. My dad's in Winnipeg
       and my mom's not an option.

> ME: If you do get out, you can live with me until you find a
>   place.

I send the text without really thinking about what I'm offering. I've lived alone for years. I'm used to living alone . . . but I
don't take back my words.

> ME: Though if you get out of the loop and I don't, who will
>   I be in your reality? Will I remember you? I might have
>   no idea who you are. And if I do get out, but a day or
>   two later than you, how does that work? It makes my
>   head hurt.
> ME: But seriously, if I know who you are, you can stay
>   with me.
> AVERY: Thanks. What about you? How's Cam?
> ME: I need to step up my game.

The following morning, I once again start my day by adding
Avery to my contacts, as well as posting on a bunch of forums,
though I'm less hopeful than I was yesterday.

Then, dressed in a different blouse than the previous times, I
head to the tea shop, ready to execute my plan for a meet cute.
However, when Cam looks over at me and says, "Have we met
before?" I start to doubt myself.

I feel like I'm using him. Meet cutes aren't supposed to be
engineered; they're supposed to be spontaneous. Plus, it seems
wrong to spill a drink on this nice man.

I have to try something, though. I can't be stuck in June 20
forever.

Better to injure myself, I decide.

"I don't think so," I say, "but I come here every now and then."

"That's probably it." He smiles at me.

It's nice when people are predictable. One of the few perks of reliving the same day.

"I'm Noelle."

"Cam."

We lapse into silence. I don't ask if he wants to go on a date.

"Number thirty-two?"

I reach for my order. "Thank you."

Then I turn, take a step, and force myself to trip on a table leg. It doesn't come naturally, especially since I have half a liter of tea and tapioca balls in my hand. But my future might be at stake here, so I do it. I fall, my tea hitting the floor and covering it in liquid right before my knee makes contact. My arms come up to cushion my face.

"Shit!" I cry.

"Oh my god," Cam says. "Are you okay?" He crouches before me, just like he did that time at the market.

"I, um . . ." I stammer. "I think so?"

Ideally, this is when he tells me that I shouldn't put weight on either of my legs, then sweeps me into his arms, and when I look at him like he's my hero, he kisses me. (My imagination isn't usually prone to romantic flights of fancy, but I've watched a lot of movies in the last forty-eight hours.)

Alas, this isn't quite what happens.

He offers me his hand. "Can you stand up?"

"Y-yes. I think so."

Turns out, I'm a liar. I put one foot flat on the ground, but then my feet slide apart, perhaps owing to all the liquid and bubbles on the floor. I'm heading toward the splits despite the fact that I cannot, well, *do* the splits.

My recently acquired expertise in romance has led me to believe that some men find clumsy women irresistible, but Cam might not be one of those men. Besides, although some people manage to look cute while being clumsy, I'm positive I look more like a drowning raccoon. I doubt anyone would want to kiss me in my current state, but since I need help getting up, I take the proffered hand. It's warm and strong, and for a second, I think it's a pity that I've both sworn off dating and found myself trapped in a time loop. Maybe if life were different, I'd want something *real* to happen.

I swear Cam holds my hand a split second longer than necessary, but maybe that's my imagination.

"You okay?" he asks, stepping back once I'm standing.

"Just peachy," I lie.

—

When I get home, I'm in no mood to watch more rom-coms. Instead, I buy a novel that promises "treachery via time loop," hoping that, despite the story being set in the distant future, it will give me some ideas for sorting out my problem.

After reading a quarter of the book, I conclude that this is unlikely, but I'm quite enjoying the novel. It's nice to be able to read and watch movies on a weekday afternoon, rather than being at the office. Just in case, I fill out the contact form on the author's website, asking if it was based on personal experience. After all, aren't writers often told to write what they know?

Avery finally breaks up with Joe, and we arrange to meet for a celebratory dinner. I suggest we avoid the market—the thought of running into Cam again is too humiliating to bear—and we eventually agree on a burger joint.

Although my attempt at a meet cute didn't lead to a kiss, I'm a little inspired by the feeling of Cam's hand around mine. I think it's worth trying that again, but this time, I'll spill it on *him*, even if the idea makes me feel rather guilty. I tell Avery about my plan, and she approves.

The next day, Avery is still in the loop, and I'm simultaneously disappointed that changing her love life didn't work and relieved that my friend is still here.

In an attempt to mix things up for my encounter with Cam, I put on my favorite drop earrings and a sundress. The dress was one of my rare impulse purchases a few years ago. Occasionally, I wear it to the office with a cardigan, but mostly, it just sits in my closet.

I spin around and the skirt flies up. Oops. Better not do that when I'm in public or I might flash someone.

Before heading to the tea shop, I take an empty plastic cup and practice turning around and knocking into the refrigerator (i.e., Cam). After nearly bruising my forehead, I decide to stop practicing. I'll just have to cross my fingers and hope I can pull this off. Improvise.

Hahaha. Improvisation is *way* outside my skill set.

Still, I'll do anything to get out of this stupid loop, so I march into the tea shop and place my order, as usual. Cam enters at the same time as always.

"Have we met before?" he says when he turns to me.

Now, spilling my drink is the main part of my plan, but I figure a touch of flirtation beforehand wouldn't go amiss.

"I don't think so. I'm sure I'd remember if we had." I shoot him a smile and do something with my head, something that's supposed to look like I'm tossing my hair over my shoulder in a sexy way, though I'm not sure that's what happens.

He smiles back, but he's a rather smiley guy, from what I've observed, so it's hard to read how he feels about this.

"I'm Noelle," I say.

"Cam."

There's a moment of silence.

"Number thirty-two?" says the woman behind the counter.

"That's me! Thank you!" I sound artificially upbeat.

As I reach for my cup, I make a point of sliding closer to Cam. Then I spin, the hand carrying the bubble tea rather far from my body. It's at this moment that I remember I wasn't supposed to spin, and in a panic, I try to shove down my dress with both hands so no one sees my underwear. Rather than knocking into the hard refrigerator—I mean, Cam's chest—the cup spills on his crotch before falling to the ground.

"Shit!" I cry, more vehemently than I did yesterday.

"Don't worry about it," Cam says, even though bubble tea is running down his legs. A tapioca pearl clings to his shorts, very close to . . .

Well, it's fallen to the floor now.

"No big deal," he says. "I was going home to change before work anyway, and it's hot outside, so I won't be cold." He's definitely much calmer than I'd be in such a situation.

Just as I'm debating what to do next, since a kiss doesn't appear to be forthcoming, the door opens, and a middle-aged woman walks in with her small dog. Before she can stop him, the pup lunges toward the tapioca pearls.

Now, I suspect tapioca pearls are not as bad for dogs as grapes—despite being somewhat similar in appearance—but they're probably not an ideal part of a dog's diet. I manage to step in front of Cam and the mess on the floor, and the dog laps at my bare leg, making the situation even more awkward.

There's a banging sound behind me, and an employee comes around the counter with a mop. I feel embarrassed at the extra work I've made for him, as well as the scene I've caused.

All I can do is flee—and this time, it's without any mentions of my private jet.

Okay, I think I need to call off Operation: Get Kissed. This really isn't going well, and I don't think the truth would go over well either.

Hi, I'm stuck in a time loop and I think a kiss might help get me out of it. Want to do me a favor and stick your tongue down my throat?

Yeah, no. That sounds utterly ridiculous. In fact, everything I've been doing lately has sounded utterly ridiculous, but when you're stuck in a ridiculous situation, what else are you supposed to do?

It occurs to me that I could simply just . . . kiss him. Make the first move, without giving him a chance to pull back. But I want him to consent to kissing me.

Or maybe, while he was dripping in Iron Goddess milk tea, I should have leaned toward him and puckered my lips and hoped it was clear what I wanted . . . and he could do it. Or not.

But the idea of going through all that again is almost physically painful to me. As is the idea of kissing another man, for some reason. My brain has fixated on this easygoing guy, who doesn't look like he's held together by duct tape—but what do I know? I've only seen this brief snapshot of his life.

I find myself wishing I knew more. Wishing I knew how that smiling mouth would feel against mine, that strong hand on my back or around my waist.

I shake my head. Nothing will come from dwelling on such things.

Once again, I meet Avery for dinner. We go to a Greek restaurant on the Danforth, and I don't hold myself back from ordering two appetizers.

"You know," she says, as we're waiting for our food, "we could try kissing each other. I'm straight—"

"Me too."

"—but what if we need to kiss someone else who's in the time loop? It seems unlikely, but it could be worth a shot, if you agree."

"Yeah, why not."

"We'll do it after our meal."

———

Outside an unbusy subway station, Avery presses her lips to mine. It's not unpleasant, but it doesn't do anything for me, and cartoon bluebirds don't start singing or anything like that.

When I wake up to my alarm on June 20 again, I'm not surprised.

The two of us spend the next week or so—is it weird to think of time in weeks when it's all the same day?—attempting to find a way out of our predicament. I post in more forums and subreddits without success. I try to contact a few more authors to see if their time-loop books were based on experience, but I don't hear back. A discussion with a physicist leads to a lot of jargon I don't understand and no good suggestions—I don't think he truly believed us but treated it as a theoretical question.

I'm starting to lose hope.

After yet another fruitless conversation with a scientist, I go home and turn on the TV. I want to stay indoors for a few days, and the great thing about a time loop is that I can eat the same food in my apartment over and over again. (See? I'm finding the silver lining where I can.) There aren't a lot of benefits, but that's one of them.

I don't feel like watching a six- or eight-episode season of a TV show that I'd be able to finish in a day. No, I want something with lots of episodes, so I start a show that I haven't seen in years. Since I have time, I'm going to binge-watch in a way I've never allowed myself to binge-watch before.

9

Noelle

June 20, Version 29 (I think? I wish I could carve lines in the wall like a prisoner, but alas, my lines would disappear overnight)

I've been watching *House* for four days—or is it five? It's hard to keep track when the date doesn't change. After finishing an episode, I make myself the same bag of popcorn that I've consumed several times before and settle back on the futon.

As I watch Gregory House solve yet another medical mystery, I realize what I need to do: I need to go to my family doctor and explain the problem. Surely my case is interesting and serious and someone will want to solve it.

The next morning, I call the doctor's office first thing and say that I would like an appointment today. They're able to squeeze me in at 2 p.m.

When I arrive, there are a few other people in the waiting room: a mom and her little boy on a Nintendo Switch, an elderly man who sounds like he's hacking up a lung, and a middle-aged woman who sits quietly with her hands folded in her lap. I've only been here twice before. My previous doctor retired, and it took me forever to find a new one. Like last time, she's running about half an hour behind, but finally, I'm called in.

"What brings you here today, Noelle?" Dr. Connelly is about fifty and has a kind smile.

"Well," I say, "I'm living the same day over and over."

She nods as if she understands.

I'm positive she doesn't.

"I don't mean every day seems the same," I say. "I'm literally reliving June twentieth. Wordle is 'happy' today, right?"

"I don't know. I haven't done it yet."

"Sorry for ruining it for you. I've done it something like thirty times, and it's always 'happy.' Happy, happy, happy. But I'm not. I've stopped going to work because whatever I do disappears overnight, so I just have to repeat it. What's the point?"

I can tell that Dr. Connelly doesn't believe me. She thinks I'm depressed and delusional, even when I mention having found someone else who's experiencing the same thing. In fact, that seems to make her think I'm more delusional. She gives me a referral to a psychiatrist.

"How long will this take?" I ask.

"A while—"

"You don't understand. I have to see someone today because tomorrow—my tomorrow, which will be June twentieth again—you'll have forgotten all about this and the referral won't have been made."

"If you think you're a danger to yourself," she says, "go to the ER."

Instead, I head home. I'm not feeling optimistic about what would happen if I went to the hospital, to be honest. I've read articles about how the healthcare system is overwhelmed and close to its breaking point; I ought to be grateful my doctor was able to see me today, even if nothing came of it.

Not in the mood to watch more *House*, I scroll through the contacts on my phone and stop at my sister's name. Madison and I aren't close. Whereas I got a degree and started working in the same field—well, it took five months to find a job, but I managed it eventually—she switched majors four times, schools once, and has never worked at the same place for more than eight months.

Her lack of stability stresses me out.

She's also struggled with her mental health more than I ever have, and I know she's sought help, but nothing seems to work—at least not well. Right now, she's living with her boyfriend and working at a tutoring center.

I feel like I understand what she's gone through more than I ever have before.

ME: How long does a referral to a psychiatrist usually take?
MADISON: hahahaha
MADISON: Months. Maybe a year. It's a mess.
MADISON: Wait. Are you asking for yourself?
ME: yeah

A minute later, I get a call, which is weird because Madison hates talking on the phone.

"What's going on?" she asks.

"I. Um. I'm living the same day over and over." As proof, I tell her about the news stories that will break later in the day.

Amazingly, she believes me, without waiting to see if my predictions come true.

"You wouldn't make something like this up," she says, "and I can hear the desperation in your voice. How long has this been happening to you?"

"I don't know. I'm starting to lose track. Thirty days, maybe?"

"Do you go to the office?" she asks.

"No."

"See, this is how I know you're not lying. You wouldn't stop going to work otherwise."

"You once said I'd work through the apocalypse."

"I don't remember that, but it sounds like something I'd say."

I tell Madison about my attempts to get out of the loop. About my failed efforts to engineer a meet cute at the bubble tea shop. It feels like the tension that has long existed between us isn't there anymore.

"I'm sorry," I say.

"Sorry?" Maybe it's my imagination, but there's an edge in her voice now.

"Yeah." I swallow. She won't remember this tomorrow, so if I don't get it right, I can try again. "I judged you for the decisions you made. Your difficulty with keeping a job and . . . other things. I'm sure you were dealing with stuff that I didn't understand, as well as a system that often doesn't provide the help people need."

"Thank you," she says quietly.

When I get off the phone, I start watching *Suits*.

But a few hours later, I wonder if that conversation with my sister will help get me out of the loop. In one of the books I read, the main character had to make amends, and I didn't see how that could apply to me, but maybe this was it? The thing that would get me unstuck?

Unfortunately, at six forty-five the next morning, I conclude that it didn't work.

AVERY: Did you escape June 20? Is that why I haven't heard from you?

I stare at the text. Even while I was bingeing *House*, I made sure to text Avery every morning, but I forgot today, and I feel too discouraged for human contact. I'm about to put my phone aside and start another episode, but then I decide I should answer.

Better to respond now than to let weeks go by and feel like it's too late to reply. I won't let what happened with Veronica happen with Avery, especially since she's the only person who's stuck here with me. I'll make an effort with our friendship.

My thumbs fly over the phone as I detail how my visit to the doctor went and what happened with my sister.

———

I spend the next several days watching *Suits* and occasionally going out to eat expensive food. I also teach myself to crochet—something I've always wanted to try but never got around to doing—with the help of YouTube videos. It's probably for the best that my not-terribly-pretty efforts disappear overnight. I text Avery every morning, and sometimes we meet up for dinner.

To be honest, it's kind of nice to have to veg out like this. I never take all my vacation days at my job.

But eventually, the workaholic in me gets hard to ignore. I feel like I have to start being productive. There's no point in going to the office, but I should put more effort into escaping the loop.

My mind turns to Cam and then to dumplings. I should try to learn more about dumplings. *How* was I sent to this weird reality? And if I eat the right dumpling, will I get out of it?

Of course, "Toronto + dumplings" yields endless search results. Adding "time loop" results in significantly fewer, not surprisingly, but nothing seems promising.

Next, I search for "Toronto + magic + dumplings" and come across a dumpling shop in Chinatown called Magic Dumplings. It's quite likely that when someone thought of this name forty years ago—it's been around for a long time—they didn't mean it in the literal way that I'm hoping for. However, it's worth a shot. I can also ask questions. Inquire if they've ever heard of dumplings sending someone into a time loop.

Having decided to go to Chinatown tomorrow, I find other places to try in the area. A place on Spadina (Tasty 8 Dumplings) will be my second stop, followed by a restaurant with soup dumplings that one reviewer claims "can cure any ailment." I doubt @tangyass had my particular ailment in mind when they wrote that, but I'm getting desperate. I'll try anything. Besides, stuffing myself with dumplings is no hardship.

Actually, I'm rather looking forward to it.

August

Cam

"Okay, that's it. I'm beat." I brush my hand over my forehead and make an exaggerated "phew" sound.

The flower girl, fortunately, lets me off the hook. She's had me literally spinning in circles for the last twenty minutes. I sit down as she pulls her mother up to dance. A slow song starts playing, but that doesn't affect her energetic movements, and I chuckle.

On the other side of the dance floor, Darrell and his new wife, Keysha, are lovingly staring into each other's eyes. Nearby, Justin is dancing with his new boyfriend.

This is the first time I've had more than a minute to myself all day, and I can't help thinking of the fact that I always assumed I'd be married by this age. Not that I thought too much about the future—I mean, we have plans for our business, but that's different—but I did idly assume that much. However, I'm not seeing anyone, and I haven't dated for a little while. And as I step out of the big white tent, a sudden fear seizes me.

What if I missed her?

What if I was supposed to have met her by now, but I made a different decision that I thought was inconsequential at the time? Maybe I just left my apartment five minutes too late?

Not that I believe in fate, or that there's only one person out there for everyone, but I can't help wondering now.

Or maybe I should have danced with Darrell's cousin, the one who seemed interested in me earlier?

I shove my hands into the pockets of my pants. Nah, that didn't feel right, and I like to go with my gut.

I look up at the sky. There are more stars than I'm used to seeing. Darrell's reception is at a brewery owned by one of our friends. It's a little north of the city, and they have a lot more property than we do—it's a better venue for a wedding reception than Leaside Brewing, though we've hosted a couple of small wedding receptions. As I'd hoped, it's a beautiful day for a wedding. Not excessively hot and humid. Some clouds, but no hint of rain, and out of Toronto, the air seems to move better.

What if I missed her?

As I continue to look up at the stars, the thought won't leave my head.

I try to picture a woman in my mind, but I can't. I just have the general impression of someone who's a little quieter than me, whose default expression is a little more serious—but she looks absolutely luminous if you make her smile.

I really don't know what I'm looking for, but I hope I find it nonetheless.

"Cam!" shouts a high voice behind me.

I turn and see the flower girl.

"Mama's tired," she announces. "Will you dance with me again?"

10

Noelle

June 20, Version 45-ish

Bright and early—which is now ten in the morning for me—I head downtown, armed with a notebook and pen just to prove that I'm taking this research business seriously.

I meet Avery at Magic Dumplings. The interior of the restaurant looks like it has seen better days—well, no. It probably always looked like this, but I find it reassuring. It's the sort of place that my grandparents might have frequented.

I hold up two fingers to indicate that we want a table for two, and an older woman in a faded apron takes us to a table by the window. We peruse the extensive menu, written in both English and Chinese, each item labeled with a number, and I select the pan-fried pork-and-chive dumplings. Using the pencil left on the chipped table, I write down the number on a slip of paper. Avery chooses something as well. The lady takes our order and sets down two small teacups and a teapot. Aside from a few older women near the back of the restaurant, we're the only customers.

As I sip my tea, I look out the window. The air conditioner makes a loud rattling sound, but I can't complain. It's cooler than it is outside.

The server returns with two plates containing twelve dumplings each, and my mouth starts to water from the smell. I pick up a dumpling with my chopsticks, then remind myself that I'll probably burn myself if I eat it now, so I reach for the vinegar and wait a couple of minutes.

Finally, I lift the first dumpling to my lips and inhale deeply before taking a bite. It's just as delicious as the aroma suggests, and it doesn't take us long to polish everything off.

When the server comes to clear the table, I take a deep breath and ask, "Why is this place called Magic Dumplings?"

"Wah, don't ask me," she says. "I didn't name it."

"Have you ever heard of dumplings with magical properties?"

She frowns.

"Like, dumplings that could make you fly." *Yeah, great example, Noelle.* "Or, random thought here, make you repeat the same day over and over."

"Why do I need magic for that? I go to work. My son doesn't call. Same every day."

"No, I mean *exactly* the same. Like, say, the air conditioner breaks at noon. Then when you come to work the next day, it's working again . . . but it breaks at noon. And the date on your phone never changes."

After a moment of thought, she says, "I don't know what you're talking about. Maybe you should see a doctor, get head checked." She taps her temple.

"I tried that." I manage a chuckle. "Could we get the bill?"

I don't come down to Chinatown very often. I live in North York, and there's no shortage of Chinese food there. On the walk to Tasty 8 Dumplings, I stop a couple of times, examining businesses that have changed since my last visit.

The second dumpling place is newer. Sparkling floors. Black tables and chairs. The server is younger than I am.

Our shrimp-and-vegetable dumplings arrive in a bamboo steamer. They're not quite as good as the dumplings at the first place but still quite tasty, as their name would suggest.

"Excuse me," Avery says to the server when he returns to clear our dishes, "have you heard of dumplings that make people travel in time? Maybe repeat the same day over and over?"

"Uh, no." He seems to brace himself, as if expecting some unpredictable behavior on our part, or at least a second weird question.

"Just wondering," Avery says with a smile. "Can we have the bill?"

By the time we get to the third restaurant, I'm rather full, but I remind myself that my future might depend on consuming the right dumpling, and so I persevere and order some soup dumplings.

After the meal, I don't bother asking my server if she knows anything about magical dumplings. Neither does Avery. We're too embarrassed to do it again. All I can do is hope that one of these dumplings did the trick, even if none of them tasted quite like the ones at the night market.

However, as I'm exiting the restaurant, I pass a group of young people—university students?—having an animated conversation at a table near the door.

"And then he swore that time slowed down and started going backward," someone says.

I reduce my speed as much as I can without drawing too much attention to myself.

"I'm serious!" a man exclaims. "That's what happened. Then it started feeling like I had, like, chronic déjà vu."

I come to a stop. Does this have something to do with dumplings?

"Really?" someone else says. "That's never happened to me, and I've done shrooms a bunch of times."

Hmph. How unhelpful.

———

Back at home, I pull up Google on my phone and make another attempt at finding the dumpling lady from the night market. I look at vendor listings and photos for other markets, but I can't find any evidence of her existence. I contact the event organizers, who have no idea what I'm talking about.

Are Avery and I the only ones who saw her?

Was she some kind of ghost? And if so, how do you look for a ghost?

I wish I could spray a little WD-40 on my life to get time moving again, but alas, that's not how it works—or is it? I consider it for a few seconds before rejecting the idea. WD-40 would probably irritate my skin, and what else could I spray it on, other than myself? No, that seems more far-fetched than my other ideas.

And—not for the first time—a more disturbing possibility seizes me: Am *I* a ghost?

I try to push that idea out of my head by watching too much reality TV.

Unsure what else to do, I spend the next few days eating dumplings. I go to a few restaurants in Scarborough. Avery joins me at a place in North York. Eventually, I—and I seriously can't believe I'm even thinking this—become a little sick of dumplings, but that doesn't make me give up.

One day, I attempt to make dumplings myself, something I've never done before. They taste reasonably good, though they look an utter mess.

The next day, it's June 20 again.

Wanting to do something a little different, I text my sister. I tell her that I'm taking a "mental health" day from work and ask if she'd like to hang out. After Madison gets over the shock of me taking a day off—I'm not in the mood to explain the time loop again, even if she'd believe me—she agrees, and we go to a restaurant on Bayview, not too far from where she and her boyfriend live. The restaurant is rather run-down, and it looks slightly out of place between a pâtisserie and an organic butcher.

"Are you sure you're not sick?" Madison makes a show of peering at me after the waiter has taken our order. She's wearing jeans with holes that are probably supposed to look cool and a T-shirt for a band that she's mentioned in passing before. We have similar facial features, though her physique is rounder, closer to our mother's than our father's.

"I'm not sick." I pause. "I work sixty hours most weeks. I deserve a break every now and then, right?"

"I mean, yeah, but it's not like you to say that. I'm just glad you realized that work is never gonna love you back."

I shrug. "One of my coworkers . . . I'm supposed to be mentoring him, but he never does his work properly, no matter what I tell him. I keep having to redo his stuff. He's the owner's nephew, so if I complain—"

"Oh no," Madison says. "Yeah, I can see how that might not go over well."

"What about you?" I ask. "How's your job?"

"It doesn't make me want to slam my head into a brick wall every day, so it's better than the last one, I guess. Low bar, though."

Unlike usual, I don't make any comments on her job-hopping.

"We should do this more often," I tell her. "Hang out. Just the two of us. It's nice."

The fact that I'm 99.99 percent sure she'll forget what I said—unless these dumplings do something that the others haven't—makes it easier to say things like that.

But I'm hit by a pang of melancholy. Madison won't remember our lunch; I'll be the only one with the memory. Sure, we can do it again, on some other iteration of June 20, but it won't be building on anything we've done before.

I'm not much of a gamer, but it's like my sister—my own sister—is a non-player character in my life, a character fully run by the game's software. Avery is the only other real player. Everyone else might appear to be here, but at the same time, they're not truly here.

The server sets two steamers of dumplings in front of us, and I mumble my thanks.

Madison leans forward. "You look like you really needed a mental health day. If that guy at work is getting you down so much, you should tell your boss, even if it might not go well. Maybe he'll surprise you."

"And if he doesn't?"

She shrugs. "Yeah, he probably won't, but you'll get another job. You've got lots of experience, right? If you feel stuck . . ."

Ha! She has no idea.

After lunch, Madison has things to do, and I walk around aimlessly.

What is the meaning of time? What is the meaning of life?

Am I trapped in a video game?

Why can't I figure this out?

With everything I try, I feel like I'm grasping at straws, not making any real progress, and I fear I'll be stuck here forever.

I stumble upon a brewery, and in my odd mental state, beer seems like a good idea, even though I'm not much of a beer person. A cold drink could be nice after being outside in the June weather. According to the sign, the taproom opens at three, which was two minutes ago.

When I step inside, the first thing I note is the singing. I look around. There are no other customers here, which isn't surprising, since it just opened and most people are at work. Two men stand behind the bar with their backs to me. They're singing something about winds and the sea. A sea shanty?

The one on the left is a thick white guy with shaggy brown hair. His voice is lower. The other man, who's writing the tap list on a chalkboard, is smiling as he sings. I can hear it in his voice, even though I can't see his face. There's something very charming about it all, and I almost find myself smiling too, despite my worries about being trapped in a video game.

The first man stops singing when he sees me. "Hey. Take a seat wherever you like." He gestures grandly around the taproom.

As I pull out a chair at the bar, the other man finishes the song. Then he turns around, and my heart speeds up. Unlike the other times we've met, he's wearing a T-shirt that says "Leaside Brewing."

"Hey." He smiles. "Have we met before?"

11

Noelle

June 20, Version 51-ish

It's Cam. The guy from the tea shop. After he finishes his bubble tea, he must come here for work. Then after work, he goes to the night market.

Why am I running into him again? What does it mean?

Maybe it means nothing. It's just a coincidence.

But I can't shake the feeling that it isn't.

"We have," I say at last, replying to his question. "Cam, right? Cameron?"

"Actually, it's short for 'Canmore.'"

"Did your parents name you after the place where you were conceived?"

I'm repeating a conversation we've had before because I'm thrown off by his appearance here and there's comfort in the familiar, even if it's a ridiculous question. I should know better than to ask such things. After all, my name sometimes leads people to ask if my parents are obsessed with Christmas—and that's not nearly as awkward.

The other guy laughs.

So does Cam. "I hope not. They just said they looked at a

map of Canada for inspiration." He pauses. "I'm sorry, I don't remember your name."

"Noelle."

"Nice to meet you. Again."

"You used to be a journalist, right?" I try to follow the script, even though it's an odd question in this situation. It's easier than figuring out what else I should say to him. Sure, it's been a while since we had this conversation, but I haven't forgotten how it goes.

"No, you must have me mixed up with someone else."

"Ah, I remember. Secret billionaire."

"And you're the heiress, right?" He winks at me, like he did the last time he said those words. There's that dimple again.

The other man slaps Cam on the shoulder before exiting the taproom. Cam and I have nearly finished our script. It was at this point in the conversation that my bubble tea order was ready.

"Where have we met before?" he asks. "It's strange that I can't remember."

I name the tea shop. "We've talked there a couple of times. I occasionally stop in before boarding my private jet."

He laughs. "Of course. Any good heiress has a private jet in case she has to make a quick escape—or an impromptu trip to Paris."

"Exactly."

"I ordered the Iron Goddess just an hour or two ago, but I hadn't been in a while." He shakes his head. "I guess that's why I can't remember, but it's still odd."

Yeah, it certainly is.

I tell myself to just go with the flow. After all, Cam is unlikely to recall the details of any conversation we have.

"Why is it so odd?" I ask with a tilt of my head.

"Because you're a very striking heiress," he says with a smile, and I can sense him trying to feel me out, trying to figure out where to go with this because he doesn't want to overstep.

"Is that so?"

He gestures to the chalkboard. "What do heiresses like to drink?"

"We usually go for wine of very exclusive, uh, vintages. I'm open to trying something new, but I don't know much about beer."

"Hm." He picks up a small glass and pours me a tiny amount. "Try this."

I knock it back and make a face before I can stop myself.

He chuckles. "Okay, no pale ales." He gives me something else to try.

I take a sip. "That's not bad."

"It's the Annex Pilsner." He points at the chalkboard and grabs another small glass.

I hold up a hand. "The pilsner's good. I'll have that. I'm sure your boss wouldn't like you giving away more beer. Or I can buy a flight. I'm an heiress, remember, so I have money to throw around."

"I'm the boss. It's fine."

"Yeah? Do you own this place?"

He nods. "With my friends. I'm the taproom and events manager—and I do various other things too," he adds with a laugh. "Whatever needs to be done."

Opening a brewery. Wow. That's the kind of risk I can't imagine taking. I'd rather just be an employee, though as Madison pointed out, being an employee at a different engineering firm might be something to think about.

He hands the third sample to me rather than putting it

on the surface of the bar. When our fingers brush, my breath hitches.

"What's this?" I ask.

"The Corktown Hefeweizen."

I take a tentative sip. The beer is a bit cloudy and has a slightly odd taste—I don't have the words to describe it—but it quickly grows on me. "I like it."

"Better than the pilsner?"

"Yeah. I'll have a pint of that."

He smiles and starts pulling me a pint of the Corktown.

"The p-pale ale really wasn't that bad," I stammer. "I'm sorry I insulted your beer."

"You didn't insult it."

"I think my facial expression did the work for me."

"It's fine. Everyone has different tastes—I'm sure heiresses have quite particular ones."

Music starts playing, and the other guy returns with some glasses and coasters. He sings along to the Matchbox Twenty song, which I haven't heard in a while. Cam joins in a moment later, pretending he's holding a microphone. I admire his ability to be a little goofy, to not be too self-conscious or take himself seriously.

And since I'm the only customer, I feel like it's a show just for me.

The song ends, and I clap. The other guy smiles as he exits the room, leaving Cam and me alone once more.

"You have a nice voice," I say.

"Thanks."

"You ever been in a band?"

"I was in an all-Asian Matchbox Twenty tribute band."

Okay, that's not what I was expecting. "Did you have many gigs?"

"A bunch, but it wasn't a full-time job, and unlike you, I don't have all those billions to fall back on."

I decide to tell him something true about myself. "I'm a mechanical engineer."

"Yeah? How do you like it?"

"It's fine. It . . . pays the bills."

"You sound a little unsure."

"It's the people I work with, not the actual work itself, which is part of the reason I'm taking today off. I feel like nothing I do matters." I mean that more literally than he knows. "But it's okay. This afternoon, I'm here with you."

I flash him a smile that I hope is a little seductive. Not because I'm scheming to get a kiss, but because I like him, and if I make a fool of myself, no one will remember but me.

Cam pretends he's strumming a guitar for a few seconds. Some kind of '90s or early 2000s alternative rock song is on now, though I don't recognize the band.

"Do you play?" I ask.

"A little."

I've never been a woman who dreams of dating a musician, but today, that's changed. I want this guy. He might not be winning any awards for his air guitar, but he's fun and sincere, even when he's joking about me being rich. He seems like the kind of man who's not afraid of showing his feelings.

The door opens behind me, and I try not to be annoyed. I have no right to be irritated that I don't have the bartender to myself anymore.

"Sit anywhere you like," Cam says, "and order at the bar when you're ready."

I'm relieved when the couple chooses the table farthest from the bar.

"You still like it?" He gestures to my pint.

"Yeah, I'll have to grab some cans for the jet."

"Are you taking off somewhere soon?"

"I've got a few hours."

I swear he looks at my mouth, then snaps his gaze back to my eyes. "Any plans for the rest of the day?"

I wonder if he wants to see me whenever he's done here. Or maybe he's just making conversation.

Probably the latter. I'm not great at reading these situations.

By four thirty, I'm almost done with my second beer, and the taproom is fairly busy. There's a group of seven guys at a table just behind me, and an older couple by the window. A few men in their twenties sit at the bar and ask a bunch of questions about the beer, which Cam gamely answers.

I consider ordering a third Corktown, then decide against it. I don't feel like getting drunk, and the only reason I want to stay here is Cam, who's now occupied.

"Can I get you another?" he asks me as I knock back the rest of my pint.

"No, just the bill, thanks."

He nods, and it's not long before I've tapped my credit card and am ready to go.

"Noelle. Wait." He slides a scrap of paper toward me.

"Your number?"

"You can toss it. No pressure. But I'm going to a night market tonight. Gotta talk to someone—I want them to bring their food truck here in August—but after that . . . No pressure, like I said."

"I'll see if my busy heiress schedule allows it." I'm tickled that this sea shanty–singing brewery owner wants to see me again. I lean forward and touch his wrist. "I'll text you. I promise."

After I get home and grab a snack, I add Cam's number to my contacts, then spend a good five minutes typing and deleting potential messages before sending something simple.

> **ME:** It's Noelle. You still want to meet up tonight?

I don't immediately get a response, but that's okay. If he's working behind the bar, he won't be able to check his phone.

About half an hour later, he replies.

> **CAM:** Hey! Good to hear from you. How about I meet you there at eight?
> **ME:** Sure! I'll let you know when I arrive.

I set down my phone and practically squeal. I have a date tonight, and it's not because I engineered a fancy—or messy—meet cute.

I'd forgotten what this feels like.

12

Noelle

"Dumplings?" Cam asks, gesturing to a booth.

"Not tonight," I say. "That's what I had for lunch." *And it's been the main food group in my diet for a while now.* "Feel free to get them for yourself, though. Those ones are pretty good."

"Yeah?"

"I had them at a festival, um, earlier this year."

Yes, it's a little awkward that I can't tell the entire truth about my life, but it's nice being at the market with Cam. I've been here countless times before, yet it feels different tonight. Like I'm seeing it with fresh eyes. There's an older couple dancing to the music. I vaguely remember them from before, but now the sight makes me smile. I examine the cupcake booth, wondering which flavor Avery would enjoy most. Perhaps I shouldn't wait until I escape the loop to do something for her birthday.

We turn down another row. I place my hand on Cam's arm so we don't get separated in the crowd. He doesn't seem to mind, which is excellent, because now that I've started touching him, I don't want to stop.

Cam is no longer wearing a Leaside Brewing shirt: he's put on a plain navy T-shirt instead. Nothing fancy, but this is just a casual date, even if I am an heiress.

He comes to a stop. "How do you feel about bulgogi poutine?"

"Could be weird, but I'd definitely try it."

"Okay. I'll get it and you can taste some of mine."

He smiles. Even though he smiles a lot, that doesn't dim the impact. I feel like he's just glad to be here with me.

"Sounds like a plan," I say.

"What are you thinking?"

I look around, and my gaze lands on a place selling samosa chaat. I gesture to the picture.

"How about we get our food, and I meet you over there"— he points to the benches—"when we're done?"

I nod my assent and give his arm a squeeze before standing in line. I watch the young woman deftly assemble my dish with chickpeas, samosa pieces, yogurt, two different chutneys, and small pieces of crispy noodle. Then I grab a napkin and head to the benches. Cam isn't here yet, and since I'm at the market at a different time from usual, there's seating available. I sit down and wait for him.

A few minutes later, he still hasn't arrived, and I start to worry. What if he's abandoned me? What if there was a beautiful woman next to him in line, one who actually knows something about beer, and—

"Hey." He's suddenly standing in front of me. "Something wrong?"

"Nope! All good." I don't want to admit that my brain had started spiraling. "Your poutine has cheese curds."

"Of course. It wouldn't be poutine without them."

"I'm not sure it goes with bulgogi and everything else there."

He shrugs. "We'll find out."

I recall the first time I met him at the market. He was carrying a tray of food then—was it also the poutine? Or does he eat something else on June 20 if he's not on a date with me?

Cam sits beside me, his leg brushing mine, as though we've

tacitly agreed to conserve space so that someone else can use the other end of the bench.

Or, you know, we just want to touch each other.

I release an undignified giggle.

"What's up?" Cam asks.

"I'm just, uh . . ." I decide to be honest. "I'm happy to be here. So much good food—though I still have reservations about yours—and good weather."

"And good company, I hope." He winks at me.

"Yeah. It's not often that I get to socialize with regular, down-to-earth people who . . ." I don't know much about being rich, to be honest. "Don't own multiple vacation homes."

I'm running this joke into the ground, but he doesn't seem to mind, and he'll forget this tomorrow anyway.

Actually, I prefer not to think about that. Even if I'm acting this way because there are no consequences, a part of me still hates the idea of him forgetting it.

I use some hand sanitizer, then dive into my food. I start with a little piece of samosa and chutney, which is deliciously tangy.

"Good?" Cam asks.

I'm still chewing, so I merely nod.

The smile slides off his face, and he pauses with a fry halfway to his mouth. "I just had the strangest sense of déjà vu. Like, I've been here before, at this market with you."

I stiffen and think of the first time I saw him. I was crying on this very bench.

"Yeah?" I say with a casualness I don't feel.

"But I have the sense it wasn't happy."

"Do you know what causes déjà vu?"

"I think it's due to processing errors in the brain. I guess you just made my brain misfire."

In his case, I suspect the déjà vu is caused by something different, though I don't understand exactly why it's happening.

"Well, I'm honored," I say, not sharing my suspicions.

He laughs, and I marvel at the fact that I'm sitting here with him, after all those failed attempts at kissing.

He eats a fry and a piece of bulgogi dotted with green onions and some kind of sauce. Then he holds the paper tray of fries toward me. I help myself, making sure I get both bulgogi and a cheese curd.

"Not bad," I say, "but mine's better." I hold it out so he can sample.

We eat our food in contented silence for a minute. Although we're not making conversation, there's lots of noise around us: food sizzling on a grill, children shrieking, K-pop in the background. The aromas of many different cuisines mingle together . . . and then there's Cam's clean, soapy scent.

"What did you do before the brewery?" I ask.

"I have a degree in life sciences."

"Were you planning on going to med school? *Did* you go to med school?"

"Nah. For a while, that was my plan, but I didn't have the marks for it. Worked in a lab for a couple of years."

I tilt my head, trying to picture him in a lab.

He chuckles. "Yeah, I didn't love it. Then my friend Darrell got into brewing, and I became interested too. Quit my job to work at a brewery in the east end, took some classes, and a few years later, this happened." He gestures at his shirt. "Oops. Forgot I changed."

"You put on a fancy outfit for your date."

He holds my gaze for a long beat, and eventually, I have to look away because it's too much. I've lived this day numerous times, yet it's never been like *this*. It makes me wonder about all the other routes my life might have taken, if one day had gone a little differently. Maybe some random choices on a March 7 could have altered my path.

"You've got some chutney . . . there." He points to the corner of his mouth.

I reach up to wipe it away.

"No, other side." He leans toward me, his face just a few inches from mine.

My heart thumps quickly in anticipation. My skin prickles in awareness. He's so close, his lips parted ever so slightly.

This is it. He's going to kiss me.

But then he hands me a napkin, and I paper over my disappointment with a smile and an overzealous "Thanks!"

Once we toss our empty trays in a nearly overflowing trash bin, we continue walking around the market. Night is starting to fall, and now it feels more like, well, a night market. Strands of lights twinkle against the darkening sky.

"Dessert?" Cam asks.

We survey the options, and I settle on halo-halo, something I've never had in my many trips to this market. He considers getting cheesecake but ultimately goes with red-bean taiyaki.

The benches are full now, and I hesitate before leading him up the stairs and around the civic center. Despite the busyness of the market, it's not crowded here, but there's no place to sit, so we lean against the wall instead. We're not alone, not really, but it's as good as we can do before my ube ice cream melts.

The ice cream is delicious, but the flan—oh, the flan is possibly the best thing I've ever eaten in my life, and I close my eyes and groan. It feels unfair that I'm enjoying this by myself, so I pick up a tiny piece with my spoon and hold it to Cam's lips. He tastes it, and I try not to be jealous of a fucking plastic spoon for the contact it gets with his mouth.

Once we've finished eating, he steps away to throw out my cup, then returns to the wall. I'm leaning with my shoulder against the brick, and he mirrors my pose.

"This was a really good day," he says.

"Yeah, it was." My favorite iteration of June 20 so far.

He doesn't say *because of you*, and I don't either.

But I can feel it, unspoken in the air.

"I'm glad my jet touched down in Toronto today," I say.

Cam chuckles before his expression turns serious. He lifts one hand to cup my cheek, slowly moving it higher until his fingers slide into my hair. There's lots of opportunity for me to pull away, if that's what I want.

But I don't.

When I wrap my arm around his waist, he sets his mouth to mine.

The kiss is a little awkward at first, and I'm probably the one to blame for that. It's been so long since I kissed someone—not counting that brief attempt with Avery—and we both angle our heads the same way and bump noses. But I persevere—and then it's exactly right. His arm is secure around my back, which is good, because I feel off-balance.

Again, I blame it on the fact that I haven't properly kissed anyone in years, but even if I had . . . I think it's him, and the wonder of this day. He tastes faintly of sweet red bean, and joy, and magic.

"Noelle," he murmurs.

Before I can string any words together, he returns to kissing me. My hands toy with the bottom of his shirt, eventually slipping underneath so I can touch his warm skin. God, he feels amazing. I kiss him like there might not be a tomorrow, like this is the only night we have.

"How did you end up at the brewery today?" he whispers.

"I don't know. I was wandering . . . and I just did. Even though I'm not much of a beer person. Except for that . . ." My brain can't recall the style of beer that I liked. It starts with an *h*, but that's as far as I get.

It doesn't matter, though, because his lips are on mine again, as if he can't get enough. With Cam, I'm not just some person who fades into the background, who keeps her head down and does her work. I don't know exactly how he sees me, but I like it. I like—

My phone buzzes insistently in my purse.

"Ignore that." I grab a fistful of his shirt and pull him closer. I'm not used to feeling so greedy, but—

It keeps buzzing.

"Look," he says, "as much as I'd like to stay here with you, it's almost ten o'clock, and I've got a busy day tomorrow. I should head home, but if you can keep your jet in the city a little longer, I can spend all of Sunday with you. If you're interested, that is."

I try to ignore my disappointment. "Yes, I'd like that very much."

Which is the truth. I just don't know if Sunday is a thing that can happen to me. The existence of something as mundane as a Sunday in June? It seems like a miracle now.

But maybe the kissing will break me out of the loop, and I hope it's this version of June 20 that he remembers. I don't want to be a stranger to him.

Sure, kissing Avery didn't work, but that could be because she's not my true love. After all, in fairy tales, it's always true love's kiss that causes a transformation. I can't believe I'm thinking those words to myself, but there it is.

As we walk to the subway, I circle my hand around Cam's upper arm, like I did earlier. This time, it's not so I don't lose him in the crowd; it's just so I can maintain our connection a little longer.

Before we head to opposite platforms, he plants a kiss on my cheek.

"See you soon," he says, and I don't know how to respond, but he's walking away already, hands in his pockets.

While waiting for my train, I check my phone to see who interrupted my kiss, but since I've never had a text at this time on June 20 before, I have a pretty good idea of who it is. My suspicions are soon confirmed.

> AVERY: I broke up with Joe again. But this time, I phrased it
> differently, and I guess it set him off.
> AVERY: OMG I can't believe I was with him for so long.
> Do you know what he told me? He said I'd come
> crawling back because I'd soon realize that I can't
> do any better.
> AVERY: That I was LUCKY he even took a second look
> at me
> AVERY: That ASSHOLE

Despite the dreamy night I've had, it doesn't take long for fury to build up in my veins. I can't remember the last time I was so righteously angry on a friend's behalf, perhaps because it's been a while since I've had a friendship like this.

> ME: Ugh. He's a piece of shit. Do you want to come over
> so you don't have to stay there tonight?
> AVERY: Yeah. If it's okay with you?

Avery arrives at my apartment half an hour after I do. Her face is red, and I pull her against me and give her a hug.

"I hope the breakup gets me out of the loop," she says. "It better. If I wake up next to him again, I might be tempted to smother him with a pillow."

"I don't blame you. I hope we both get out of it." I pause. "I kissed Cam tonight, so maybe that'll work."

"Really? I thought you'd given up on it."

"I walked into a brewery, and there he was, behind the bar. We started talking, and . . ." I shrug. I don't want to talk too much about me. Avery's the more important one right now—she just ended a long-term relationship.

"That's good," she says. "I hope us both changing our love lives will do the trick. I'd hate to get out of it by myself, only to find you had no idea who I was." She covers her face with her hands and releases a very emphatic "*Fuck*."

"Would some food help?" I gesture to the coffee table, where I've laid out bags of sour cream and onion, ketchup, and regular chips. I also have Cheetos and Oreos, since I wasn't sure what she likes. I stopped at a convenience store on the way home.

She hesitates.

"If I don't have anything you like . . ." I begin.

"No, no. Just deciding since I can't eat everything."

"You could," I say. "We could dump some of everything into a bowl." The time loop has made me think of wacky things that never would have occurred to me before. After all, tomorrow—

Well, it might actually be June 21. I want to move forward in life—and I definitely want Cam to remember me—but I still feel a pang at the thought of having actual consequences and not being able to buy any food I like without a care for the cost.

"Nah, I'll just stick with the sour cream and onion." Avery grabs a few chips, then offers the bag to me.

I shake my head. "What do you want to do? Do you want to, um, talk about it more?"

God, that sounded awkward.

"Not now. Maybe tomorrow. You said you're watching *Suits*, right? Let's do that. Whatever episode you're on works for me."

We watch two before turning in for the night. We fold down the futon, and I get some extra pillows and blankets from the closet. She's lucky I have them; I've never had an overnight guest at this apartment before.

"Noelle?" she says. "No matter what happens, I'll talk to you tomorrow, okay?"

I nod, then head to my room and turn out the light.

What day will it be when we wake up?

13

Noelle

June 20, Version 52-ish

My alarm goes off at 6:45 a.m. Though I know what I'll find when I go to the living room, I check anyway.

Avery isn't here, as expected. It's June 20. Again.

Some foolish, romantic part of me feels a keen sense of disappointment, different from the disappointment I've felt dozens of times before. I thought that part of me had long been extinguished, but apparently, I was wrong.

I guess Cam isn't my true love.

Of course, he still could be. There's no reason this time-loop curse should be broken by true love's kiss, just because it broke Sleeping Beauty's curse.

I'm shaking my head at my silly thoughts when I get a text.

AVERY: I woke up next to Joe. Goddammit.
AVERY: Are you still in the loop with me?
ME: Yeah. I'm still here.
ME: Want to meet up in a few hours?

Avery dumps a bunch of sugar into her coffee. We head to the patio at the coffee shop, managing to snag a table under an umbrella.

"I really thought that might work," she says. "For both of us. You kissed Cam, I broke up with Joe—and spoke my mind, unlike before. Or maybe it was more that I desperately hoped it would work." She sips her coffee. "How did I not realize that Joe sees me as beneath him? That he thinks he's the one who settled? Now I have to live through yet another disappointing birthday, and . . ." She leans closer and lowers her voice. "Is it your period?"

I wasn't expecting this change in topic. "Uh, no."

I haven't gotten my period since I started this time loop, and I *know* it's not because I'm pregnant. Sure, unlikely things are happening to me now, but immaculate conception seems a step too far.

"My body completely resets each morning," Avery says. "It's *always* my period."

My eyes widen in horror. She definitely has it worse than I do.

"On the plus side, I never run out of tampons." She chuckles ruefully. "The ones I use reappear each morning."

I take a peek around the patio, making sure that no one is listening to the very bizarre conversation we're having.

"There must be some way to escape the loop. I can't keep doing this. I *can't*," Avery practically wails, and I cover her hand with mine.

"We'll get out of it," I say, with more confidence than I feel. I quickly try to think of ideas. "What about travel? Neither of us has had a real vacation in a long time, right? Maybe that's what we most need."

"So we'll spend all day on a flight to Rome, check into the hotel, then wake up in our own beds?"

That does seem likely, but . . .

"What if the time loop only happens if we're in the Toronto area? Our hypothesis is that it's worldwide, but we should do an experiment to test that. We'll go somewhere closer than Europe, so we don't spend all day in transit."

Avery nods slowly. "I suppose that makes sense."

"What about New York? Do you have a passport?"

"Yeah. And I've never been to New York."

"Perfect!" I inject enthusiasm into my voice, in an attempt to cheer up my friend. "There are lots of flights to New York, which is good because we can't buy a ticket in advance. How about we meet at the island airport tomorrow around nine? With any luck, we'll be out of Toronto by noon."

"Worth a try," Avery says.

"Yeah, I think so."

"If this is the thing that ends the loop, we'll both get out of it." She pauses. "I'm glad we're in this together."

"Me too."

I spend a few hours researching what we can do in our presumably limited time in New York. I went once before—with my mother and Madison—but it's been years.

Around dinnertime, I return to the market. There are still lots of vendors that I haven't tried. I purchase some dry pho and sit on the bench beside the man and his young son, and . . .

I freeze.

Cam is standing nearby. His gaze snags on me, and he walks over.

"Hey," he says. "You look really, really familiar, but I can't recall your name."

I suck in a breath. I knew this would probably happen, but it's still a bit of a shock. Someone who had his mouth on mine ought to remember me, yet he doesn't. I'm the only one with memories of our date, and now I realize I'd hoped that, at the very least, our kiss would cause him to remember more than before.

Alas, that doesn't seem to be the case.

"You must have me mixed up with someone else," I say, forcing a smile.

"Sorry, my mistake."

I watch him disappear into the crowd. I could have continued our conversation. Introduced myself. Made that terrible comment about his name, only to have him forget it all tomorrow.

Some other time, perhaps, but I have something else to do tonight. I had an idea while looking at a map earlier.

I make my way to the nearby cemetery. If the dumpling woman is a ghost, maybe I can find her here. The sign says that visiting hours end at eight, so I'll make sure I leave by then, in case they lock the gates.

The large cemetery is very, very quiet, aside from the distant sound of traffic. Nobody else is around. The busy night market isn't far from here—lots of people jostling for dumplings and mochi and noodles—but I can't hear that now.

It's just me and the tombstones.

A little unnerved, I grip my keys in my left hand. I keep my gaze moving, looking for anything that could be a ghost capable of selling magical dumplings, but I see nothing. A gust of wind rustles the leaves in the trees, but that doesn't bring out any ghosts.

I think of my grandparents. My grandfather died in my last year of high school, and my grandmother in the summer after my third year of university; they've both been gone more than ten years. I last went to their graves—in a different cemetery— on Tomb Sweeping Day.

I hear another rustle, but it's not due to the wind.

And there it is again.

Slowly, I approach the nearest bush. I see a flash of white among the leaves, followed by a hissing sound, and my heart kicks up another notch.

Is that a shoe?

I step closer.

Oh, crap.

I don't know much about skunks, but in the past ten minutes, I've significantly increased my knowledge base. Apparently, they don't like spraying but do it when they're frightened. It must have felt threatened by my skulking about the cemetery.

A little further research on my phone informs me that instead of tomato juice, I should try a mix of hydrogen peroxide, dish soap, and baking soda to get rid of the odor. Fortunately, I have all of those things in my apartment, so I won't have to stink up a store. I decide to walk home instead of taking public transit or an Uber, to avoid being in an enclosed space with another person. According to Google Maps, it'll take just over an hour.

There are few pedestrians on the streets, and I'm not used to walking so far at dusk. It's probably fine, but I keep gripping the keys in my pocket. Sure, the fact that I smell like absolute shit might scare off some people, but no guarantee it will work on everyone.

My legs are tired when I reach my apartment building, but I take the stairs rather than the elevator to the seventh floor—less likely to run into someone that way—and begin my attempts to de-skunk myself.

By the time I climb into bed, I still stink, but not quite as badly, and with any luck, tomorrow will be June 20 again and I'll smell like a normal human being.

———

I've never been happier to wake up to my alarm and discover that Wordle is, once again, "happy." I breathe in deeply. Yep, the skunk odor is gone.

I add Avery's contact info to my phone and send a text to confirm our meeting time. After a quick breakfast and coffee, I pack a large purse. I add a cardigan and pajamas, but I don't pack any more clothes.

It's a long trip down to the airport, but we manage to get there around nine. We investigate the flight situation and discover there's one at eleven thirty with available seats. I take out my credit card and wince as I pay. I don't fly often, and when I do, I usually book far in advance and get a good deal. We're probably only going to spend twelve hours in New York, and it seems extravagant to do this. Even with all my experience of credit card purchases not existing the next day, it still makes me grimace.

It's instinctive for me to save money. The memories of my parents' anxious whispers about mortgage and car payments . . .

In some places, teachers don't make much at all, but here, they do okay, which means many people think they're overpaid. Most years, Dad taught summer school for extra money. Mom usually worked part-time, but there were years when she was the main caregiver for my paternal grandparents. My father's younger brother frequently needed to be bailed out of one thing or another, so with all that, my parents had trouble paying the bills at times. These were problems they tried to keep from us, and my siblings usually didn't know—but I did. I heard their conversations, and I saw the differences in our lifestyle. I wouldn't say they were really careless with their money, but they didn't always make the best decisions, and they felt obligated to help people even when they couldn't afford it.

It stressed me the fuck out.

I swore that when I grew up, I'd be better at saving and living below my means, so my finances wouldn't cause such stress—and I'd be able to help my immediate family without sleepless nights. Though if my siblings ended up being as foolish as my uncle—which I highly doubted—I had no intention of repeatedly assisting them.

Housing prices in Toronto have skyrocketed and I still haven't bought a place of my own, but I hope to within the next five years. I'm careful to put aside a decent amount each month. I don't own a car. I don't travel a lot. I don't go out much. I'm frugal when it comes to my wardrobe. I've lived in the same small one-bedroom apartment for eight years, and the rent isn't terrible.

My repeats of June 20 have been a little different, though, and when we get to New York, I continue to spend money that I wouldn't normally spend. Even a modest hotel in Manhattan isn't cheap, especially with the exchange rate. Once we've checked in, Avery wants to see the Empire State Building, and we pay to go up and look out at the city. Luckily, June 20 is quite a nice day in New York. Hot, but not completely disgusting, and with the clear skies, we have a good view as we stand among all the other tourists.

By the time we finish with the Empire State Building, it's almost dinnertime. The flight—and getting into the city from Newark—took much of the afternoon. We see Times Square on the way to Central Park, where we wander around before deciding that food really is a necessity.

"What do you want to eat?" I ask Avery.

There's a dizzying array of possibilities, but we end up just getting cheap pizza on paper plates. We eat in the park, entertained by a man playing a saxophone, and then we mosey down the streets.

"You know what we should do?" Avery says. "The next time we come here—"

"The next time?"

"Yeah. I have a feeling this isn't going to break the loop, which means we can come back for free and buy expensive last-minute Broadway tickets. I think it's too late for that today."

"Sounds like a plan."

"If I knew how much longer the loop would last, it would be easier to enjoy. Like, another twenty or thirty days? Fine. I'd spend it watching shows and eating good food and trying different hair colors. But when you worry it might go on forever, it's hard to live in the moment."

"I agree."

"But I'll try," she says, lifting her chin. "For tonight."

"What do you want to do?"

"Top of the Rock, so we can see the city at night?"

We go up our second skyscraper of the day, and as we look out at the glittering lights, I feel tiny and insignificant. Toronto is a large city too, but it's been a long time since I've seen it from up high; I haven't been up the CN Tower in over a decade.

Yet of all those people, I'm the one who's stuck in a loop, remembering repeats of June 20 that no one else but Avery seems to recall. Are there others out there that we haven't been able to find? Is our time loop unimportant, in the grand scheme of things? Does stuff like this happen regularly and we just don't know about it?

I feel like I don't have the answers to anything.

Afterward, we have cocktails at a rooftop bar. Then I convince Avery to order cake at a late-night café—it's her birthday, after all. Once we've split a large piece of salted caramel cheesecake, we return to the hotel and collapse into our beds.

When I wake up, I'm back in my apartment.

14

Noelle

June 20, Version 54-ish

The June 20 after our trip to New York, I'm well rested, despite the fact that yesterday was very busy. Still, I decide to have a leisurely day: I rebuy the ebook that I was reading on the plane and finish it with my morning coffee, absently thinking that while it was annoying not to have more time in New York, it was nice to only have to deal with the airport once.

By midafternoon, however, I feel the need to get out, and I find myself heading to Leaside Brewing. When I step inside, Cam and his colleague are singing a sea shanty once again, though it's a different one from last time—I assume that's because I'm a few minutes later.

"Hey." Cam smiles at me. "Have we met before? You look really, really familiar, but I can't recall your name."

I tamp down a prickle of irritation. "You're Cam, right? Cameron?"

Our conversation proceeds the same way it did last time, and my annoyance fades. This is rather comforting, actually. I'm reliving a good day; I bet many people wish they had the ability to do that. I don't recall the exact words I said, so there are little differences here and there, but it's more or less the same, until he asks what heiresses like to drink.

"We usually go for wine," I say. "Preferably ones that cost at least two hundred a bottle. I'm open to trying something new, but I don't know much about beer."

"Hm." He picks up a small glass and pours me something. "Try this."

I'm prepared for it to taste terrible. Last time, the first beer he gave me was a pale ale, and I didn't like it. But this is really good.

It's the hefeweizen.

I don't say that, though; after all, I just told him that I know nothing about beer. Also, I'm struggling to gather my thoughts. It's like he knew the beer I prefer, even if he doesn't remember that day. When he forgot my name, I thought our date didn't make a difference . . . but apparently, it did, however small.

"I'll get a pint of this," I say at last.

"I had a feeling you'd like it."

"A feeling. What do you mean, exactly?"

He shrugs, then goes to pull a pint. "I don't know. Just did. It's the oddest thing."

Is Cam the key to sorting out the time loop? He remembers the beer I like, he keeps thinking I look familiar—and I've stumbled across him in three different places on June 20.

Or is this a sign that we're meant to be, even if the kiss didn't work?

I shake my head. *Meant to be? What's wrong with me?*

But at the very least, I should spend more time with Cam and try to figure this out. That's only sensible. What else might he remember? Will it lead me to any answers?

As it gets busier, I admire the easy way he talks to people, his fluid motions behind the bar. I recall what it was like to have those arms around me.

After I pay, he slides me a scrap of paper with his number. No pressure, he assures me, but I can text him if I like.

And I do.

We meet up at the night market again, and once again, he suggests dumplings.

"No, I've had a lot of dumplings lately. I'll try something else." I tilt my head. "But speaking of dumplings, have you ever heard of dumplings that make you travel in time? Or, random example here, relive a day over and over?"

"Uh . . ."

"Forget it. It's just a story one of my heiress friends told me, but she was high on designer drugs at the time."

We get our food and sit on the same bench as before.

"You know," Cam says, "I just had the strangest sense of déjà vu. Like I've eaten bulgogi poutine here with you before."

"Yeah?" I hesitate. "What did we do afterward?"

"I saw someone eating taiyaki, and that sounds good to me." He leans in, his breath tickling my ear. "But I also . . ."

There's a very, very intense pause. He's feeling me out, trying to figure out what *I* want. There are lots of people around us, but I'm most aware of him, of how close he is to me.

With another man, before this time loop, I wouldn't have been so sure. So bold. But it's Cam, and I've already kissed him, even if he doesn't remember.

And maybe, once he feels my lips on his . . .

I shift my tray of food to one hand, and I dance the fingers of my other hand over his shoulder. "What about after you eat dessert?"

"We'll see." He winks at me.

This time, I get taiyaki too, and once again, we end up behind a building as we eat. After he throws away our paper bags, I say, "Good thing my jet touched down in Toronto today."

"I agree."

When he lifts a hand to my cheek, I know what's coming next. I breathe rapidly in anticipation as I wrap my arm around him and pull him close.

He sets his mouth to mine, and it's . . . different. I can tell that immediately. There's no initial awkwardness, and I don't think it's just because my last proper kiss was only three days ago, rather than years ago.

No, there's something different in *him*. As if he remembers. He doesn't say as much, but his body tells me that he does. He knows what I like the most. It's mere seconds before I'm softly moaning against him. My hands slip under his shirt, and he hisses out a breath.

This time, I know we won't be interrupted by my phone because, first of all, Avery's actions aren't on the same schedule every day, and second of all, I've set my phone to silent.

He presses me against the wall, and when I arch against him, his mouth slides to my neck. God, how am I so sensitive? One of his hands slips down to grip my ass, and I can feel his erection against my thigh.

"How did you end up at the brewery today?" he whispers.

I don't answer; I just keep kissing him.

When his lips leave mine again, I squeak in protest. He turns, and I follow his gaze.

"Is that a skunk?" I ask.

"Looks like it."

Goddammit. I wonder if it's the same one who sprayed me in the cemetery. Thankfully, after watching us for a moment, it scurries off.

"I should go," Cam says, "much as I'd like to stay here with you. I have a long day ahead of me tomorrow, but I'm free on Sunday. Does that work for you?"

"Yeah, it does."

I feel a touch of sorrow that he won't remember me tomorrow. There's a chance he'll remember a little more than he did today, but he probably won't *really* remember.

I try to focus on the fact that I can repeat this day with him. I swore off relationships after Dave, but this isn't really a relationship. How can it be, when I have to keep telling him my name? It's just a little fun, and I deserve that, don't I?

Besides, he might be important to figuring out the time loop.

When Cam and I part, I pull out my phone and text Avery to ask where she's staying tonight. I should have done that earlier.

She informs me that she's broken up with Joe again, although this time, she's insisted he spend the night at his parents' so she can have the apartment to herself.

The next day, Avery and I meet for coffee again. We sit outside, the weather as pleasantly warm as it always is on June 20.

"Yesterday," she says, "I donated a thousand dollars and volunteered at a food bank—I *insisted* they let me come in that afternoon—to see if doing good deeds would help. But they didn't. I don't know what to do." She pauses. "You're an engineer. Could you, like, build something to get us out of this?"

"I can't fix a problem if I don't understand it at all, and we haven't made much progress in understanding this."

"I'm just so tired of being stuck."

"I know."

Here I am, getting the chance to relive a great first date and first kiss, and she keeps waking up next to her ex and has a never-ending period.

I'm not sure I'm doing a very good job at this being-a-good-friend business, but I don't know what I can do other than listen and perhaps offer suggestions, however unlikely they might seem. Anything that might give her a bit of hope.

"Traditional Chinese medicine!" I say suddenly. "What if this is happening because our qi is blocked? If we restore balance, maybe the passage of time will become unblocked for us too."

"Do you mean acupuncture?" Avery asks.

"Yeah, but there are other things as well. How about you get acupuncture, and I'll go to an herbalist?"

"It's worth a try."

The next day, I make a trip to a Chinese herbalist. I explain my problems to a man who's at least eighty-five and doesn't look at me like I'm batshit crazy. He confesses it isn't something that he's personally treated before, though he's heard of such a case. Unfortunately, he can't provide any details about that case, but he gives me a concoction of interesting-looking herbs to try and explains how to prepare them.

At home, I soak and boil them for the prescribed amount of time, in a clay pot that I bought along with the herbs. As I wait for them to be ready, I recall there was a subtle flavor in the old woman's dumplings that was unlike any dumpling I'd had before. I couldn't figure it out, but maybe it's one of these herbs? And maybe tasting it again will break the curse?

I try the liquid. It tastes like it ought to be good for me—by which I mean, it's absolutely foul. No hint of anything that was in those dumplings.

Not feeling terribly hopeful, I text Avery.

ME: How was the acupuncture?
AVERY: Great. I'm definitely more relaxed now. Maybe it did
     help to unblock my qi.

Once again, we'll just have to wait until morning.

15

Noelle

June 20, Version 57-ish

When I wake up, it's still June 20. As always, I add Avery to my contacts and text her to confirm that she too is still in the loop.

We decide to make another attempt at traditional Chinese medicine, but our efforts are unsuccessful once more.

The following day, Avery suggests we go to a fancy salon and get makeovers. I opt for a pixie cut again, and at her insistence, I also have my hair dyed pink.

"You look really good," she says as we look in the mirror.

"Are you sure?" I ask doubtfully.

"It's a great look for you," the stylist says.

To be honest, I'm not sure it's *me*.

But that's okay. It'll disappear tomorrow.

"Time to see Cam?" Avery asks.

"Yeah." I pause. She wants to meet him, and the plan is that she'll accompany me to the brewery, but I'm not sure I want to do the initial flirting in front of her. "Maybe it would be better if I get there first, and you arrive later?"

She decides to pop into a store, and I head to Leaside Brewing alone. Once again, I'm met by a sea shanty. I smile, but then my worries get the best of me.

What if Cam doesn't like women with short hair? Or women with pink hair? Maybe he liked me as I looked before, but—

"Hey." He tilts his head. "Have we met before? You look really, really familiar, but I can't recall your name."

"Cam, right?" Deciding to mix it up a little, I say, "I've come here a bunch of times before, though it's been a while. I'm Noelle."

I say nothing about being an heiress, and it makes me a touch nervous—I'm going further off script. But I don't want to have exactly the same encounter every time. Although we may only have the one day, I can still use it to learn different things about him.

He shakes his head. "I can't believe I forgot. I'm usually good with names. Especially . . ."

"Especially what?" I ask, leaning forward.

The silence that follows is heavy, and I'm very conscious of how much I like the look of him. His easy smile and those gently sloped shoulders.

He laughs and shakes his head again.

"When it comes to women with bright pink hair?" I supply.

"Yes. Exactly."

"I only got it done today. Perhaps it's throwing you off."

"Perhaps." He gestures to the chalkboard with the tap list. "What would you like to drink? I seem to think that last time you had the Corktown."

"Can't remember my name but you remember my beer," I tease.

I could never flirt like this before my life started repeating. Knowing he won't remember tomorrow—not fully, anyway— is a double-edged sword. If I screw this up, I'm the only one who has to live with the embarrassing memory beyond the next twelve hours. And if I don't screw this up and we go out, I'm the only one who will remember our date.

"So it seems," he says as he starts filling a pint glass.

"The important things in life."

He returns with my beer. "I think names are important too, but I won't forget it now."

Oh, but you will.

"Do you serve food?" I ask, suddenly realizing I haven't eaten since breakfast. After getting my hair done, I was too focused on arriving here at three to think about the food situation, but now, my stomach is growling. I hope he doesn't hear it.

"We've got a few things." He motions to a QR code for me to scan. "On the weekends, I try to arrange a food truck around the corner—going to talk to someone about that later, actually—but this is what we have now."

I take a quick look. "The meat pie sounds good."

According to the menu, it's made by a company that special-izes in pies. I've had their pies before and enjoyed them, though it's been a while. My stomach growls even louder than before.

"Sorry," I say.

"How about this? The pie will take twenty-five minutes, but it comes with chips. I can get those for you now."

"That would be great. Thank you."

He leaves and returns a moment later with a bowl contain-ing some kettle chips.

"Can't have anyone dying of hunger in the taproom," he says.

"Yeah, that would be unfortunate." I scramble for some-thing else to say, and somehow land on, "Though I don't think there's much danger of that happening. Before I die of hunger, I'd shape-shift into a, uh, bear. Then I'd eat all your customers, which would probably be, uh, worse for you."

Oh god. What is wrong with me?

I can't think of clever things to say on the spot. Sometimes I just make things awkward. Like when Dave gave me a cute card with koalas, and I wondered aloud whether these particular koalas had chlamydia because apparently a lot of wild koalas do. I don't think that was quite what he'd intended to discuss on Valentine's Day.

I consider running out of the taproom and writing this day off as a loss—I can try again tomorrow—but I really am hungry, and I want to eat those chips. And that pie. Hopefully the rest of my food arrives soon, and then I can scarf it down and meet Avery at another location.

"Luckily," Cam says, "you're my only customer right now."

It takes me a moment to figure out what he's talking about. Wow, he actually responded to my bizarre comment about turning into a bear. He might just be trying to keep his only customer happy, but maybe I should keep talking. After all, flirting is mostly about confidence, right? And I can hardly hide in the corner when I have bright hair.

"Very true," I say smoothly. "I guess I'd just have to eat you instead." I give him an assessing look. "Yep, I think you'd do nicely. So it's lucky for you that I have these." I point to my chips before grabbing a handful. I wash them down with beer.

At that point, his colleague returns, and they start singing "Unwell." A moment later, Avery enters and takes a seat beside me.

"That's him?" she whispers, nodding toward Cam.

"Yeah."

He's bopping his head along with the music. When they finish singing, Avery and I clap. The other man heads to the back again, and Cam asks Avery what she'd like to drink.

She shrugs and points to my glass. "I'll have that."

"Good choice," he says.

"What would be a bad choice?" I ask.

"Deciding you don't like anything here and going to another bar."

"Don't worry, I'm not doing that," Avery says.

He pulls her pint, then says to me, "I'm going to get your pie. Can't have you turning into a bear."

When he leaves, Avery turns to me. "What was that about?"

"An inside joke."

"An inside joke? You only—well, *he* only just met you."

"What do you think of him?" I ask.

"After what happened with Joe, you should know I'm a terrible judge of men's characters, but he seems nice. Fun."

"And cute," I say.

"And cute."

But hearing her repeat those words makes me bristle.

"Don't worry," she says with a laugh, "he's all yours. He's not my type, but I understand what you see in him." She tastes the Corktown and makes a face. "Really? You like that?"

"Try the Annex next time," I suggest.

Cam returns with my meat pie, and I eagerly dig in. I'm not quite as ravenous after finishing the chips, but I'm still hungry, and the pie is full of rich braised beef and veggies.

As he serves other customers, I watch him out of the corner of my eye. His fingers curled around a glass. His easy laugh. The dimple that occasionally makes an appearance.

At one point, he catches me looking and shoots me a smile that would make my knees weak if I were standing.

"What do you want to do now?" I ask Avery.

"Well, you're going to get his number and meet him tonight—"

"I don't have to do that. I can spend today with you instead."

"Nah." She shakes her head. "Have fun. I'll be fine."

This time, I slip Cam my number rather than waiting for him to provide his.

Once again, we meet at the market, but as I look around at the crowds and the familiar booths, I can't find any enthusiasm for it. I've been here so many times before. Yes, there's lots of good food, but I've tried much of it, and the benches aren't the most comfortable places to sit.

"How about we grab something small here?" I suggest. "Maybe taiyaki? Then we can wander up Yonge and find somewhere else for dinner—a place where we can sit at a table. Heiresses are too refined for crowded markets." I attempt to toss my hair over my shoulder, then remember my hair is too short for that.

He furrows his brow. "What?"

Right. There were no heiress jokes today. He has no idea what I'm talking about.

"Ignore me. But what do you think of finding a restaurant?"

We buy some taiyaki and walk up Yonge. The first restaurant we enter is small and has nothing available, but a bustling izakaya miraculously has a table on the patio. I select a cocktail with plum wine, and Cam goes for one with yuzu and sake. We order a bunch of food.

"So, what do you do, Noelle?" he asks.

"I'm a mechanical engineer."

"An engineer who doesn't work on Fridays?"

"I banked a lot of vacation days, so I'm working four-day weeks this summer."

We talk a bit about our jobs, and I learn some things I didn't know before: Cam's plans for the brewery and how you go about getting the LCBO to stock your beer, for example. I've never given much thought to what it takes to run a brewery, but it sounds difficult to survive in this crowded marketplace. Cam's easygoing temperament belies the fact that he has a wealth of knowledge.

Our drinks and edamame beans arrive.

"Cheers," he says, clinking his glass against mine.

"Cheers."

He takes a sip of his drink. "Mm. That's good. We have a yuzu wheat beer. It's not on tap right now, though we do have cans. You might like it."

"I'll get some the next time I come in."

"You should. Or I can bring you a can sometime." He pauses. "If you didn't give me your number, I was planning to slip you mine."

"Is that something you do a lot?" I tease. "Handing out your number to cute women who come into your brewery?"

"No," he says, uncharacteristically serious.

My skin tingles, and I swallow hard.

Why am I special? What exactly does he see in me?

"I really can't believe," he says, "that I met you before and forgot your name."

I could attempt to tell him the truth, but that seems too weird. Instead, I say, "What would you do if you were stuck reliving the same day? Like, June twentieth, for example."

"What's everyone else doing in this scenario?"

"They're not aware that the same day is happening over and over. Only you remember the previous iterations of it."

"Sounds like a video game."

"Yeah. Except you don't die. You just keep waking up in the same day."

He gives me an odd look.

"I'm reading a novel," I say, "in which something similar happens."

He taps his chin. "Hm. I guess I'd find the best possible day, and I'd just keep living it again and again. This one, for example?" He gestures between us. "It's pretty good."

I roll my eyes. "You're such a charmer."

"No, just with you."

"See, there you go again!"

He chuckles. "Today *is* a pretty good day. I wouldn't want to relive Tuesday."

"What happened on Tuesday?"

"Oh, what didn't happen on Tuesday? Our air compressor had a leak. Then there were supplier problems . . . accounting problems . . . raccoon problems . . . It wasn't a fun day. And Darrell desperately needs another assistant brewer/cellarman." But Cam's smiling now. "It would probably take a little while to find the best version of the day that I could, but then I'd repeat it over and over."

"You wouldn't get sick of it?"

"I'd change it up a little," he says. "I wouldn't eat exactly the same meals every day."

"Now let's say, hypothetically, that this first date was part of that day, but when you woke up the next morning, I didn't know who you were."

"Then I'd get to know you all over again. It doesn't sound like a hardship."

I don't ask how many times the day would have to repeat for him to see it differently.

No, I just smile at him over my drink.

And when he kisses me later—in a parkette this time, rather than against a building—I sink into the moment and enjoy that I get to have a first kiss again.

The next day, after Cam and I eat at the market, I suggest mini-golf, something I haven't done in a long time. We take an Uber to a place in the suburbs.

"You are *so* going down," I say before the final hole.

Big talk from someone who's losing, but we've been playfully smack-talking each other the entire time.

He grins. "Is that so?"

I set up my shot. My ball goes under the kraken and bounces off the edge of the pirate ship, then off a plastic wave. I cheer as the ball stops remarkably close to the hole. Despite my confident words, I didn't expect to get this one in fewer than three shots, but I'll be able to manage it.

"Well, I can do better," Cam says.

He spends even longer preparing and shoots with a flourish. The ball goes beneath the kraken . . . and doesn't come out.

"Dammit," he says good-naturedly.

"Told you."

"You still haven't won yet. Pressure's on."

I make a show of shaking out my limbs, getting myself ready for this very important—and easy—shot. My ball manages the six inches to the hole without any difficulty, and I whoop.

Cam lifts his hand for a high five, and when our palms make contact, he pulls me into his embrace. Then he places his putter along the green and jabs under the kraken. The ball emerges, just barely, and it takes three more shots for him to get it in the hole.

Which means I'm the winner. Apparently, that earns me a kiss on the cheek.

"Congratulations," he says. "What do you want to do now?"

We didn't eat a lot at the market, so we go out for poutine. The regular kind, with just cheese curds and gravy. No bulgogi or green onions. We claim a picnic table outside in the darkness and sit on the same side of the bench.

It's a very cute first date.

"I'll text you tomorrow," he says as we begin our trip home.

"Yes." I swallow. "Tomorrow."

The next day, I find myself wondering how Cam starts his June 20. I've never seen him before noon. When does he wake up? What does he do before bubble tea?

I have no idea, but I do know where to find him at 3 p.m.

That evening, we go bowling, and Cam beats me handily. I haven't bowled in years, and my performance is honestly embarrassing—it certainly doesn't hold a candle to my mini-golfing—but I don't care. It's just fun to hang out with him.

I settle into a new routine of sorts, where I see Cam every day. I also get rather good at crocheting and start to find it frustrating that my creations don't survive the night, but I enjoy the act of creating something with my hands, however fleeting.

Though I'm often occupied with Cam, I make sure to devote time to Avery each day. Sometimes she breaks up with Joe, sometimes she doesn't—I understand it would be exhausting to keep doing that. We brainstorm ideas to get out of the loop and give them a try, but we're completely unsurprised when none of them work. We discuss whether it would be cheating if she were to kiss someone else, if she hadn't officially broken up with Joe that day—I say that the fact that she's broken up with him multiple times already (and never taken him back) has to count for something.

I find I'm not too bothered by our inability to escape the loop anymore. I start to feel relaxed for the first time in . . . I don't know how long. My life consists of first dates, talking to a friend, reading novels—mostly Avery's recommendations—and crocheting in front of the TV.

"What do you think happens when we get out of this?" she asks one day when we meet at a coffee shop.

"I assume it'll be June twenty-first," I say, "and the version of June twentieth that everyone else remembers will be the most recent one we lived." After all, that's what happened in the last book I read.

"That's what I figured, but what if the rest of the world is proceeding without us?"

"I don't know. Somehow, it just makes more sense to me that we'd wake up on June twenty-first."

But Avery brings up a good point. What *is* happening with the rest of the world while we're stuck? Is everything else frozen?

September

Cam

Although I've eaten more than enough food, my grandmother deposits an egg tart on my plate. The whole family has gathered for dim sum at a crowded restaurant near my parents' house, and on the other side of the round table, my father and aunt are having an argument about . . . something or other.

Unlike my parents, my grandma wasn't disappointed in me when I decided to quit my stable job to do something related to beer. Or when Justin, Darrell, and I opened the brewery a few years later.

Honestly, I was shocked. I'd expected her to be unhappy, but she even gave me the money she'd been saving for when I got married. I just had to promise that I wouldn't expect a big wedding gift.

"How is my investment?" she asks me now. She likes to jokingly call it an "investment" even though the money was a gift.

My father, who wasn't thrilled she gave it to me, makes a face. The two of us have never been particularly close, and his relationship with his mother has always been tense too, for reasons I don't fully understand.

"It's going well," I say.

"You meet any nice girls lately?"

"No, I've been busy." An excuse. I don't tell her that sometimes I wonder if it'll never happen for me, if I've missed my chance somehow.

"Ah, don't worry, you will find someone." She pats my hand, and I feel like she can read my thoughts.

And then I feel a strange prickle on my skin, and I have the overwhelming conviction that I just told a lie. That I've already met someone.

A moment later, it's gone.

"Mom tried to set me up with the daughter of one of her friends the other week," I say. "You think I should have agreed to that?"

My grandmother shakes her head. "No, you just wait. It will turn out."

"If she's not Taiwanese, is that okay?"

To my surprise, she doesn't even hesitate before nodding. "You are getting old."

"I'm not that old," I say with a chuckle. "Is that the only reason it would be okay now? Because you're desperate?" I tease.

"No, you are—aiya!" she exclaims as a piece of tripe escapes her chopsticks and falls to the ground. She's been dropping things more often lately, I've noticed.

Before she can bend over, I swipe it off the floor with my napkin.

"I know you are very busy," she says, "but come over soon, yes?" She lives with my parents now. Although she and my father often don't get along, he takes his duties as the eldest son seriously. "I will buy the mooncakes you like."

"Don't worry, I can bring them."

"Good boy," she says, even though I'm thirty-four. She leans closer to me, and I think she's going to add something more, but she just sips her tea.

16

Noelle

June 20, Version 80-ish

"What do you want to do now?" Cam asks, his hand around mine as we leave the market.

"Maybe a movie?" I suggest.

We take the subway to an indie theater. By the time we arrive, there's only one movie that hasn't started yet: a low-budget horror film. It's been ages since I've watched a horror movie on the big screen, and I nearly jump out of my seat at one point, spilling the remaining popcorn onto the floor.

When we see it for the second time a few June 20s later, I'm better prepared, but when we step out into the warm night air at eleven thirty, I'm still half-convinced that something is lurking in the shadows. After all, given how strange my life has become, it doesn't seem that far-fetched.

But a kiss from Cam wipes away those fears.

Another night, we watch an action movie together at a VIP theater with incredibly comfy seats. The next night, we opt for a raunchy comedy. Well, Cam suggests the action movie, but when I tell him I've already seen it, he's easily persuaded to see something else.

Seeing the trailers before the feature presentation is a strange experience. It feels like a message from a future that doesn't exist for me. I'm intrigued by an opulent historical drama that's supposed to come out at the end of the summer, which seems endlessly far away.

I live in such an odd reality.

Soon, I've watched every movie in theaters in the Greater Toronto Area. We've also watched a few movies back at my apartment, from *While You Were Sleeping* to *The Day After Tomorrow*—a day that seems like an impossibility in my life.

While spending so much time with Cam, I discover quite a bit about him.

I learn that his parents grew up in Taiwan and came to Canada in the eighties.

I learn that if I nibble at *just* the right place on his neck, he absolutely loses his mind.

I learn that it doesn't matter what I wear, or how I style my hair. The important thing is that when I get to the bar, I make conversation. Any kind of conversation will do. One time, we spend a rather long time discussing traffic and whether the Gardiner Expressway should be torn down.

He still gives me his number.

He never remembers my name, though. I've now told him my name forty-seven times. He does remember my preferred beer and how to kiss me. Once he learned those things, he never forgot them, even if he doesn't have clear memories of who I am. Unfortunately, spending more time with Cam doesn't cause him to develop any new knowledge of me, and I'm stumped as to how he could be related to the time loop.

But I do learn that when he sings "I've Got You Under My Skin," it's almost enough to make me cry.

———

One day, I feel like doing something different. After we've eaten at the market, I suggest we go down to the lake.

He looks at the time. "Now?"

"Sure, why not?" I'm carefree Noelle. "Don't worry—I won't keep you out all night."

Cam considers it for a moment. "All right."

We take the subway to Union, walk south to Lake Ontario, and wander down the trail by the waterfront. At one of the WaveDecks, I run down with my arms outstretched and feel like some kind of manic pixie dream girl who's supposed to help the hero learn to *live*.

Cam doesn't need my help with that, though.

We follow the sound of classical music toward the Music Garden, where we catch the tail end of a performance by a string quartet. Even though I've lived this day about a hundred times, there are still things happening in the city that surprise me. While I might never see the movies in those trailers, there's still more to discover.

We sit on a bench and look out at the dark water, my head on his shoulder.

"I'm not usually this spontaneous." The words are out of my mouth before I've thought them through.

He shifts, and I straighten up to look at him.

"You're not acting this way because you think that's what I want, right?" he asks.

"No. Today is just . . . a special day."

A dog, out for a stroll with its owner, woofs as if in agreement, and I chuckle.

"It's the longest day of the year," Cam says.

He doesn't realize how right he is, and it's more than I can handle. I laugh until I have tears streaming down my face.

He looks at me, eyebrows raised, as if waiting for an explanation.

"It sure feels that way," I say at last, wiping my eyes.

"Did something bad happen this morning?"

"You could say that, but I don't want to talk about it now. I'm here with you, and I can deal with it tomorrow." I feel like I'm all over the place; my feelings are a yo-yo.

"To tomorrow," he says, lifting an imaginary glass into the air and clinking it against my imaginary champagne flute.

To tomorrow, indeed.

In the mornings, before I go out to meet Cam, I do research. I read about him on the Leaside Brewing website—it's how I learn that his last name is Huang—and I teach myself about beer. I didn't know the difference between lagers and ales before, but I do now. Most beers are supposed to be clear, but I discover that hefeweizens are meant to be hazy. I learn about hops and IBUs. I learn a bit about the process of making beer, what must go on behind the scenes at Leaside Brewing. I don't use any of this knowledge to impress Cam; when I go to the brewery, I always say I know nothing about beer. But it makes me feel closer to him, somehow. It also makes me feel like a lovesick teenager.

I look him up on social media, and I laugh when I see a picture of him next to a "Welcome to Canmore" sign. I had wondered if he'd been there.

Occasionally, I take the day off from seeing Cam and go somewhere with Avery. We rent a car and drive to Prince Edward County, where we go to a couple of wineries and sunbathe on a sandy beach. Another time, we head up to Collingwood and swim in Georgian Bay.

I show her the trailer for the historical drama, and she agrees it looks interesting, a sad smile on her face. I read her favorite fantasy serics and encourage her to write fanfic, which she told me she used to do.

Our attempts to get out of the loop—a little half-hearted on my part—continue to fail. She goes to four different walk-in clinics to see if she can find a doctor who will believe her story.

She can't.

I haven't been neglecting my friend, but something I have been neglecting?

My family.

One night, when I'm lying awake at midnight and replaying Cam's goodbye kiss in my head, I decide that will change in the morning.

17

Noelle

June 20, Version 110, or thereabouts. I'm losing track

ME: Any plans for the day? How about I come over?
DALTON: Aren't you working?
ME: No, I have the day off.
DALTON: Sure! Whenever you're free. Lenora usually naps
    at two.

I arrive at my brother's apartment just as Lenora is finishing lunch. My fourteen-month-old niece has some jam on her nose and peanut butter below her ear. There's a half-chewed stick of cucumber on the tray of her high chair.

Dalton takes her out and wipes her off.

"Can you say hi to Auntie Noelle?" He waves in my direction.

Lenora waves at me, then buries her head against her father's shoulder.

"It's been so long," I say, leaning in to hug them.

Dalton frowns. "We saw you at Mom and Dad's last weekend."

Oh, right.

"Well, uh, it's been a long time since I visited your place." I'm pretty sure this is correct. The problem is that I'm starting to forget details of my life before June 20.

"Very true," Dalton says, and I breathe out a sigh of relief. I don't sound *too* confused.

Dalton is two years younger than me. Since his wife finished her mat leave, he's been a stay-at-home father. He's wanted kids of his own ever since he was a small child himself; when Madison came home from the hospital, he was enamored with her. He was so excited to have a little sister. He gave her toys and tried to comfort her when she cried, whereas I was indifferent. He also enjoyed pretending to be the parent of his stuffed hippo and beloved Ninja Turtle.

When my brother heads to the living room, I follow. One side of the floor is covered in a colorful alphabet play mat.

"How about you sit here with your auntie while I clean up?" He sets Lenora down and walks away.

"Daddy!" She starts bawling and runs after him.

"Okay, okay, I'll do it during your nap." He sits cross-legged on the mat and brings a few toys closer for her inspection.

"Am-ee," she says.

I have no idea what that means, but Dalton reaches for a plastic wrench and sets it in front of her.

"Am-ee!" She smacks it against a yellow plastic toy, which starts singing the numbers.

I wonder how many times he hears that every day.

As we watch Lenora whack a plushie with her wrench, Dalton says, "Mona's pregnant."

"Oh my god!" I say. "Congratulations." I give him a hug. "Do Mom and Dad know?"

He smiles. "We're going to tell them next weekend."

I mime zipping my lips. "How far along is she?"

"Thirteen weeks. At the end of the year, you're going to be a big sister, aren't you, Lenora?"

"Daddy! Up!"

He pulls her into his lap.

Eventually, she's distracted enough that Dalton is able to disappear into the kitchen without her noticing, but when she realizes he's gone—about four minutes later—she wails like she's been grievously betrayed. She scampers off with her wrench and stuffed monkey in hand . . . and she trips on the edge of the tile floor, which is slightly higher than the parquet. I see it happen as if in slow motion, but I'm not close enough to stop it. Her head hits the leg of the coffee table, and she wails even louder.

Dalton is there in a flash, scooping her into his arms and examining her injury. No blood, but I suspect she'll have a bruise.

"It's okay," he murmurs, and within two minutes, she's running around again.

Next time, I promise myself, I'll stop that accident from happening.

———

On the bus, I pull out my phone to text Cam. It's not until I fail to find his contact info that it hits me.

Cam Huang doesn't know who I am. The man who's watched several movies with me, beaten me twice at bowling—and lost to me at mini-golf—doesn't know who I am, even though he's kissed me dozens of times.

If I text him right now, he'll assume I have the wrong number.

I don't know how I forgot. After all, this has been my life for quite a while. But it also happened when Dalton told me about Mona's pregnancy: I failed to realize that as long as I'm stuck in this loop, I'll never meet their new baby. I'll never see Lenora get older.

I feel a keen sense of anguish.

Yes, I can try out different hair colors. I can eat expensive foods. I can even travel to New York and go up the Empire State Building.

But nothing can change, not really. Anything that happens is washed away at three in the morning, existing only in my and Avery's memories.

And even then . . . everything is blurring together.

———

I head to Leaside Brewing rather than going straight home.

"Hey," Cam says from behind the bar. "Have we met before? You look really, really familiar, but I can't recall your name."

I force myself not to wince.

"No." I don't introduce myself. "A pint of the Corktown, please."

"Somehow, I knew you were going to order that."

I shrug as he sets it in front of me.

He doesn't attempt any more conversation; he's respecting the fact that I clearly want to drink my beer in peace.

I can't believe you don't know me. You had your tongue down my throat last night!

This has happened countless times before, but it hurts. Any comfort I derived from the predictability of our interactions is fading. I'm irrationally annoyed with him, even though it's not his fault. I wish I could shake my world, like I could shake one of Lenora's toys, in the hopes of getting all the moving parts working again.

I remind myself that when it comes to Cam, I like the time loop. In fact, it's the reason I've allowed myself to spend so much time with him, even once I realized that kissing wouldn't get me out of the loop. As long as he doesn't remember me, we can't have a *real* relationship, just a fun first date.

Now, however, I'm not so fond of it.

Yet how can I want a relationship? That's the one thing I wished to avoid.

You think you know someone, after five years . . . and then they break your heart, and there's nobody to help you pick up the pieces. People do unexpected, irrational things, and a romantic relationship is orders of magnitude riskier than a dramatic haircut—and I didn't even try a new haircut until I got stuck on June 20.

I remember crying over Dave, wishing he hadn't changed and ended our relationship. And now I'm dating a guy who can't change, and it's not all I'd thought it would be. Of course, this is an unusual situation; it's certainly not what I had in mind when nursing a shattered heart.

Cam comes over and gestures to my almost-empty pint. "You want another?"

Today, he's just a bartender to me. Maybe he thinks I'm attractive, but he isn't going to do anything about it.

"Give me a minute to decide," I say.

Sure, it hurt that Dave dumped me out of the blue, but a whole bunch of other things are hurting me now. The man I'm falling for literally doesn't remember my name . . . and I fear I'll never meet my new niece or nephew. Did I think that by swearing off relationships, I'd completely avoid emotional pain?

Rather than getting something on draft, I scan the QR code for the bottle/can list and quickly find the one I want.

The yuzu wheat beer.

I ask Cam for one of those, and he soon brings over a cold can and a glass. As I take my first sip, I recall sitting on the patio with him, the warm evening air on my face, and I grimace. It's almost physically painful to me that he's forgotten all our dates.

I do like the beer, as he thought I might, though it's hard to truly enjoy it.

He doesn't properly remember me, but I've become attached to him.

I've never tried to go further than a kiss. It seems wrong, when he doesn't know the truth about our "relationship," but maybe I could try telling him.

I've been to the brewery enough times that I have a pretty good idea of who comes in and what they order. Now, I pay closer attention, and I write it all down in the notes app on my phone.

> 3:25: Man and woman in their forties, both wearing Jays jerseys. He orders the stout. She orders the IPA.
> 3:40: Group of four men in their twenties and thirties. They order nachos with no green onions. Two get IPAs. The other two get pilsners.
> Etc.

Of course, this document won't exist tomorrow, so when I get home, I do my best to commit it to memory. Then I text Avery.

ME: Went to see my brother today. What did you do?

I don't get an answer.

———

The next morning, Avery and I exchange our usual morning texts. She tells me that she was too despondent about doing the same things over and over to reply yesterday. Concerned, I suggest that we do something together today, but she declines and asks how it's going with Cam.

I hesitate before explaining my plans to tell him the truth. She's skeptical it'll work—the proof I have isn't enough to make up for the unbelievability of the situation—and I don't blame her, but it's worth a shot.

Then I text my brother again and ask if I can come over.

When we're all settled on the play mat, Lenora says, "Am-ee!" and I instinctively reach for the plastic wrench.

"How did you know what she meant?" Dalton asks.

"You mentioned it the other day," I say brightly, hoping to cover up my mistake.

"Oh, right. I probably did, but she's had a few terrible nights of sleep, and sometimes my mind is like a sieve. Also . . ." He smiles. "Mona's pregnant."

I act appropriately surprised and delighted, and I try not to betray any fear that I'll never meet Lenora's sibling.

And when my niece scampers toward the kitchen, I grab her before she can hit her head.

———

Once again, I don't introduce myself to Cam. I just sit at the bar with my beer and type out everything that I think will occur. And then I watch it happen.

I'm all ready for tomorrow.

October

Cam

I pull my coat tighter around me as we stand in front of the restaurant after dinner. I wish I'd worn a warmer one.

"Look, Delphine." I sigh, running a hand through my hair. "I'm sorry, but I just—"

"I know, I know," she says. "The vibes weren't there."

"Yeah."

I'm not sure if she would have been that honest if I hadn't gone first—some men don't take rejection well, after all—but I'm glad to have it out in the open.

Keysha had insisted on setting me up with her friend. I took Delphine to a casual place, and there were lots of awkward silences, followed by us speaking at the same time.

This isn't like me. I can usually keep conversation going easily with someone I just met, but the entire meal, I couldn't shake the feeling that this was *wrong*, that I shouldn't be on this date. I guess that's why I was distracted and couldn't make proper conversation.

Weird.

Now that we've gotten that out of the way, we smile at each other, and I walk her to the subway in the crisp autumn air. Once I'm alone in my empty apartment—Justin is at his boyfriend's—I spend an hour planning my upcoming trip to New York with another friend.

But no matter what I do, I still can't rid myself of that odd feeling. Something is off, but I have no idea what.

Well, hopefully, whatever it is, it'll be gone by morning.

18

Noelle

June 20, Version 112-ish

"Hey," Cam says with a smile. "Have we met before? You look really, really familiar, but I can't recall your name."

"We have," I say. "Cam, right? Short for Canmore?"

A notch appears between his brows. "And you are?"

"Noelle."

"What would you like to drink, Noelle?" He gestures to the tap list.

"I'm not sure. I don't know much about beer."

"Hm." He gives me a sample. "Try this."

I do. As expected, it's the hefeweizen.

"I'll get a pint," I say.

"I had a feeling you'd like it."

"Yeah? What do you mean, exactly?" I'm repeating a conversation we've had before, knowing this will lead where I want.

He shrugs, then goes to pull a pint. "I don't know. Just did. It's the oddest thing." He sets the beer in front of me.

Okay. Here it goes. "We've actually met dozens of times. That's why you knew my beer."

"*Dozens?* No. You seem familiar, but there's no way I could have met you dozens of times and not remembered your name."

"You forget our encounters, but I don't." I grip the cold glass in my right hand as I prepare to tell him the truth. "I'm trapped in a time loop. I'm reliving June twentieth over and over again."

He laughs, but it quickly fades. "Wait. You're serious?"

"Yeah. I'll prove it to you." The words come out in a rush. "There won't be any other customers until 3:25, at which point a man and a woman in their forties will walk in, both wearing Jays jerseys. He'll order the stout. She'll go with the IPA."

When the couple enters at exactly 3:25, Cam serves them with a smile, but his gaze keeps darting toward me.

"So, who's next?" he asks after they've claimed a table.

I tell him about the group of men two minutes before they enter. I predict their outfits. Their beer orders. Their food order: nachos without green onions.

Once they've been served, Cam returns to me. His usual smile is absent. "How are you doing this?"

"Like I said, I'm stuck in a time loop."

"Is anyone else stuck with you?"

"I've found one other woman in the same situation. Her name is Avery. Once, I brought her here to meet you."

He regards me for a moment. "Maybe you just know all these people and told them when to come in and what to order."

"They're not acting as if they know me, though."

"True. But you could have asked that they not say hello. I know it's far-fetched, but . . ."

"Not as far-fetched as me repeating the day? Yeah, I get it." I consider what else I can tell him. "Earlier today, you got Iron Goddess milk tea." I name the tea shop. "I also know quite a bit about you because we've been on lots of dates. If I introduce myself to you and we get to talking, you slip me your number and we meet up later at the night market at Mel Lastman Square, where you're going to talk to a vendor. You get bulgogi poutine and taiyaki."

"Those do sound like things I'd order. What else do you know?"

"Your parents are from Taiwan. You have a degree in life sciences. You used to be in an all-Asian Matchbox Twenty tribute band."

"Holy shit," he whispers.

When he says nothing more, I wonder if I've screwed this up. Is he really creeped out? I might have to try again tomorrow. Ease into it a little more, though it's hard to ease into something like this.

"The news," he says at last. "If you've lived this day over and over—"

"Well, a Canada goose will cause a power outage in Scarborough later today. Also, a very famous actor who's known for being devoted to his wife? His affair with a makeup artist will become public around four forty-five on social media. You'll see. The taproom gets busier, but there will be a lull at that time. Pull out your phone then and check."

"I can't believe we've gone on so many dates and I don't remember them."

"Your subconscious seems to remember a few things. The first time I said I didn't know much about beer and you gave me something to try, you started with a pale ale, then a pilsner, before going to the Corktown Hefeweizen. But now, you always start with the Corktown, like you did today."

"Huh. I'm sorry, I'm just having trouble wrapping my head around this."

"I know. When it first started happening to me, it was a struggle to accept it."

"How many times have you lived this day?" he asks.

"A hundred and twelve, give or take."

"And how did you get into this loop?"

"I'm not sure, but I think it has something to do with magical dumplings I ate at the night market the first time I was there. I've been unable to find the vendor since, though everything else about the market is the same."

"You really think it was caused by dumplings?"

"Yeah." I pause. "Sometimes, I think you must be pivotal to understanding all this because you're the only person who subconsciously remembers the other June twentieths. Also, I keep running into you. First at the market, then at the bubble tea shop. It feels like it has to mean something."

He holds my gaze but doesn't say anything.

"So." I swallow. "Do you believe me?"

He remains silent and the seconds tick by. I know there are seven minutes until the next customers arrive, and that seems like a vast amount of time right now.

Finally, he answers. "Yes. A time loop sounds impossible, but you've provided me with pretty solid proof."

I release a breath. *Thank god.*

"Have you ever told me before that you're stuck in a loop?"

"No," I say, "though I did ask you some hypothetical questions, like what you'd do in such a situation."

"How did I respond?"

"That you'd find the most perfect version of the day and live it over and over."

"And going out with me—is that perfect?"

Why him?

That's the question that pops into my mind. I mean, I think

he's cute and kind and goofy in a sweet way, but that doesn't feel like enough of an explanation. Am I drawn to him in part because I keep seeing him and he has subliminal memories of me?

Rather than saying all that, I reply, "It's pretty good."

"Pretty good." He waggles his eyebrows. "But?"

"It's tiring to introduce myself to you over and over. I love all the iterations of our first date, but I wish we could get beyond a first date."

"Have we ever kissed?"

"Many times."

His gaze drops to my mouth, and for a moment, I forget to breathe. It's just the two of us, and a connection that seems to defy the rules of my world.

"It's a shame," he says quietly, "that I have no memory of those kisses."

"It is."

"They were good, were they?"

"The first time was good. The other times were amazing." My cheeks flame as I speak, but Cam is the kind of guy you can talk to about anything. I wonder if other people feel that way with him, or if it's just me. "As if you remembered exactly what I like."

My skin feels hot and prickly as I recall our kisses. Against a wall, in a parkette . . . The whole world shrinking to his lips against mine, the need blooming inside me.

I try not to squirm on my stool.

"The thing is," I say, "before I got stuck in this loop, I swore off romance. I'd had a bad breakup and felt it just wasn't worth it. I hated the uncertainty of trusting and depending on someone who could pull the rug out from under me at any time. I wanted to avoid that despair. But with you, I felt safe because we couldn't really have a relationship, not when I kept needing to reintroduce myself to you. Except now I wish we could have June twenty-first together. June twenty-second."

He rests his arms on the bar and regards me. "Have we ever . . . ?"

"No. It didn't feel right, when I hadn't been honest with you—like I said, this is the first time I've told you about the time loop. And you—"

I snap my mouth shut when the next group of customers enters. Cam taps the bar in front of me twice before he goes to serve them.

He believes me.

If I've gotten him to believe once, I can get him to believe again. I wouldn't want to do it every day, but it's nice to know that.

Cam returns. "Have you tried to get out of this loop?"

"Yeah. Without success, obviously. It's hard to know what to try when I don't really understand how it happened."

Considering everything I've told him, he doesn't seem terribly rattled. A little, yes, but not nearly as much as I'd be in his position. Is it another sign that he's special, that he's somehow the missing piece in this time loop? Perhaps his subconscious's vague memories of previous June 20s made it easier for him to believe me.

I down the rest of my beer. "It'll get busy in here soon, but I know you're only working the bar for a few more hours. I'll text you and we can meet up at the night market, okay?"

"You need my—oh, you must already have it in your phone."

"No, because it resets every morning. But I've got your number memorized, having entered it into my contacts dozens of times."

"It's still hard to wrap my head around how this works."

"Yeah, it takes a while. Even now, I occasionally forget." I set down a twenty.

"Let me get you some change."

"No need. The bill will be back in my wallet tomorrow morning."

And with that, I exit the brewery.

19

Noelle

"I guess I should try something else today," Cam says when we meet up at the market, "since I always have the bulgogi poutine."

I sigh. "I'm sorry. Maybe I shouldn't have told you. This is weird."

"It's fine, I promise. You know, I'll just get the poutine. It's not like I remember what it tastes like, after all."

I smile weakly. "It might be easier if we pretend this really is our first date."

"But surely there are conversations you're tired of having by now. What don't you want to talk about?"

"My career. I have a degree in mechanical engineering. I do HVAC, fire protection, stuff like that for buildings. But I haven't bothered working in a while now, since it's pointless when everything I do gets erased. Uh . . . that's the main one. My family, my childhood, my travels, my education—I guess those are up there too. We've covered the basics a bunch of times."

Yeah, there's no way to avoid this being weird.

But Cam simply says, "Okay, got it. What are you going to eat today? Surely you haven't tried every single food here."

I decide to go for tteokbokki.

Food in hand, Cam regards the benches. "Is there some-where else to eat around here? Somewhere less crowded?"

"If we wait about a minute, some space will open up."

"But nobody looks like they're close to finished eating."

"Trust me."

He does, and soon we have a seat.

"Okay," he says as he picks up a fry. "Let's see. What might I not have asked you before . . . okay. What's the very best thing you've eaten? *Ever.*"

"That's an impossible question."

"Fine. What do you do for work, Noelle?" He waggles his eyebrows, and it shouldn't be enough to make me laugh, but it is.

I consider my answer to his previous question. "Some of the foods I've eaten here have been pretty amazing. The halo-halo, for example, especially the piece of flan? Delicious." Yeah, I'll definitely need to get that again.

But part of the reason it was so amazing? Because I ate it with him, on our very first date. The food is entwined with that precious memory.

I don't say this out loud, even though I've been honest with him today.

The dumplings I ate the first time I came here were incred-ibly delicious as well, but that's a more complicated memory because of what came next.

"Now I'll ask you a career question," he says, "but some-thing a little different. What was the first thing you wanted to be when you grew up? When you were, like, in kindergarten, what did you want to be? I'm guessing it wasn't a mechanical engineer."

"I waffled between teacher—like my father—and zookeeper. What about you?"

"It was either an astronaut or clown for me. Or clown astronaut."

"What happened?" I asked. "You flunked out of clownstronaut school?"

He laughs. "Yeah, I didn't do well with those big shoes in zero gravity training. It was such a pity." He releases an exaggerated sigh. "If I'd succeeded, I could be up there right now, circling the planet in a red nose and rainbow wig."

The image makes me giggle.

"I'm guessing we've never had this conversation before?" he asks.

"We have not."

"What about you? You could have been . . . a zeacher?"

"A zeacher?"

"A zoo-teacher. You could have taught camels the alphabet. Encouraged leopards to learn their multiplication tables. I probably asked you this before, but what does your dad teach?"

"He's retired, but he taught high school English."

"You could have taught Shakespeare to baboons." Cam sits up straight and puts a hand—the one not holding the bulgogi poutine—to his chest. "To be a baboon, or not to be a baboon," he says solemnly. "That is the question."

"Indeed. A very important question. The question that all clownstronauts on the moon are pondering at this very second."

"Shh. Don't mention that. It's a sore subject for me."

"My apologies," I say grandly, then turn my attention to the tteokbokki.

I keep smiling around my food. I'm here with Cam, the weather's nice—and now that I've told him the truth, I'm more relaxed than usual.

He spears a piece of meat and a fry on a fork, then holds it toward me. "I bet you've tried it before, but try it again."

I lean forward and eat the proffered food. "Not . . . bad."

It's hard for me to get the words out when my mouth is so close to his.

"I really wish I could remember kissing you." He brushes his fingers over my cheek, and I nearly shiver in the warm air.

I want to sink into his touch and learn every inch of him.

"So do I." My breath hitches, and I trail a fingertip over his jaw. Does this feel familiar to him? "We'll make new memories soon."

Memories that he'll have for just a few hours before they disappear, leaving only the faintest impression behind.

The thought is bittersweet.

———

This time, we don't have dessert. No, we end up away from the crowds, against a brick wall, as soon as we finish our tteokbokki and poutine.

Cam leans forward, then pulls back. "It's odd, knowing I've done it before, but . . ."

"It's okay." I smile at him reassuringly. "I keep coming back for more. I keep choosing to kiss you over and over—"

His mouth crashes down on mine, and he presses me against the wall. Despite how many times we've kissed, often right in this very place, I squeak in surprise before I wrap my arms around him and pull him close.

"It seems impossible that I could forget this," he murmurs.

"You kiss like you remember."

He nips at my throat, in a way he discovered I like about a dozen days ago, and I groan. My desire to get closer to him is even stronger than usual. I paw at his clothes and finally slide my hands up his chest.

It's still not enough.

Cam's hand slips below the neckline of my shirt and into my bra, and I nearly see stars.

"More," I plead. While he knows the truth, I want to experience everything I can with him. We don't have all the time in the world; no, there're only about six hours until he forgets again.

Frustratingly, he pulls his head back, just enough for me to see that this usually cheerful man has a decidedly wicked smile on his face. His thumb brushes over my nipple, and I gasp. I want those fingers between my legs.

And for the first time, he obliges.

He unbuttons my jeans, and I swear he's lowering that zipper in slow motion. I'm so desperate that I can hardly stand it. At last, he slides his hand into my panties.

"I've never done this before?" he asks.

"No."

One finger penetrates me. Then another.

Oh my god.

With his other hand, he slides down the top of my shirt and bra, just enough to bare one nipple to the night air. Faintly, I can hear music and laughter from the night market, but here, it's just us. I'm wouldn't normally want to be so exposed in public, but I'm beyond caring. Cam has his mouth on my breast, his fingers inside me, and it's bliss. I arch against him, trying to get more. *More.*

I've wanted this for so long, from this man who gives me his number no matter what I look like, no matter what weird conversation we have about me being an heiress or stuck in a time loop . . .

I squirm as his fingers slide in and out, his thumb on my clit.

"Fuck. Noelle," he says.

My nipples stiffen even more as a light breeze caresses my skin.

I wish I could come from being touched like this, but unfortunately, knowing my body, no matter how skilled he is, this won't quite be enough.

"Do you . . . do you want to come home with me?" I ask.

"Yes," he says immediately.

My body sings with joy, but I need to be sure he understands. "The next time you see me, you won't remember. You're okay with that?"

"It's not ideal, but yes. Whatever tomorrow brings, I just want you . . . tonight."

I nod because I'm suddenly incapable of speaking.

This is finally going to happen.

He steps back from me, and I fix my clothes. Then I pull out my phone to look at the time and discover I've missed some texts. My stomach drops as I start reading the desperate messages.

> AVERY: I can't do this anymore. Living the same day over and over, waking up next to Joe each morning. It's like being trapped in a nightmare.
>
> AVERY: Even the thought of doing it one more time . . . it's unbearable.

Oh no.

My lust fading, I look up at Cam. "You know how there's another woman in the loop?"

He nods.

"She needs me, and there's no one else because, well . . ." I gesture feebly with my hands. "I have to go to her. I'm so sorry, but—"

"It's okay. I understand." His hand slides into my hair. "Besides, she'll remember tomorrow, whereas I'll forget this ever happened." He pauses. "When do I usually say I'll see you again?"

"You're busy tomorrow, but you're free on Sunday."

"But Sunday has never come for you."

"Correct."

There's a long, melancholy silence.

"I'll see you soon," he says softly. "Text me tomorrow to see if I remember, but if I don't, you know how to find me, whenever you want me."

And then he's gone, and I hurriedly ask Avery for her address.

20

Noelle

Fifteen minutes ago, I was having a hot-and-heavy make-out session with Cam, but that feels very, very far away now. My desire has been completely replaced with worry.

Avery lives in an old building in the west end. I take an Uber to save time, and when it comes to a stop, I practically sprint inside, following a delivery person into the lobby. We get into the elevator together, and I distantly register the smell of pizza.

Avery answers the door in pajama pants and a large T-shirt, her hair—not dyed today—unkempt. Her eyes are red.

"I'm sorry," she says. "You were with Cam, weren't you?"

"Nothing I haven't done many times before," I say lightly, even though it's a lie. I don't want her to feel bad about needing to talk. I sit down on the couch with her. "Do you want me to get you anything? Food, water—"

"You're at my place. I should be offering those things to you."

I shake my head. "Tell me what's happening."

I hope I'm doing a half-decent job of this. It's been a long time since a close friend has called me while in distress because, well, I don't have any close friends in my regular life. My pre-loop life. Veronica was my closest friend, but I didn't talk to her all that much; I spent a lot of my time alone.

And honestly, I like spending time alone, but I'm realizing I isolated myself more than I should have.

"I'm just so *tired*," she says, "of seeing Joe's stupid face on my birthday."

"Did you break up with him today?"

She nods. "Yeah. I told him he better not be here tonight. Then I ran outside because I can't stand to look at him anymore, not when I know that he thinks he's too good for me and no one else will have me. I couldn't bear to hear him say, once again, that I'd come crawling back sooner or later, that I didn't realize how lucky I was."

She releases a sob-hiccup, and I pull her into my arms. I pat her back in a way that I hope is reassuring.

"And I've had my period," she says, "for, like, four months straight."

"Yeah, that sucks. Nobody should have a four-month-long period."

"Yet here I am, and I've just . . . had it. With everything." Her voice is flat. "I can't live in this time loop any longer. I considered going to an overpass and—"

"Avery—"

"But I doubt that would even work. I'd just lose the rest of the day, then wake up on the morning of June twentieth again."

"We don't know that for sure," I say. "It's likely, yes, but maybe that's the one thing that would be permanent."

"It sounds better than being trapped." She shakes her head. "You don't seem to care as much as me. You're calm, and I don't understand it." Her voice is still flat, but a trace of bitterness has crept into it.

Yeah, a part of me was enjoying the break from work, and I've been having fun first dates with Cam, though it no longer feels like enough.

I don't know how to make this better. What can I say?

I glance around the room. My gaze lands on a plant by the windowsill. Avery told me that it's supposed to be watered every week, but she hasn't watered it since June 18, which feels like a lifetime ago. Yet the plant is still perfectly healthy.

What Avery needs, I assume, is hope—and to spend as little time with Joe as possible.

"From now on," I say, "every morning, when you wake up, just leave. Come to my apartment. Spend all day there."

She nods.

"We'll figure this out. We'll redouble our efforts."

"But how?" she asks. "We've tried so many things."

"There has to be more. There's always something to try." I feel like I'm talking out of my ass, but it's the best I can do. "We'll devote all our time to getting out of this."

"What if we're stuck here for eternity?"

"I can't believe that's the case. Not yet." I pause. "Your day is worse than mine, but I want to get out too. Everyone in my family is frozen in time. My niece has been fourteen months old for *months*. My sister-in-law is pregnant, and at this rate, I'll never get to meet my new niece or nephew. And it's getting really frustrating that Cam doesn't remember who I am." I pull up the notes app on my phone. "So, what haven't we tried?"

"We haven't tried dying. What if that actually gets us out of the loop alive?"

"Err, let's save that for later, since it could have serious consequences," I say. "We could travel farther, somewhere outside of this time zone. Seems like a long shot, but we're going to try it regardless." I type it into my phone. "What about our jobs?"

"Our jobs?"

"You know, those things we haven't done in a long time.

Maybe we're supposed to fix them somehow. I don't know much about your job, but I could, I don't know, refuse to keep doing the work of two people. Lodge a proper complaint about Tyler."

I still feel like I'm talking out of my ass. Just saying whatever comes to mind, in the hopes that something will resonate with Avery so she doesn't test death.

I'm all she has. Therapy won't help when it's unlikely she'd be able to make an appointment for today—and no therapist will remember what she said last session.

Unless . . .

"We need to look harder for other people who are stuck in a time loop—or who have been stuck in one before and gotten out. I've posted about it in lots of places online, but we can look in person." I shoot her a smile that expresses more confidence than I feel. "Does that sound like a plan?"

When she nods, I exhale in relief.

———

In an effort to cheer Avery up, I suggest we go to New York the next day and see something on Broadway. If someone is truly depressed, they might be unable to get pleasure from anything, but I figure it's worth a shot. The thought that she considered jumping off a bridge, even in our weird reality, makes me desperate to improve her life.

Before I leave for the airport the next morning, I text Cam, as I promised, and I soon get a response:

CAM: Sorry, you've got the wrong number.

I'm not surprised, but I'm disappointed nonetheless.

In New York, Avery and I get tickets to *Chicago*, and even if she isn't bursting with excitement, she seems to enjoy herself, at least a little.

The following day, we meet at Pearson Airport and see what last-minute flights out of the Eastern Time Zone we can arrange. We end up flying to Vancouver. Avery has been before, but I haven't. I appreciate that the weather is different in Vancouver on June 20 than it is in either Toronto or New York.

Rain! It's been a long time since I've felt rain on my skin. I didn't bring an umbrella with me, but I don't mind. It's refreshing.

Avery is less enthused about the rain, but after we walk around Stanley Park, she suggests an izakaya that she enjoyed the last time she was here. As we sit down at a cramped table, I think of that meal I had with Cam.

I wonder what he's doing now. I look at the time on my phone. Toronto is three hours ahead, so he's probably heading home after talking to the vendor at the night market.

I miss him, but he won't miss me . . . or will he feel an ache in his chest that he can't explain? There's so much I don't know.

Avery and I get an expensive hotel room in downtown Vancouver. She falls asleep at 11 p.m., but I'm determined to stay up until midnight. Midnight in Vancouver is 3 a.m. in Toronto. Is the reset always at 3 a.m. Toronto time? Or is it 3 a.m. wherever I am? I don't truly expect our travels to break the curse, but I can try to get a better understanding of how it works.

Just before midnight, I'm reading the paperback I bought at the airport. I read for the entire flight, and I've only got one chapter left. I'll learn who the killer is and—

I wake up in Toronto to my alarm.

21

Noelle

June 20, Version 115-ish

After I make my morning coffee, I buy the book I was reading last night—the ebook, this time—and finish it as I eat breakfast.

Ha! I was right about the killer.

Next, I post in a bunch of different subreddits, trying to focus on ones that I don't think I've posted in before, and text Avery.

> ME: Let's focus on finding other people who've been in a time loop today. I'll make a sign and stand at Yonge and Dundas for a while before going to Mel Lastman Square for the start of the market.
>
> ME: Do you want to join me? Or do you have another idea?
>
> AVERY: I'll see you at Yonge and Dundas.

I grab a piece of cardboard and a marker.

Have you ever been stuck in a time loop? Am trying to find others like me.

There are lots of things I want to add, but it should be short. That's the sign I'll use at Yonge and Dundas, but I make another for the night market.

**Help! I ate some dumplings at this market and
have been stuck living June 20 over and over.
Did this happen to anyone else?**

———

Avery and I stand outside the Eaton Centre with our signs,
not far from two people promoting Bible classes. They try to
get us to sign up, but we decline.

Yonge and Dundas is a very busy intersection. Tons of
people hurry by; most are careful not to make eye contact. I
don't like the fact that many people are probably—definitely—
questioning my sanity.

But I have to try. Maybe someone else has had experience
with this, and maybe they know how we can get out of it . . . and
then Avery can wake up without her ex-boyfriend next to her in
bed, and Cam will actually remember my name.

The first person to speak to us is a middle-aged man, and it
quickly becomes clear that he's trying to hit on Avery. When
we finally get him to leave, she releases a weary sigh.

The second person is an older white woman.

"Both of you are stuck in this time loop?" she asks.

I nod. "We've both lived June twentieth over a hundred
times."

"I see," she says, in a way that suggests she very much does
not see. "I think you should seek medical intervention. Go to
the ER, I mean."

There's something about her tone that grates on my nerves.
It's patronizing. Like she believes I couldn't possibly think of
such a reasonable idea by myself.

"It's not all in my mind," I say. "It's really happening."

"I'm sure it feels like that."

I bite my tongue so I don't yell at her. "I've already seen a
doctor. Believe me, I tried. I got a referral to a psychiatrist, but

that'll probably take months. I mean, it would take months if I *weren't* reliving the same day, but as long as I'm stuck in June twentieth, it'll never happen."

She takes a step back. "You should go to the hospital," she says before quickly walking away.

The next person who approaches is a man of indeterminate age. He's wearing clothes and shoes that have seen better days.

"Can you spare any change?" He holds out an empty cup.

I give him a twenty.

"Thank you," he says. "God bless."

Well, that was certainly better than the previous two interactions.

Three hours later, my feet are aching and my faith in humanity is low. Some of the looks we got were unpleasant, to say the least.

"The night market starts soon," I say to Avery. "I'll head there now. What about you?"

She shakes her head. "I'm exhausted. I guess I'll stay here another hour, then head home . . . except Joe will be around. I didn't break up with him today."

"How about this?" I take out my keys and hand them to her. "When you leave, just go to my apartment, okay?"

At the market, I stand on the north side, where people might pass me when exiting the subway station. I recognize some people from my previous trips to the market, and I try to pay careful attention to the times that they come and go. I plan to return tomorrow, and I want to be aware of anything that's different. That could be a sign.

However, my feet are aching. My arms hurt from holding this stupid piece of cardboard, which I taped to the end of a broom because it was the most suitable object in my apartment.

A few minutes later, a familiar man approaches the market. It's Cam.

My face heats as I remember what we did, not far from here, and what I wish we'd had the chance to do.

"I know I've seen you before," he says, "but I can't remember your name."

"It's Noelle."

Every time he forgets my name, something inside me dies. I should be used to it, but it hurts more than it did before.

"Noelle," he repeats. "Yes. I remember now."

"You do? What do you remember?" I feel a spark of hope.

"I don't recall you telling me your name, but it just feels right."

I deflate.

He scratches his head and studies my sign. "I swear someone else told me a very similar story, once upon a time, but I can't remember when or where." He pauses. "If I recall the details, I'll let you know."

"Thanks," I say. "I'll be here for another two hours."

But I'm pretty sure the story is familiar because his subconscious remembers our conversation the other day. It's not someone else he's thinking of; it's me. And he likely won't recall any more than he currently does. I want to scream in frustration, but I won't take it out on Cam. He's not responsible for any of this.

"Do you need some food?" he asks. "I can give you some cash, and you can buy whatever you want." He gestures toward the vendors.

I shake my head.

When he walks away, my sign feels even heavier than it did before.

I stay at the market for two more hours, like I said I would, and the only people who talk to me are a family looking for a washroom and a man asking if I've found God.

Before I leave, I buy some cupcakes from the place that I considered too expensive on my very first trip to the night market.

———

Avery has made herself comfortable in my apartment by the time I arrive. She's scarfing down pretzels and watching TV.

"Any luck?" I ask, but I know the answer. If she'd gotten anywhere, she'd have texted.

She shakes her head. "What about you?"

"Nothing. But I got you a treat." I hold up the box in my hand and open the lid. "Happy birthday." I considered buying her a present as well, but it would have disappeared overnight anyway. Food, at least, is meant to be consumed.

She gives me a faint smile, and that's enough for me. "Thanks. What are the flavors?"

"Salted caramel, candied ginger calamansi, chocolate raspberry, and lemon rosemary."

"Ooh."

I'm not surprised when she reaches for the salted caramel. I try the ginger calamansi, the swirl of perfect, pale buttercream topped with thin slices of candied citrus and ginger.

Well, now I understand why the cupcakes cost so much. *Holy shit, that's good.*

As I savor my treat, I pull out my phone to see if there have been any helpful comments on my Reddit posts. Nothing worth mentioning.

But right before bed, I get a direct message.

dustypeony: I swear my mother told me a story—a real story—about a woman experiencing the same day over and over. I'd ask her about it tomorrow, except I'm not sure how that'll work for you. Here's my email address. Email me first thing when you wake up, whatever day that happens to be, and hopefully I can talk to her that afternoon.

I can't believe it. After all this time, I've finally got a real lead! I commit the email address to memory.

The next day, I send the email as I make coffee. After remaking my sign, I head to Yonge and Bloor. Rather than holding the sign on a broomstick, I've fashioned a stand—also out of cardboard—so I don't have to hold my arm up.

Once again, I'm not successful. Some people pick up their pace after reading the sign.

I'm not delusional! I want to shout.

I'm sure that wouldn't help, but even if I were hallucinating this entire situation, I'd deserve compassion, right?

I obsessively check my email all day, but it's not until the evening that I get a response from dustypeony.

My mother says that when she was a girl in Japan, she knew someone who got stuck living the same day. The woman said that after the thirtieth time, it simply ended, and it never happened again. She thinks it was supposed to repeat for a fixed number of days. I'm sorry I can't tell you more.

I groan. This is the closest I've come to finding anyone who's gotten out of a time loop, and it's just a vague story about someone who knew someone decades ago. It's no help to me. And thirty days? If only! I've been stuck for a lot longer than that.

———

I try yet another Chinese herbalist. These herbs aren't quite as bitter, but they don't help with my problem, and I sigh when I wake up to my alarm yet again.

As long as I'm stuck on June 20, life isn't real. There are no true consequences.

Yet in a way, life is very real, isn't it?

I certainly have more feelings. Before, I was on autopilot, but now, I'm definitely not, even if I'm repeating the same day. I experience lots of disappointment and frustration and sadness . . . and the beginnings of love.

Then there's Avery. It feels like she's slowly becoming hollow. A shell of her former self. I make another attempt to encourage her to write fanfic, but she just sighs and asks what the point is.

Have we been cursed for a set number of days? It's clearly not thirty, but what if we're destined to live like this for 365 days, no matter what? And why us?

I've made no real progress, so I figure we've got to do the other thing that I mentioned to Avery. If it's *not* a set number of days, and it's related to a change we need to make in our lives, we can't avoid this any longer.

One night—she spends every night at my apartment now— we're halfway through a pepperoni pizza when I say, "Tomorrow, we're going back to work."

22

Noelle

June 20, Version 120-ish

The first day back at the office, I don't plan to do anything unusual. I'm just trying to get the lay of the land, so to speak. Sure, I've lived this day at work more than once, but it's been a while.

"Good morning," I say to Eloise, one of the drafters.

"Good morning," she says, as though it's just another day. As though I haven't been gone for months.

I head to my cubicle, where I email Tyler—who's not in yet—a reminder about the proposal, as I remember doing before.

It takes a couple of hours to get into the swing of things, but by eleven, I feel like I've adjusted. In all honesty, it's kind of nice to be back, despite the sterile décor and rather harsh overhead lighting.

At lunch, I eat with Fernando and ask about his family. As he's telling me about his summer plans, I get an idea.

If anything is going to change about my job, I need to gather some information.

The next day at lunch, I open my mouth to ask Fernando about his salary, then snap it shut. I don't think this is something he'll want to discuss while we're at the office, even if we're in the break room and nobody else is present. I'll wait until later.

"Last one here again?" Fernando says as he heads to the door at six.

"Actually, I was about to pack up," I say. "Could you wait a minute? We'll head out together."

"Sure." He smiles, but he looks a little puzzled—this is out of character for me.

When we're on the street, walking toward the subway station, my heart rate speeds up. It's time for my question.

"What's your, uh, salary?" I ask.

He stops on the sidewalk and gives me a look.

"As a woman in engineering, I'm concerned I'm being underpaid. We graduated in the same year, with the same degree. We have the same job title." And I think we're equally competent.

"Okay," he says. "Just don't tell anyone that I told you."

My eyes widen at the number. I think of all the extra money I could be saving with that salary.

Since he told me his, I tell him mine, though I suspect he had some idea based on my reaction.

"They should definitely be paying you more," he says.

"They should," I agree.

———

That night, I text Avery, who has returned to her job in comms, as she calls it. She has a master's degree in the field and studied psychology in undergrad.

Communicating is, in fact, something I need to research. Specifically, I need to figure out how to ask for a raise. I've never done that before, but maybe being assertive at my job will get me out of this time loop. Even if it doesn't, knowing my boss's response will be useful information to have, if I escape the loop at a later date.

The articles I read tell me to be confident, to focus on my accomplishments. I shouldn't mention how long it's been since I had a raise—two years, in my case—or that I know a coworker makes more than me. (I promised Fernando I wouldn't mention it anyway, although he won't remember our conversation.) I do look up job listings for comparable positions at other companies, so I have some numbers at my disposal. My current salary isn't below the range I find online, but it's below average. Some listings don't mention a salary range at all, which is bullshit. Not just because it's completely unhelpful for my research purposes, but this is information you should have before applying for a job, isn't it?

One article recommends not asking for a raise of more than 5 percent, but screw that. (Also, who's writing these articles? Can I trust their expertise?)

The more time I think about it, the angrier I get. I have more work dumped on my plate than Fernando does, yet I make less. I've kept my head down and done it all without complaint, believing I'd be rewarded eventually. But *why* did I think that? It seems so naïve.

I'm not sure if it has anything to do with my gender, though. Apparently, new hires often get paid more, and this is Fernando's second job after graduation—he's been here for four years—whereas it's my first. Job-hopping can increase your salary, which is frustrating. Shouldn't employers want to reward loyalty?

The next day, I email my boss first thing in the morning, asking if I can have fifteen minutes of his time. He responds that we can speak at two thirty.

It's a good thing I've done all these tasks before. I'm struggling to concentrate, and I'm annoyed with myself for being so nervous. I've been stuck in this loop for ages; I'm used to the fact that what I do doesn't have real consequences.

And yet.

For a split second, I consider not doing it, but then I think of Cam and my family. I have to try.

At two thirty on the dot, I knock on the door of Lee's office. "Come in," he says.

I enter. My boss is a thin white man in his sixties, his sandy brown hair tinged with gray. He has a mustache that overwhelms his face and glasses perched on his nose.

I sit down across from Lee, and after a brief exchange of pleasantries, I launch into the speech I've prepared about why I deserve a raise. I'd meant to ask for a raise that would have me making the same salary as Fernando—not that I'd mention it—but I chicken out and ask for a bit less.

Despite my anxiety, I try to be confident. My voice wavers a couple of times, but I think I do a decent job. Lee's expression, however, is inscrutable.

When I stop talking, he doesn't immediately answer. No, he takes his time arranging a few things on his desk, including a stress ball emblazoned with the company's name.

Then he says, "I'll give you two percent, but no more."

The old me—well, the old me would never have asked for a raise, to be honest, and if she did, she certainly wouldn't be complaining about this.

But I'm not that woman anymore.

I begin outlining the research on salaries that I've done. I don't say *I could make more elsewhere*, but I strongly imply it.

Lee sighs, takes off his glasses, and pinches his brow. "I know you don't know much about the finances of the company, but I simply can't afford it, and if I give you a raise—"

"How much would it cost to replace me?" I ask. "I do more than one person's work."

I don't think I expected this to be successful, despite all the anecdotes I read about people who negotiated decent raises—though women asking for raises aren't always treated the same as men. Yet a part of me still hoped, and now, I feel like my world is crumbling. It's not as bad as when I discovered I was in a time loop, but still. This company clearly doesn't appreciate what I do for them. I worked sixty hours most weeks, and for what?

"Thank you for your time," I say, then return to my desk and glare at the bland motivational poster on the wall.

For the first time ever, I leave at exactly five o'clock.

If there were consequences, I wouldn't be quitting my job on June 20. No, I'd quietly start looking for a new one. The idea of being without a source of income is distressing—financial stability has always been important to me—and besides, I've heard that it's easier to get a new job while you still have one.

But I'm *pissed*.

Although I usually don't make waves, preferring to observe drama rather than be the center of it, the next day, I march into the office determined to, well, not be myself.

In some ways, the day starts just like any other. I say hello to Eloise, I get my coffee, I send an email to Tyler. I also send an email to Lee, asking for a meeting this afternoon.

At the appointed hour, I knock on his door and enter. He's wearing the exact same button-down shirt that he's worn in all iterations of this day.

"What can I help you with today?" he asks.

I launch into a speech that's a little different from the one I gave yesterday. I don't expect it to make a difference, but I figure I'll mix it up just in case.

Once again, he says, "I'll give you two percent, but no more."

"That's unacceptable."

"I know you don't know much about—"

"I work longer hours than anyone else here," I say. "Especially since I'm expected to mentor Tyler . . ." I trail off as I ponder an awful question: How much does Tyler make? How much would it piss me off if I knew? "No matter what I tell him, his work doesn't improve. I've tried to be patient—"

"It's your job to figure it out."

"Then you should at least pay me an appropriate salary," I say, my anger building.

"As I've tried to tell you—"

"Fuck that. It's not my job anymore. I quit." I savor the shock on Lee's face. "I deserve better."

I walk out of his office with my head held high, not waiting for a response. For the first time in my life, I've quit something, and it feels great.

I go to my desk and grab my stuff. What's the point in staying?

As I'm heading down the hallway, I nearly bump into Tyler. I clap him on the shoulder. "Good luck on that proposal. It's all yours now."

"Wh-what do you mean?"

I leave him stammering as I get on the elevator. He'll be fine—he's the owner's nephew, after all—but I'll enjoy the moment while I can.

———

Leaside Brewing isn't close to the Woods & Olson office. There are many more convenient places to drink, but I head there anyway. Since I arrive later than usual, I'm not the only customer in the taproom, and I've missed the sea shanties. Still, Cam does his usual *you look familiar* thing before I ask for a pint of the Corktown.

"Somehow, I knew that's what you were going to order," he says.

There's a pain in my chest as I introduce myself to him yet

again. Though he doesn't consciously remember any of the kisses and meals we've shared, I still felt the need to seek him out today, for some reason.

When there's a lull, I say, "I just quit my job."

"Yeah? Does it feel good?" he asks.

"It does, but it's a little terrifying at the same time."

Cam nods. "I know what that's like."

"I have nothing else lined up, but I couldn't stand it anymore, not once I knew how little they valued me." I pause. "I'm a mechanical engineer."

While I've never had this exact conversation with Cam before, I know that if we were out for dinner, he'd ask more questions. Ask me if I want another engineering job, or whether I want to switch fields completely. But right now, he's working. He'll listen, but I won't ramble too much.

I take out my phone to text Avery, but she's already messaged me.

AVERY: I quit my job today too.
ME: Why don't you meet me at the brewery?

While I'm waiting for her to arrive, I scroll through my contacts and stop near the end.

Veronica.

I start to text her, asking if she knows anyone who's hiring, then stop. Everything will probably reset tomorrow. Rather than making this all about work, shouldn't I just talk to her as a friend?

A not-very-good friend, that is. I've been terrible at keeping in touch with her.

ME: Hey! It's been a while. How are you doing?

I don't get an immediate answer, but that's okay. I'm sure she's got a busy life, and she's probably at work.

Avery arrives and orders a pilsner from the man who has replaced Cam at the bar.

"Did you tell your boss to fuck himself?" she asks.

"Ha! I did drop an F-bomb, but I didn't go quite that far."

"You could have. After all, you'll still have a job tomorrow, unless this is what gets us out of the loop." She has a sip of her drink. "That's why I quit: to see if it would break the curse. It didn't feel quite right to me, like it did to you, but I had to try."

"I thought you weren't entirely happy at your job."

"I'm not, but I think it's my feelings about my relationship bleeding into work, more than anything else. I've started to wonder about switching to a slightly different role in the same company, though."

Terror suddenly seizes me. If I do get out of the loop and this is the "true" version of June 20, then I quit my job for good. Even though I have savings, the idea of being without a job freaks me out. But at least time would be moving again, right?

"You know what?" I say. "Let's get drunk tonight."

———

A few hours later, I have my elbow propped on the bar, head resting on my hand. I've consumed five—or is it six?—beers.

However many, it's enough to give me the hiccups, and I'm currently reading articles about how to get *rid* of hiccups, wondering if they will lead to more success than my attempt to ask for a raise. (Well, I suppose I did get a raise, but it was a lot smaller than what I asked for.)

I've already attempted drinking lots of cold water and sucking on a lemon, with no success. I would try breathing into a paper bag, except I don't have one.

Avery—who has consumed less alcohol than me and/or is

less of a lightweight than I am—is flirting with a tall white guy at the other end of the bar. Good for her.

I ask the bartender for the bill, and he looks a little relieved—I think he was afraid I'd ask for another beer and he'd have to cut me off. Or something. Everything is a bit hazy right now.

"Noelle?" says a familiar voice.

I attempt to execute a fancy turn on my barstool and somehow end up on the floor instead, Cam's face above me.

"You're not supposed to be here," I mumble.

He frowns. "Why not?"

"Your shift finished," I say as I pull my knees to my chest. That's apparently another way to stop hiccups, but it was hard to do on a barstool. I take advantage of my position on the floor and try it now.

"Dammit!" I say when it doesn't work.

Cam takes my hand and helps me up. Our faces are very, very close, and his is creased with concern.

Don't kiss him don't kiss him don't kiss him

"Why are you here?" I ask.

"Because I was worried about you," he says.

"But *why?*"

"I don't know," he admits. "You hadn't had a lot to drink when I left, but you said you'd just quit your job, so I guess I worried . . ." He shakes his head. "I just had a feeling, so I called to ask if you were still here, and when I heard you were . . ."

He sounds distressed that he doesn't entirely understand the situation.

I decide to explain it to him. "I'm stuck on June twentieth. I've lived this day over a hundred times, and on many of them . . ." It takes me a moment to remember where I was going with that. "Right! On many June twentieths, I've seen you. At the bubble tea thingy-ma-bob. At the night market. Here. You don't remember. Not really, but your sub-whatsitcalled . . . Your *sub-conscious* seems to remember me. I think. I don't know." I hiccup.

"Uh . . ."

"Really. I'm not that drunk. Well, maybe I am, but that's the truth. Avery will tell you." I turn to seek out my friend. The room seems a touch wobbly. "Avery!" I have to shout at her a few times before she comes over. "Tell Cam that I'm stuck reliving the same day."

She gives me a look that says, *You told him? Really?*

Or possibly: *How fucking drunk are you?*

This is the wonderful thing about having a close friend, I'm learning. You don't need words to communicate.

After a long hesitation, she says, "She's telling the truth. The two of us are living the same day over and over."

"You see?" I say.

"Right." Cam scrubs a hand over his face. "How about I call you a cab, or get you to the TTC—"

"It's okay," Avery says. "I'm staying with her tonight. I'll take care of her, don't worry."

I start laughing. I've lived June 20 so many times before, yet *this* has never happened. It's amazing how many possibilities there are in a single day. You can quit your job . . . or not. You can go to Vancouver and feel the rain on your skin. You can eat three types of dumplings and get sprayed by a skunk when you go hunting for ghosts in a cemetery. You can . . .

Huh. I've been bundled outside, and Avery is trying to make sure I walk in a straight line.

"Why am I so drunk?" I ask.

"I don't know," she says, "but hangovers don't seem to happen on June twentieth, so you'll be probably be as good as new in the morning."

"Avery, you're my best friend. If we ever get out of this, I promise I won't forget it." With that proclamation, I trip on the sidewalk, but she catches me before I fall.

"But what if, when we get out of this," she says, "we don't remember all the repeats?"

"That's not possible. We have to remember. Otherwise, what's the point?"

"Maybe there *is* no point."

Hm. That's interesting.

I'll think about it tomorrow.

———

I wake up to my alarm. It's six forty-five, and the morning light filtering through the window doesn't hurt my head. Once again, it's June 20, and I'm simultaneously relieved—I didn't *really* quit my job—and pissed off. Pissed off that I can't change my life.

What else is even left to try?

Halloween

Cam

I smile as I look out at the crowd gathered in the taproom and on the small heated patio. Our Halloween event is a bigger success than last year's, and I enjoy seeing all the people mingling, laughing, drinking. In the corner, someone in a donut costume is dancing. Several witches have congregated on the other side of the bar.

Yet even though everything is going well, I'm hit by the strange feeling that something isn't quite right. It's like I want someone to be here—twining her fingers with mine, pressing a kiss to my cheek—but she isn't.

How can I miss someone without knowing who she is? This isn't just my romantic heart wanting a relationship; no, it feels different. A yearning for someone in particular, even if I don't know her name.

It makes no sense.

I hear laughter to my left, and I turn. There's a middle-aged woman wearing a box that is clearly supposed to be a Rubik's Cube. Specifically, one that hasn't been solved yet.

"Love your costume," she says to me.

For some reason, I look down at my chest, as if I don't know what I'm wearing, even though I spent hours making my red Pocky box outfit. "Thanks."

She grabs the arm of her companion—who's dressed as a ghost—and tows her toward the bar, just as my phone vibrates in my pocket. I ignore it and continue to survey the room. Darrell has no interest in brewing a pumpkin beer, but we have some spiced pumpkin ale on our guest tap, and it's been fairly popular all week.

I decide to check in with Miriam behind the bar, but before I can get there, my phone vibrates again. Pulling my phone out of my pocket when I'm wearing this costume is no small feat. I head into the employees-only area, slide my arm back through the armhole of the Pocky box, and reach into my pocket. By the time I've successfully retrieved my phone, it's stopped ringing, but it starts again a few seconds later, "Dad" flashing across the screen. It's almost 10 p.m., which is an unusual time to hear from him. He rarely calls me, and never this late.

This can't be good.

There's a tightness in my chest as I answer the call, bracing myself for whatever news I'm about to receive. Is this why I had that peculiar feeling earlier—did some part of me already know?

No, that was something else, though I can't explain why I'm so sure.

"Cam." Even in that single syllable, my father's voice sounds all wrong. "You have to come to the hospital."

23

Noelle

June 20, Version 135-ish

I sit on my futon with my morning coffee and listlessly watch the viral squirrel video yet again. For the last several days, I've been focused on getting out of this stupid loop. I was already scraping the bottom of the barrel when it came to ideas, but now, I'm truly out. Since the night I got drunk, I've quit my job multiple times and stood in Times Square with a sign. If those didn't do the trick, what will?

I'm an engineer. Surely I can figure out a time loop.

At that thought, I start laughing. I've figured out nothing, except the fact that Fernando makes more than me and Lee won't give me the raise I deserve. And I don't think my engineering background has helped me at all with this situation.

I need a day off from this.

ME: I think I'm going to spend the day with Cam.
AVERY: Sounds good. I might meet you at the brewery.
ME: You want to see the guy you were flirting with the
    other day?
AVERY: maybe?

I do some reading, consider sending Lee an email that says *Fuck you* before ultimately deciding against it, then call the hair salon.

———

I've gotten this exact haircut nine—or is it ten?—times now, and I love it. I love how my head feels lighter afterward. It's just annoying that I can't keep it.

I give the stylist a generous tip, then walk out the door of the salon. Sure, my life is just as ridiculous as before, but I feel rejuvenated. Taking a day off was a good idea. I—

"Shit!" I cry as I tumble to the ground. I rub my sore knee as I look up.

"I'm so sorry. Are you okay?"

From this angle, the sunshine is like a halo around Cam's head, and I stare at him, entranced. I guess I wasn't paying close enough attention when I walked out the door, and I ran into him. He's on his way to the bubble tea shop a few doors down.

"I'm fine," I say.

His concerned look morphs into a smile that's powerful enough to make me tingle, even though I've seen it many times before. He extends his hand, and I take it.

"You look really familiar," he says, "and I feel like I ought to know your name, but I don't. That seems impossible, though, because if I'd learned your name, I'm sure I wouldn't have forgotten it."

We're still holding hands.

"And why is that?" I ask with a flirty tilt of my head.

He chuckles. "You busy right now? I could buy you some bubble tea as an apology for knocking you down."

"I think that was my fault." I pause. "But I accept."

"Wait a second. Your name—it has something to do with Christmas?"

I wait for his next words, heart thumping wildly. This is new.

"Saint Nick," he says. "Nicky? Nicole?"

"Noelle."

He still didn't get my name, but it's progress, however small.

"I'm Cam," he says as we head to the tea shop. He opens the door and gestures me ahead of him.

As we wait in line, I consider how I want today to go. It's been a while since we spent much time together.

Weirdly enough, this is exactly the sort of situation I'd hoped to engineer when I first got stuck in the loop: a meet cute that would have him asking me out, with the hopes that he'd kiss me.

But I'm not the same woman that I was back then. I'm also encouraged by how close he got to guessing the right name.

"You're going to order the Iron Goddess milk tea with pearls, aren't you?" I say as the customer in front of us orders.

"How did you know that?" Cam asks.

I shrug. "I'll tell you in a moment."

We place our orders and stand off to the side to wait.

"This is going to sound cheesy," he says, "but I mean it honestly—I feel like I already know you, even though I can't remember anything about it."

"That's because you do know me. We've met dozens of times before."

"That's not possible. I'd remember—"

"You never do, not really, and it breaks my heart every time. Think of it like this: we met in an alternate reality."

Our drinks are ready, and we take them to a small table by the window.

"What do you mean?" Cam asks as he sits down. "I'm confused."

I explain the situation. As "proof," I tell him about his plans for the day, and a few tidbits I know about him. Since I've never stayed in the tea shop this long, I can't predict the customers like I can at the brewery—other than the woman and her dog—but he believes me. It doesn't take much to get him to believe me; it feels like he's primed to do so.

"So you don't know why you're in this loop," he says, "or how to get out of it."

"I've tried. I quit my job. I traveled across North America. I ate a disgusting number of dumplings—"

"I'm not sure there's such a thing."

"—I kissed you." I cover my mouth after I say it.

"Wait a second," he says. "Is that the only reason you kissed me? To see if it would break the spell, so to speak?"

My cheeks heat. "I admit that's why I kept returning here." I gesture around the shop. "At first, I mean. I didn't know you well, but you were nice to me the first time we met, and I thought perhaps it meant something that I'd seen you in multiple locations."

"We didn't meet here?"

"No, the very first time I saw you . . . it was soon after I'd gotten into the loop. I was crying at the night market, and you asked if I was okay."

"Ah."

"But eventually, I felt weird about trying to orchestrate a cute meeting, and I gave up on that. Then I just happened to walk into Leaside Brewing, and you were singing a sea shanty. We got to talking and . . . yeah. You gave me your number and we met up later. I've lived variations of that day many, many times. Often, we go to the night market together, and you get the bulgogi poutine."

"Sounds like something I'd do."

"Other times, I try to mix it up."

He regards me from the other side of the small table. "What do we do on those days?"

"One time, I beat you at mini-golf. Too bad you don't remember that."

He laughs, then slides his hand forward. "I really wish I could remember. Everything."

"I wish you could too," I whisper.

This feels like too much—it's too serious—for a first date. But I have no concept of what is normal anymore. How can I?

I take comfort in the fact that some part of him seems to remember me. When he moves his hand up my wrist, there's something in his expression that says, *This is familiar.*

"So, what happens after we leave the bubble tea shop?" he asks.

"I don't know. We've never talked much here before. Usually, I just meet you at the brewery. There are no other customers for the first twenty-five minutes, so we talk then."

He nods.

"You're extremely chill about this whole thing," I say.

"I am, aren't I?"

"Some strange woman—whose name you don't quite remember—tells you that you've gone on many dates with her before, all on a single day in June. It shouldn't be easy to accept."

"I don't know. It just feels right." He leans forward and presses a single kiss to my mouth. It's over way too soon. "You want to come to the brewery with me?"

———

The taproom isn't open yet. Cam uses a key to let us in. The big white guy is behind the bar, and nineties music is playing.

"Hey," Cam says. "Justin, this is Noelle."

They exchange a few words about lager while I stand there rather awkwardly. Then "I Don't Want to Miss a Thing" starts playing, and Cam pretends to hold a microphone and lip-syncs. He steps out from behind the bar and comes over to me . . . and now he's quietly singing instead of mouthing the words.

Goose bumps break out on my skin, and the words seem to echo inside my chest.

The song is eerily appropriate. Cam will keep missing things, as long as I'm trapped like this. Maybe that will change one day, or maybe we'll always be stuck in this weird place.

But I can feel his wish that we could have more.

He makes a show of setting down his microphone, and through the tears that are threatening to fall, I chuckle. He walks over to me and sets his hands on my waist.

"I'm sorry," he says, "that I have to ask for your name each day."

That's part of what I always liked about him: the earnestness, the sincerity. Was he ever a sullen teenager who was too cool to put together an answer of more than two words for his parents? I can't imagine it.

As the song ends, I tilt my head up and kiss him. One of my hands goes to his shoulder while my other palm is pressed against the left side of his chest. I can feel his heart beating, and it's reassuring.

His lips meet mine again and again, and it's like we're trying to express something that's beyond words. Beyond reason.

"I didn't want a relationship," I whisper. "And I kept telling myself that with you, it wasn't a real relationship. How could it be, if you couldn't even remember my name? Yet I still . . ." I trail off, frustrated with my inability to express myself.

He doesn't rush me, just sways us gently to the song that's now playing—something I don't know. I keep thinking that he ought to be more freaked out by my declarations, yet he's not. Some part of him *knows*.

"I've come to really like you and care for you." I hold back from saying I love him; I'm not sure I can truly love him until I know who he is outside of June 20. "Each time you don't remember, it hurts more than the time before."

"I'm so sorry," he says feelingly.

"You have no reason to apologize."

"I feel like I should be able to make myself remember. Like if I just say your name to myself enough times . . ." He dips his head closer to my ear. "Noelle, Noelle, Noelle."

Each time, he imbues it with a slightly different feeling.

Wonder.

Desire.

I kiss him and hold him as tightly as I can.

His hand slips below my shirt, and I hiss out a breath.

"What are you remembering?" he murmurs. "Have we ever—"

"No. It didn't feel right, if I didn't tell you about the time loop. And the time I did—my friend needed me. I had to go to her. But before that, you did . . ." I move his hand so it's on the button of my jeans. "Are you sure? After everything I've said?"

"Yes." He leads me through a door, then through another. It's a small office, and there are papers in disarray. He lifts me onto the desk. "I'm going to tell Justin to open the front door at three. I'll be back."

He presses a kiss to my cheek, and when he leaves, I'm half-afraid that he won't return. That, once again, this won't actually happen. Though I've lived with the disappointment before, it feels like too much now.

But then he's standing between my legs, reassuring me with his mouth on mine. I wrap my legs around him and pull his shirt over his head. A moment later, he does the same to me, and my bra quickly follows.

I feel a moment of self-consciousness. It's been years since I've been shirtless in front of anyone. But that feeling is wiped away as he dips his head and takes my nipple in his mouth. I roll my hips, seeking out his, but he's too far away. I groan in frustration.

"Just a second," he whispers. "I've got you." Hurriedly, he undoes my jeans. "Have I ever made you come?"

Before I can reply, he slides my pants and underwear down. My bare ass hits the cool desk, and there's something delicious about the fact that we're not doing this in a bedroom.

"No . . ." It turns into a moan as he kneels and his tongue touches my clit. I grip the edge of the desk. I need this—I need him—so badly.

I've thought about it, of course. All the nights I've lain in bed alone, waiting for the day to restart, I've thought of feeling his mouth in places it's been—and places it hasn't. Until today, that is.

His touch feels like the most important thing in the world.

He slips two fingers inside me, and when I jolt, he looks up at me with delighted wickedness. I grab his hair and push his head back down because I *need* to finish.

Cam doesn't keep me waiting. He dives between my legs with more enthusiasm than he has when singing sea shanties, and it's all focused on *me*. He touches me like today is all we have, and I press my hips against him, shameless in my desperation, and move in time with the thrust of his fingers.

There are so many things I want that don't seem to be possible. But this—*this* is something I can have.

He picks up the pace, and I urge him on. I push my hips forward . . . and hold.

My release feels like more than a simple orgasm. For a few glorious seconds, all frustrations empty from my body, and I'm completely lost in pleasure.

When I open my eyes, Cam is standing. I waste no time in unzipping his pants and sliding a hand over his cock. Touching him like this . . . it makes my breath unsteady. My other hand reaches for the condom in my purse, which somehow ended up on a stack of papers. I hold it up, and he nods. While my current life seems to be free of consequences, it still feels wrong not to use protection. I tear open the wrapper and roll the condom over his erection, my hands shaking. When he presses the tip of his cock to my entrance, I cover my face. It's too much yet not enough.

"You okay?" he asks, and for a split second, I flash back to all the other times he's said that to me, in so many different situations that he no longer remembers.

"Yes," I whisper at last.

He pushes inside, and I swear, I *growl*.

"I'm not going to last," he says through clenched teeth.

I nod jerkily. Anything to get him to move.

And then he does.

My hands are all over him. I want to touch everything I can. Burn this into my memory, bright enough for the two of us.

One thing I'll never, ever forget is the joy on his face. There's an intensity there too, but more than anything, Cam looks absolutely fucking delighted.

And I'm delighted to be here with him.

His mouth crashes down on mine, and I can still feel his smile as he kisses me. I wrap my arms around him, needing as much contact as I can with him—as though, if I hold him tightly enough, I can keep him with me, keep him experiencing time in the same way that I do.

Overcome with the urge to see his face, I pull my head back. Sweat is beading on his skin. I rest my forehead against his, and he brings his finger to my lips. After I lick it, he drops his hand between our bodies and moves his finger over my clit.

He slides his other hand under my ass and tilts my hips. That angle . . . oh my god. I bury my face in the crook of his neck so every other person in this building doesn't hear my scream.

He pushes into me a few more times and finds his own re-lease.

"We have to do that again," I say as he pulls out.

He presses a hand to my cheek. "We will."

24

Noelle

When we return to the taproom, Justin winks at Cam. He knows exactly what we were up to, and if he'd remember tomorrow, the embarrassment might cause me to flee.

"Corktown?" Cam asks when he's behind the bar.

He's fully clothed and not touching me, which is unfortunate, but for another eleven or twelve hours, he won't forget who I am and what we've done, and that's a beautiful thing.

Yeah, I can deal with Justin knowing, in exchange for that.

Cam serves me a pint, and I check the time on my phone.

"You've got three minutes," I say, "until your next customers arrive."

"Who are they?"

"Couple in their forties wearing Blue Jays jerseys." I tell him which beers they order.

"Wanna bet on that?" he asks, and we share a laugh. He really has accepted my strange reality so easily.

The next hour passes similarly to how it has in the past, but whenever Cam smiles in my direction, I remember that mouth on mine—and between my legs. At one point, he winks at me, and I almost fall off my stool.

Just before five, Avery walks in and sits beside me.

"Hey," I say.

She gives me a look. "You two did it, didn't you?"

Is my post-sex glow that obvious? I hope she's the only one who can tell.

"Shh," I hiss. "Not so loud."

"I'm whispering."

"Not quietly enough."

She chuckles and pats me on the back. "I'm happy for you. What if sex gets you out of the loop?"

I look at her, wide-eyed. "You think *sex*—"

"The old woman said the dumplings would give you what you needed most, right? It had been a while for you, so what if . . . ?" Her eyes dance.

"No," I say decisively.

But as appalled as I am by her words, I'm glad she's teasing me. It seems like a sign she's doing better than she was in some of our previous iterations of June 20.

———

When Cam and I leave the taproom to go to the night market, Avery is flirting with the same man as last time. I tell her to text me his info if she ends up going home with him. She promises me that either way, she won't come to my apartment tonight—she'll stay at her place if she needs to. Despite my protests, she insists.

I've never traveled with Cam to the night market before; we always meet there. Upon our arrival, I wander on my own for fifteen minutes, giving him time to talk to his food truck contact. As always, I walk past the place where the dumpling stand should be, but nothing's there.

Cam orders the bulgogi poutine, and I order the samosa chaat, since I want the same food that I got on our first first date. Maybe sex has me feeling strangely sentimental, I don't know.

We're here a little earlier than usual, and so we sit at a different bench than usual, his thigh pressed against mine. When he sets down his tray afterward, his arm slides along the bench behind me, and I rest my head on his shoulder.

"What do we . . ." His voice trails off as a new song starts playing over the speakers, which are quite close to this particular bench. "You want to dance?" He holds out a hand.

I shake my head. "Absolutely not."

Dancing isn't something I do, in part because I have no sense of rhythm. I slow danced with Dave at weddings a few times, but that was it. If I'd lived in Regency England, I would have been a wallflower.

I definitely won't dance to "Gangnam Style."

Cam stands up by himself. He does the dance that I vaguely remember from the video, which I haven't seen in years, and he looks like he's having fun, whereas my expression would be closer to one of terror. I never expected to find someone dancing to this song quite so sexy, but I do.

He gestures to me again, and I shake my head.

He comes closer and bends down. "No one will remember, right? Not even me."

True, but dancing isn't something I've ever enjoyed, even if people won't remember me making an ass of myself.

But . . . what the hell.

I stand up, and when someone whoops, I almost sit right back down.

I don't, though. Instead, I try to copy Cam's movements. I still don't like being the center of attention, but I enjoy laughing with him, being in his orbit.

When I take a seat, he accepts that I've done my dancing for the day. I just enjoy watching him have fun, and once the song is over, he joins me on the bench again, his arm draped over the back.

"Want to get out of here?" I ask.

Back in my apartment, we lose most of our clothes before we get to the bedroom, but we make it to bed before he slips his hand between my legs. I gasp.

"God, I love the sounds you make," he says in wonder. "How did I find you?"

How did I find you? Why do I see you in multiple places on June 20? Why does your subconscious remember me? What does it mean?

But I've asked myself those questions many times before, and I'm able to shove them aside and live in the moment.

I wrap my hand around the hot length of him. When I take him into my mouth, he groans. I crawl up his body and kiss him on the lips. The thought that we don't have much time—we don't have enough time—keeps reverberating through me.

"Cam . . ." I say urgently.

He reaches for a condom, flips me onto my back, and slides into me.

Just like earlier, he's smiling, like being with me is the most delightful thing. He lowers his chest to mine, and I arch against him, bare skin on bare skin. I kiss him with everything I have before turning us over so I'm on top. I look down at him, his dark hair against my white pillowcase.

Now I'm the center of attention—but only his attention, and I glory in it. I adjust the angle to get more friction in just the right place, and . . . there. It won't be long.

I bend down to kiss him as we climax together.

"Do you want me to stay over?" Cam asks as it approaches midnight.

"Yes" I say. "Even if . . ." *Even if you won't be here in the morning.*

He smiles, but this time, it doesn't reach his eyes. They don't crinkle; there's no dimple.

"Tomorrow," he says, "whatever that means—come find me."

"I will," I promise.

He wraps his arms around me and falls asleep, and I stay awake, eyes open in the darkness, the song he sang earlier running through my head.

"I Don't Want to Miss a Thing."

—————

A few minutes before three o'clock, I can't help pulling Cam into my arms. Maybe if I'm physically holding on to him, it'll make a difference. Doubtful, but I do it anyway. He mumbles something unintelligible and burrows close to me.

I stare at the glowing red numbers on my alarm clock. At 2:59 a.m., I tighten my hold on him, and my pulse speeds up. It's almost time.

The next thing I know, I'm waking up to my alarm.

There's no warm body next to me.

Despite it being exactly what I expected, it feels horribly wrong. I roll to the other side of the bed and try to smell Cam on the sheets, but there's no evidence that he was ever here, and I'm overcome by the loss. The bed feels unbearably empty without him, and I clutch the pillow that he slept on. It's a poor substitute for his embrace.

I wonder if some tiny part of him misses me too.

25

Noelle

June 20, Version 136-ish

I spend the morning listlessly puttering about my apartment, though I do make an appointment to get my hair cut.

I leave the salon a few seconds later than yesterday, so rather than running right into Cam, I enter the bubble tea shop behind him. He turns back and smiles at me . . . and does a double take.

"Hey," he says. "You look really familiar."

Those casual words . . . this time, they break me.

You fell asleep in my bed last night, I want to scream. *We had sex in your office.*

Though I'm not surprised, I guess an ever-hopeful part of me thought that maybe today, he'd remember my name.

Yet here I am. Again. And while yesterday, he got close to guessing the right name, he doesn't get that far today.

I don't introduce myself. No, I just stand there and stew.

"Have you ever been to Leaside Brewing?" he asks, clearly immune to my thoughts.

"Many, many times," I snap.

Then I run out the door before I can express more of my snark.

I want someone to comfort me, and before I know what I'm doing, I'm on the bus, traveling toward my childhood home. I've never been on this particular bus at this particular time before, so the passengers are unfamiliar to me.

A young woman with a baby in a stroller. The baby, holding a squeaky lion toy, gives her a gummy smile.

A middle-aged man with stringy gray hair and a six-pack of beer.

An older woman with a visor on her head and a cart of groceries next to her.

Two teenagers on their phones.

I try to focus on what I can see around me rather than the emotions that are making me hunch in my seat.

When I get off the bus, I run to my parents' house and knock on the door. I have a key, but they aren't expecting me.

My mother answers. "Noelle, what's wrong?"

I throw myself into her arms and release the sobs I've been holding back ever since Cam said I looked familiar. She doesn't ask what's wrong again, not right away, just strokes my hair like she might have done when I had a fever and had to stay home from school.

In some ways, my mother and I are very different. I've often felt like she didn't fully understand me—and that wasn't merely a teenage phase—but she's always been kind and patient.

"What happened?" she asks at last.

I shake my head. "I can't tell you."

"Why not?"

"You wouldn't understand."

I wonder what would happen if I tried to tell my mom about the time loop. She didn't believe me the first time, but I have more experience telling people now. Cam believed me. Madison believed me. But right now, I'm too tired to go through that again.

My mom isn't offended by my words; she has three kids, and she's heard them before.

"Where's Dad?" I ask.

"Would you rather talk to him instead?"

I shake my head.

"He went to pick something up at the pharmacy," she says, stroking my hair again. "He'll be back soon." She leads me to the kitchen, where she turns on the kettle and takes out some gingersnaps. "You didn't go to work today?"

"No. I couldn't. I called in sick."

She raises an eyebrow. "You're not even working from home?"

I shake my head again.

This is why I came here and not to Avery; I had to see people who knew me from before time got stuck. People who really know me. Or at least, they know the person I used to be.

I stand by my parents' wall calendar, looking at their plans for days that don't exist in my reality. My parents have always been big on building community and helping their neighbors. They volunteer at a literacy program, and they're supposed to take the elderly woman across the street to an appointment next week. With a jolt, I think of my next-door neighbor. I don't see Mrs. Santos on June 20, but I used to take down her recycling every Thursday. The first time I met her, she greeted me in a language I don't know—Tagalog?—and tried not to look disappointed when I said I didn't speak it.

My father enters the kitchen and touches my shoulder. "Is everything okay?"

I start sobbing again, and my parents exchange a look.

"You can stay here tonight," Mom says.

"No, I . . . I'll go home in a few hours. I just . . ."

I don't have the words.

———

At my childhood home, I eat a snack and watch TV—the same things I'd be doing in my apartment, but here, I'm not alone. My parents keep exchanging looks, keep opening their mouths, then shutting them.

This behavior isn't like me. I'm usually quite predictable, and as a kid, I wanted to go to school even when I was sick. If this were my sister, it would just be one of those things that happens occasionally, but the only time I ever did something like this was after Dave dumped me. And back then, I immediately told them what had happened.

I have no idea what they're assuming now. Maybe their assumptions are getting wilder with every minute I don't tell them what's wrong, yet I'm sure they haven't hit upon the truth.

Darling, do you think our daughter could be trapped in a time loop?

No, I doubt that's occurred to them.

Seeing my parents together is rather painful, actually. Some people hate the thought of being like their parents at all, but I imagined I'd be like them in some respects—and that didn't happen.

I never thought they had a grand romance, but I didn't need that for myself; I just wanted the same quiet companionship and affection that my parents have with each other. After my breakup, I shoved those desires down. Clearly, I wouldn't be like my mom and dad; the relationship I started in university hadn't lasted. And while I knew you didn't need to meet someone by twenty-one, my brother married his university sweetheart as well. I wasn't interested in making myself vulnerable again—

why subject myself to the possibility of pain?—and it felt like love was something I couldn't have.

But last night, with Cam . . .

I can't have him either, even if I yearn for it. Simply wanting something isn't enough to make it true.

My parents invite me to stay for dinner, but I refuse. Dad drives me home at five o'clock, not complaining about rush hour.

When he drops me off in front of my apartment building, he says, "If you ever need to move back in with us, it's fine. We have room."

"Thank you, but it's not a financial difficulty."

"For any reason," he says.

I give him a hug and head inside. I ask Avery if she wants to come over for dinner and which expensive food she might want to eat.

If I'm going to be stuck here, I might as well take advantage of it.

Avery arrives with macarons and truffle pizza, and I manage a watery laugh.

"What's wrong?" she asks. "Other than the obvious, I mean."

"Cam didn't recognize me. Which has happened countless times before, but this time . . ."

She nods and wraps her arms around me.

"What about you? What did you end up doing last night?"

"Made out with the guy at the brewery," she says, "then decided I didn't want to go any further, so I got a hotel room for myself. And don't you dare feel guilty that I spent a night in a fancy hotel so you could be alone with Cam. Maybe tomorrow I'll go to Winnipeg to see my dad."

We watch three episodes of a procedural drama. I wish we could have a team of experts devoted to solving our problems within forty-two minutes. Alas, it's just the two of us, and we've been spinning in circles.

Just after midnight, we get ready for sleep. I recall last night, when I had Cam's arms wrapped around me, and feel a wave of melancholy, but my emotional pain is duller than it was earlier in the day.

I feel like I can't expect anything more than that.

26

Noelle

June 20, Version 170? 180? I don't know. It doesn't matter.

Back in university, I learned about stress-strain curves. In elastic deformation, the material returns to its original dimensions when the stress is released. But once you hit the yield point, you get plastic deformation: the material undergoes permanent change until it fractures.

A little stress in your life might not fundamentally change you, but there's no way I won't be irrevocably changed by this time-loop experience, even if I escape it eventually. I wonder how much plastic deformation I can withstand.

I fear it's not much more.

I've stopped trying to count days. What's the point?

I've also stopped crocheting, too annoyed that my work disappears overnight. I do my best to fill my time with reading and watching TV. I see Avery most days. Occasionally, I go to meet Cam, but I don't enjoy it as much as I used to. One time, he remembers that my name starts with an *N*; another time, he guesses "Annabelle." But usually, he has no guesses.

Why the variation? I have no idea.

I'm lost. Despondent.

"I think we have to try dying," Avery says, one night after

we watch a movie with a lot of, well, death. "What else is there to do?"

I'm uneasy with the idea. Besides . . .

"We've read a bunch of time-loop books," I say. "Dying never ends the loop; it just restarts the day. I can't imagine it would help us."

She sighs. "I suppose you're right."

"Promise me you won't try it," I say, because even if dying has never been permanent in any time-loop book I can think of, I can't help worrying.

"I promise."

———

The next day, Avery does try something drastic, though: she attempts to mend fences with her mother, with whom she has a distant relationship for good reason.

Like everything else, it has no effect.

The following day, I want to do something nice for her, so I buy cupcakes at the market again, as well as some birthday candles. I even go to a bookstore and buy the first book in her favorite series. Inside, I write, *This is the best I can do for now. I'll buy you the newest book in the series when we escape the loop.* It's supposed to be released in August.

At home, I retreat to the bedroom and wrap the novel in some colorful wrapping paper. Then I stick a single candle in the salted caramel cupcake and light it. I head to the living room, where Avery is wasting time on her phone. When she sees the cupcake, she rolls her eyes, but she does it with a smile, which is enough to encourage me to sing "Happy Birthday," even if my singing abilities are about on par with my dancing abilities.

"Now make a wish," I say, "but don't tell me what it is."

She blows out the candle. "I'm sure you know what my wish is anyway."

"I do." But for some reason, it feels important to go through the motions.

We each eat a cupcake, and then I hand her the gift.

And that night is different.

———

I wake up at 2:50 a.m. and use the washroom. I'm in the middle of washing my hands when the light flickers three times. Weird.

Also strange: I have a bad headache, which hasn't happened in ages. Maybe the specific decisions I made today somehow resulted in a headache? I don't know. Even though I'm sure the day will reset in a few minutes anyway, I pop a painkiller before returning to bed. I watch the red numbers on my alarm clock. 2:59 . . . 3:00 . . .

Holy shit.

Am I out of the loop?

I jump out of bed again, planning to see if Avery is still on my futon.

It's 3:01 now and—

The day restarts. As always.

———

Avery pours herself some coffee when she arrives at my apartment. "Do you feel different this morning?" she asks. "I've never remembered my dreams in the loop before, but I had a restless sleep and I dreamed that a cupcake came to life and attacked me."

I tell her what happened in the middle of the night.

She stills. "Do you think we almost got out of the loop?"

"Maybe. It could be related to celebrating your birthday?"

I have to believe we can escape the time loop and cling to any sliver of hope, so that day, I celebrate Avery's birthday in an even bigger way. Rather than cupcakes, I find a bakery where I can purchase a whole salted caramel cake without placing an order in advance. I buy her lots of books and wrap them all. Balloons. Streamers. We go out for dinner, and then we return to the apartment and I light twenty-nine candles on the cake and sing with more enthusiasm than I've ever sung before.

That night, nothing unusual happens.

Nothing.

———

The next morning, I tell Avery to text everyone she knows and invite them to a party at my apartment. She also breaks up with Joe, just in case.

Due to the last-minute notice, not a whole lot of people show up, but it's still a party. I even buy cone-shaped hats with polka dots and pom-poms.

It doesn't work.

———

After that, we try celebrating Avery's birthday in a few more ways, but with less enthusiasm each time.

There are no more light flickers. No more weird dreams.

I try not to lose hope, but I can't help it.

A little research on time loops and birthdays gets me nowhere. I spend far too long mindlessly scrolling through social media, even though the same things are trending as usual. On one particularly low day, I watch the squirrel video sixteen times in a row. Then I go to Leaside Brewing to see Cam, and when he doesn't remember my name, I rush out the door, afraid I'm going to burst into tears.

Sometimes, I obsess over the night I saw 3:01 a.m. Did that mean anything? It feels like it has to, but maybe it means nothing. Maybe it's all random. Meaningless.

The days start to blend together even more than they did before. Having some hope, only to have it dashed . . . it wears on me. Makes me feel like I'm getting closer and closer to my fracture point.

June 21 seems impossibly, impossibly far away.

————

One morning, I wake up and something feels different. I can't explain it, but then I see the time on my alarm clock, and I bolt up.

8:03 a.m.

Did I sleep through my alarm? Turn it off and go back to sleep?

Huh. That never happens.

I get out of bed and pad toward the washroom. When I sit down on the toilet, I realize that I'm wearing flannel pajama pants rather than shorts.

My eyes widen, and I finish up in the washroom as fast as possible and rush to the living room, where I look out the window.

There's snow on the ground.

part two

Boy Meets Girl

27

Noelle

I stare in shock at the snow on my balcony. It's clearly not June 20 anymore, but what the hell is going on? It sure doesn't look like June 21, which is where I thought I'd be when I got out of the time loop. I grab my phone from the kitchen table and check the date.

Saturday, January 24. More than seven months have passed.

I let out a scream, then cover my mouth with my hand.

Okay, self. Calm down. You can figure out what happened.

At least it's a Saturday, which means I don't have to go into the office. I scroll through the contacts on my phone. Cam's name isn't there, nor is Avery's. I add her number.

ME: Hey. Is it January 24 for you?
AVERY: Oh thank god. You're here.
ME: I'm freaking out
AVERY: Me too

———

After arranging to meet Avery at eleven, I load Wordle. The word isn't "happy," though it does have a *p*, but not in either of those spots. I solve it in three: "plumb."

I didn't do anything special on the last June 20, so what got me out of the loop?

However, I first need to figure out what my current reality is like. I look inside my messenger bag and see my Woods & Olson laptop, which is good. At least I know what my job is, even if I don't know what else is going on.

Then I start up my home computer and look at my credit card statements. I open up the one for last June and sigh in relief that there are no expensive restaurant bills or flights to New York. The single purchase on June 20 is from a vendor I don't recognize, but it's for a small amount of money—I think it's the calamansi iced tea I purchased on my first trip to the night market. The dumplings were bought with cash, so it can't be those, but I believe the booth serving calamansi iced tea was card-only.

Okay, the first June 20 must have been the "real" one.

I write that down. I assume it won't be erased overnight—unless I'm now fated to repeat January 24. But I won't know that until tomorrow morning.

My next question is what everyone else remembers. I assume that nobody but me and Avery has any memory of those repeats, but I could be wrong. I call my parents.

Dad picks up on the second ring. "Hi, Noelle."

My father is here. That's reassuring.

"Dad, do you remember back in June, I showed up at your house in the middle of the afternoon and cried?"

"Uh . . ."

That's a no. My father would definitely remember such an unusual event if it happened within the past year.

"Never mind," I say. "Is Mom around?"

"No, she's at Zumba."

My mother does Zumba? Since when?

"Oh, right, right. Well, I better get going—"

"Is everything okay?" he asks.

"Yep, just peachy."

"You're still coming for dinner tomorrow, right?"

"Uh, yes," I say. "Six o'clock?"

"Dalton requested that we do it a little early, so if you could get here at five thirty, that would be great."

At the mention of my brother, I freeze. Has the baby been safely born? Is Mona okay?

But I've already asked enough questions.

"Okay, okay, see you tomorrow," I say.

"Madison won't be here, don't worry."

I'm not sure why I'd be worried about that, but I don't ask.

I look through my texts, starting with the ones from Dalton. His most recent message—one week ago—is a picture of a tiny baby. My new niece or nephew! I scroll up and see that he's named Cecil, and he was born a week before Christmas. I stare at the words that I apparently sent last week.

ME: Can't wait to meet him!

While I was stuck on June 20, the world moved on. It didn't move on without me; no, a different version of me was living this life, and I have no idea what she did. How does that even work?

Next, I check my text history with Madison. There's nothing in the last four months. My sister and I aren't super close, but usually we exchange at least a few texts a month, so this is unexpected. I send her a message, but she leaves me on read.

Hmph.

I almost head out without a jacket—I'm used to June weather—but as I'm about to lock my door, I remember to check the temperature. It's below freezing, so I pull out my winter coat and a hat before leaving. I make a quick stop at a bookstore before going to meet my friend.

When I arrive at the coffee shop, I get a black coffee and head to the back corner. Avery joins me a few minutes later, and I hand her the book that I promised to buy.

"I can't believe I forgot about this! Thank you." She strokes the cover, and I'm distracted by the ring on her finger.

"Oh my god," I say. "Are you engaged?"

"Unfortunately, yes," she says dryly. "I'm engaged to Joe. I have to end it, of course, but before I do anything, I'll wait to see if tomorrow is actually January twenty-fifth."

The man next to us gives us an odd look before returning his attention to his phone.

"Which version of June twentieth was the real one?" Avery asks, dropping her voice.

"The first one," I reply. "Based on my credit card statement."

"That's smart. I had no idea how to figure it out, except clearly, it wasn't one where I broke up with Joe. Although I guess we could have gotten back together." She looks at the ring on her finger and shudders. "How did you make a mess of your life in the last seven months?"

"I'm not sure yet. My sister might be mad at me, but other than that, it's hard to say. Still at the same job. Living in the same place. My sister-in-law had her baby." I show Avery the latest picture. She makes appropriate cooing noises, but I can tell she's preoccupied. I don't blame her.

"I have no idea how long we've been engaged. Or how it happened."

The guy next to us clearly thinks we're off our rockers.

When he shifts to another table, I wonder if he thinks we're contagious.

"Look through the pictures on your phone," I say. "Your texts and emails."

She covers her face with her hands. "How can I just not *remember*? It seems impossible."

"It's like how nobody else remembered the previous versions of June twentieth in the time loop."

I think of Cam. I assume he won't know my name, but will I look familiar to him?

———

After leaving the coffee shop, I wander the neighborhood. A restaurant that I liked has closed. It was there just a few days ago—well, a few June 20s ago—and now it's gone. After living so long in a world where such things didn't happen, it's disorienting. I feel like a small-town girl who's overwhelmed by the sights and sounds of the big city.

I consider going to see Cam, but I'm a little afraid of what I'll find, and I'm already dealing with a lot.

When I get home, I spend some time catching up on the news, then scroll through the pictures and videos on my phone. I come across a video of Lenora calling me "Auntie No." I smile, but there's an ache in my chest. Though I can see records of what happened, nothing can make up for the fact that I wasn't there.

Except some version of me *was* there. It's all very confusing.

That night, I go to bed in my flannel pajamas and don't set my alarm.

———

When I wake up, it's January 25.

It appears time is moving normally, but there's a seven-month gap in my memory. I assume that corresponds to the number of days I was stuck in the time loop. Though I'd lost track, the number seems about right.

Yes, I've gotten out of the loop, which is what I wanted, but I'm not as relieved as I thought I would be.

Because now, it feels like I have amnesia.

28

Cam

I turn the screen toward the man in the gray parka. He taps his credit card before hefting his beer into a tote bag.

"Have a good day," I say, forcing a smile onto my face.

It's usually not a problem to smile.

Some people have a rather romantic notion of what opening a craft brewery is like, but it's a lot of work. I thought I was prepared for all that it would entail, yet I wasn't, not fully.

Still, there's nothing else I'd rather be doing . . . most days.

Today is not one of those days.

It's a Sunday, which means that if I had a "normal" job, I could be home, but instead, I'm at Leaside Brewing. One of our suppliers suddenly went MIA, and there's a scheduling issue that I need to sort out. Normally, I don't mind the putting-out-fires aspect of the job, but now, I wish I could be on autopilot.

Which I sort of am, standing behind the bar, popping over to the other register whenever someone pulls something out of the four fridges that comprise our bottle shop, but there are lots of things on my mind. Lots of problems to solve. And I'm only in the taproom because Miriam is out sick.

"Another Dufferin Grove?" I ask the guy sitting at the far end of the bar.

He nods. He's an avid home brewer, and his wife recently

left him. They've got a couple of kids in their teens. He comes in a few times a month.

The next fifteen minutes are busy, and when there's a lull, Justin emerges from the back.

"You doing okay?" he asks.

"Yeah." I force another smile.

I'm not really okay, and I'm sure he knows it, but I'm coping.

My grandma died ten days ago, so I haven't been here as much as usual. She was ninety, and her health had started to go downhill a few months ago; it was a death we were all prepared for, grieving before the end actually came.

Still, knowing she's no longer in this world is a blow.

It seems unfair that time just keeps going. I wish it could stand still for a while, let me adjust to this new reality, but the world doesn't stop for my personal life.

A single woman comes in and sits at the bar. After removing her large coat and her winter hat, she regards the tap list.

"You don't have the Corktown today?" she asks.

"No, sorry," I say. "We only have it in the summer."

She must have been here before. I assume that's why she looks oddly familiar, like a distant memory. She has long dark hair. Dark eyes. Shoulders I can't help noticing in that wide-neck sweater.

There's something compelling about her. I can't quite describe it.

I do my usual spiel about the different beers on tap, but I stumble over my words, which isn't like me. I laugh and continue as though it's no big deal . . . which it isn't.

Yet it bothers me more than usual. Probably just because everything is bothering me more than usual today—or because she's rather pretty.

After I set down her Annex Pilsner, which is one of our

mainstays, she gives me a lingering look that makes my skin prickle. It feels like she's searching for something and hasn't found it. I have the strangest sense that I've disappointed her.

This bothers me too.

She slowly sips her beer, and I assume she's waiting for someone, but once half an hour has passed and no companion has appeared, I figure she's here alone. That's rare: we don't get a ton of women who sit alone at the bar.

"Would you like another?" I ask when she's almost finished her pint.

She shakes her head. "Just the bill."

She pays with her credit card, then puts on her hat and coat before heading out into the January weather. Maybe she had a little time to kill—between shopping and meeting a friend for a meal, perhaps?—and that's why she came in.

With a sigh, I wipe down the bar and help the next customer.

29

Noelle

He didn't remember me, just like he didn't remember me countless times before.

But this time, Cam didn't even say I looked familiar, though
I swear there was a flicker of recognition in his eyes. I considered trying to have a conversation, but I was paralyzed by fear.
Everything is real now. Presumably, he has the ability to recall
what I say to him; he won't forget tomorrow.

Well, he might forget the unremarkable woman who sat
alone at the bar, but if I'd awkwardly flirted with him, I probably would have stuck in his memory for a little while.

I'm not used to such consequences. What if I made a mess
of things, and that was it?

Unable to handle the pressure, I simply drank my beer and
left, but from the time I spent near him, I had the sense that
something was wrong. There was a heaviness to him, which I'd
never seen before; if I'd mentioned that, I'm sure he would have
been weirded out.

And he definitely would have remembered it tomorrow.

Time is advancing normally now, and it's throwing me off.
Even though this was my life for the first thirty-two years . . .

No, thirty-three years. My birthday is in September; I saw

a handful of texts wishing me a happy birthday when I went through my phone yesterday.

The advancement of time and the existence of consequences—and winter!—will require some adjustment, plus I have to make the adjustment without knowing exactly what happened in the real world in the last seven months. I feel like I ought to be happier about escaping the loop. I *am* happy about it, but I'm scrambling to piece things together.

After leaving the brewery, I take transit to my parents' house. The sun is low in the sky by the time I arrive; it'll be dark soon, and I'm not accustomed to the sun setting so early. On the porch, I stomp the snow from my boots, then use my key to open the door. It's nice to be out of the cold.

My mother and Dalton enter the front hallway as I'm taking off my coat. My mother's hair is a bit grayer than it was when I last saw her, and I remind myself not to freak out. She's not aging unnaturally fast; I—or, at least, this version of me—just haven't seen her since she was seven months younger.

A moment later, my father appears with Lenora on his shoulders.

"Auntie No!" She giggles.

I nearly lose it. I haven't seen all these people together in a long, long time. There was no family gathering on June 20, and it would have been awkward to arrange one on any of the iterations I lived through.

Lenora reaches for me. I pull her into my arms, slightly unprepared for how heavy she is.

"Baby," she says, pointing not to herself but toward the front room. I follow her finger and see Mona on the couch. She's nursing.

"What's his name?" I ask.

"Cece!" Lenora says.

"Do you like being a big sister?"

She nods solemnly.

Dalton laughs. "She's not used to sharing our attention with another kid, and sometimes that makes her unhappy."

I pat his arm. "I'm sure I was the same when you came along." In fact, based on the stories I've been told, it's pretty clear that was the case.

After my nephew finishes feeding, he falls asleep, so it's not until after dinner that Mona hands him to me. He briefly opens his eyes and gives me a look that I interpret as suspicious.

Yeah, kid, you should be suspicious of the auntie who just lived through seven months' worth of June 20s. Who knows what she could do next?

At least with Cecil, I haven't missed anything. Well, I don't remember being told that Mona was in labor, and I don't remember hearing that he was born. But this is my first time meeting him, and he's still so small.

When he starts fussing, I hand him to Dalton, who goes off to change the baby's diaper. Then I inquire about the one person who isn't here.

"How Madison?" I ask.

"She's fine," Mom says, a little abruptly.

I open my mouth to ask what happened between Madison and me, then shut it. I ought to know, and what if saying I don't has a cascade of effects?

Consequences. I can't handle them.

"That's good," I say simply.

I'll have to study my sister's social media accounts and see what I can glean, but for now, I need to focus on my job.

I walk into the office at the usual time on Monday morning. After leaving my parents' house yesterday, I spent about an hour going through my work computer, trying to figure out what projects I'm working on and what the deadlines are. Fortunately, my main project appears to be the one whose proposal was due in June, so I'm somewhat familiar with it.

Alas, my research also revealed that Tyler still works here and is just as useless as always. I can practically hear the frustration oozing out of my voice in my polite emails.

"Good morning . . ." I trail off as I realize that Eloise isn't where she's supposed to be. Someone else—a young man I don't recognize—is there. Did she quit?

I scan the room. When I find her at another desk, I breathe out a sigh of relief. There's been some reorganization, that's all.

I head toward my own desk, but stop short when I see Fernando sitting there.

"Hey," he says.

"Hi, you're . . ."

No, he's not in my seat. He has pictures of his family here. This must be his desk now.

"Oh, right." I attempt a self-deprecating laugh. "Old habits die hard."

He frowns. "We changed desks five months ago."

"Has it been that long?" I say airily. I swear I can feel multiple people looking at me, but hopefully that's all in my head.

I slink around the office until I locate the desk with my mug. Then I check my email, open up the most recent files on my computer, and pray I don't fuck this up. When Lee walks by, I glare daggers at the back of his head, but somehow, I manage to make it through the day.

Of course, I could simply quit my job. For real this time. In fact, I *do* plan to quit soon, but the idea of being without a steady paycheck is too scary to contemplate, especially when I think of how much I struggled to get work in my field after graduation. I want to find another job first, but it'll probably be a little while before I'm ready to start hunting for one. Getting back in the swing of things is my priority.

―――

By Friday afternoon, I'm exhausted. It's been a long time since I worked five full days in a row, but the biggest problem was figuring out what the hell was going on. Because I was playing catch-up, I stayed at the office past six every day, but I'll stop doing that going forward. I'm used to being the person who will get everything done, but *why*? They don't pay me enough for that—based on the last deposit to my account, my salary hasn't gone up in the past seven months—so once I've gotten a handle on my work, I'll make a point of not staying any later than five thirty.

After dinner, I make myself a cup of herbal tea before my video call with Avery. I miss talking to her multiple times a day.

"Hey," she says. "How's work?"

"It's been better," I say weakly, "but at least I'm caught up now. Sort of. What about you?"

"Work is okay. It's my personal life that's depressing me."

"Where's Joe tonight?"

She shrugs. "Out with some friends." She has a sip of something that looks like it has a lot of alcohol. "It appears we got engaged on New Year's, in front of his family."

"So you felt like you couldn't say no?"

"I don't know what I thought." She sighs. "But I assume I didn't know that he thinks he's too good for me."

"You're still going to break up with him, right?" The fact that she hasn't done it yet has planted a seed of doubt in my head.

"Yeah. That's what I want to ask you about, actually. I'm

planning to do it this weekend. Could I stay with you after I leave?"

"Of course."

It'll be different from the other times she's spent the night: she'll bring her stuff with her, and she'll actually wake up here in the morning. But I wouldn't say no.

"I promise I'll try to find a place as soon as possible," she says, "but the market is a bit rough. I'll leave my furniture here for the time being and hope he doesn't put up a fuss when I pick it up later."

"Do you want me to come over and help move your things?"

"No, no. I should be okay, but thanks for asking. What are your plans for the weekend?"

"Nothing much," I say. "Though I might go to the brewery and see if Cam's there."

I half hope he won't be. The thought of talking to him makes me anxious.

———

When I get to the brewery on Saturday afternoon, I don't see Cam. I'm about to leave when he steps out of a back room and heads behind the bar.

I take a seat at one end—not my usual place, but a man is sitting there. Cam's now busy serving a group, so I take a moment to admire him.

Cam Huang looks like he could've starred in a rom-com in the nineties, if Asian guys had starred in North American rom-coms back then. He's good-looking, but he's not some perfectly shredded specimen, which seems to be expected from young male stars these days.

His hair is a touch longer than it was in June. Too long, some might say, but I like it. Yet there's something about his expression—just like there was last weekend—that doesn't seem quite right. It's strained, though that wouldn't be obvious if I didn't know him so well.

"Hello again," he says to me.

I stare at him for a beat too long. I'm not used to him acknowledging that he recognizes me; I'm usually a vague memory he can't place. For so long, I yearned for him to have a clear memory of me, and now he does, but he still doesn't recall our dates.

I wonder if he had anything to do with me and Avery getting out of the loop, even though I didn't see him the day before we escaped it. While I can't imagine how that would have worked, I once thought he might be the key to ending the time loop.

My thoughts turn to the email from dustypeony. Maybe we were just cursed for a certain number of days, but the memory of the night the lights flickered makes me feel otherwise. I wish I understood what happened.

"Annex?" Cam asks.

"Sure."

He starts pulling my pint, while I gather up the courage for a conversation he might actually remember tomorrow.

It's a strange new world for me, and it's simultaneously exciting and terrifying.

30

Cam

I set the pint in front of her.

"Thanks." She looks like she wants to add something else, but she doesn't. I'm about to turn away when she says, "Your name's Cam, right? Short for Cameron?"

"Canmore, actually."

Unlike most people, she doesn't seem even a little surprised by this.

"Is that, um, where you were born?" she asks.

"No." I chuckle. "My parents just looked at a map of Canada for inspiration."

"It could have been worse. You could be named . . . uh . . . Lake Superior?"

"That was their second choice," I quip. "What's your name? I'm sorry I don't remember." But she probably told me, if she knows mine.

"Noelle."

When she says it, I have an odd sense of déjà vu.

"Where did we meet before?" I ask. "Was it here?"

"No." She names a place where I occasionally go for bubble tea—it's not far from my parents' house. She's silent for another few seconds before saying, "You used to be a journalist, right?"

"No, you must have me mixed up with someone else."

"Ah, that's right. I remember. Secret billionaire."

"And you're the heiress?" I say before I can think better of it. I sound vaguely flirty, but that wasn't my intention.

For the first time, she smiles, and it's brilliant.

"Yes, that's right," she says. "My private jet is parked down the street."

I can't help my burst of surprised laughter.

"What about your bodyguards?" I make a show of looking around. "I don't see any."

"Oh, they're here," she says airily. "Doing . . . bodyguard things. They're skilled at performing their jobs without being seen."

"If someone is hiding in my brewery, I'd like to know."

"Well, I can't tell you. Top secret." She winks at me, but then her expression sobers and she gulps her pilsner.

Four people enter the taproom and look around uncertainly.

"Take a seat wherever you like and order at the bar," I tell them.

They're followed by a couple of men who have been here before. I don't know their names, but I recognize them. I've been working in the taproom more than usual lately, since one of our employees quit and we haven't been able to replace him yet.

By the time I return to Noelle, she's two-thirds of the way through her beer. It's hard to explain, but there's something particularly captivating about her face. I want to keep looking at it to make sure I can remember it correctly. She lifts the pint glass to her lips and I stare at her throat for a second before snapping myself out of it.

I meet a decent number of women at my job, even if, on an average day, there are more men than women here. However, I try not to mix my work and personal life. Running a brewery might be different from, say, working in a lab—which is what

I used to do—but it *is* my job, even if my father doesn't always respect it.

One time, about a year ago, a woman slipped me her number when she paid the bill. We hooked up, but that's not something that happens often, and it's never been the other way around.

"Another Annex?" I ask Noelle.

She hesitates.

"Or the Swansea Stout?" I suggest. "It's our latest release."

"I'll try that. Yes."

"I hope it's up to your expensive heiress tastes."

"I'm sure it will be."

The taproom gets busier, and she doesn't say much more to me, other than asking for the bill. She pays with her card and doesn't write her number for me anywhere.

It shouldn't disappoint me, but it does.

Oh well. Business is good, and at six, I head home to do the laundry I've been putting off.

———

On Sunday afternoon, Justin and I have our once-a-month karaoke session. Darrell, Darrell's wife, and Justin's boyfriend all come over and squeeze into our living room. Darrell rarely sings, but he enjoys watching everyone else make fools of themselves, and once in a while, Keysha convinces him to do a song. She's the only one who can do that.

"All right, you're up." Justin slaps me on the back.

"What should I do?"

He raises his eyebrows. Usually, I pick my songs myself, rather than allowing him the pleasure.

"'Call Me Maybe,'" he says.

I grab the microphone.

Honestly, I was expecting worse from him. I like Carly Rae Jepsen, and I rather enjoy doing this song—even if, right now,

I might prefer "The Loneliest Time"—though before it begins, he gets a disturbing gleam in his eye.

"The woman you were flirting with yesterday—did you give her your number?"

I don't bother denying that I may have been flirting.

"Nah," I say good-naturedly, then start singing, acutely aware of the fact that I'm the only single one in this group. Just like I was when I looked up at the stars at Darrell and Keysha's wedding reception.

And once again, I wonder if I missed her, the woman who's right for me.

Except this time, for some reason, I'm picturing Noelle.

31

Noelle

"Hey, Noelle," says the man opening the door next to mine.

Who the fuck are you? I refrain from asking.

What happened to Mrs. Santos? Did she move? Did she die?

Since my pre-loop life was fairly uneventful, I don't have as much to catch up on as some people would. Still, there are things that throw me off, like the fact that I apparently have a new neighbor, and my usual grocery store has rearranged *everything*. Seeing Valentine's chocolate for sale—without first seeing Christmas chocolate—was also odd, but I smiled at the evidence of passing time.

A little rattled, I heave my grocery bags inside and close the door. I put everything away, then check my phone to make sure I haven't missed anything from Avery. She said she'd dump Joe this weekend, but I've yet to hear from her. A part of me also hopes for a message from my sister, but there's nothing. Impulsively, I give her a call.

Madison picks up. "I'm still not talking to you."

And then nothing.

I think of the time we ate dumplings together. We got along then, but apparently, in another reality, something went terribly wrong. I can't bring myself to ask what happened because . . . I ought to know.

Not for the first time, I search for tips to retrieve old memories. Many of the articles discuss tips to retrieve repressed traumatic memories, but that's not exactly the situation here—at least, I assume it isn't. I also try to figure out what happened to my neighbor. I can't find an obituary, so I hope that means she's okay. Maybe she moved into a retirement home.

Sighing, I attempt to think about something else, but my mind immediately turns to Cam, which doesn't help. I returned to the brewery yesterday, and unlike the previous time, I got up the courage to speak to him. Flirting with a cute guy is harder when you know he'll actually remember it, but we exchanged names, and our conversation progressed similarly to before. Asking if he used to be a journalist certainly felt awkward, but once again, he made that comment about me being an heiress, and we were in familiar territory. Except he didn't give me his number, like he did all those times on June 20. Should I have given him mine?

Or is he seeing someone now? Or did he have a bad experience dating a person he met at Leaside Brewing and swore he'd never do it again?

I hate that I won't get another chance at a first impression. As tired as I was of having the same conversations over and over with him, I felt assured of my success. Now, I have no idea what the hell to do.

But I do know one thing I want: a haircut.

When I call the salon and they say they have nothing available today, I freak out. Then I remind myself that making an appointment for next Saturday is just fine.

I'm about to start preparing lunches for the week when my phone buzzes. It's Avery—my phone actually remembers her contact info now—saying she's ended her engagement.

"I meant to do it earlier." Avery is perched on my recliner, a bag of sour cream and onion chips in her hand. Her hair is now pink, and it looks great. "But knowing I wouldn't have a chance to redo the breakup . . . that scared me."

"How did you end up doing it?"

She's been here for half an hour, and I'm finally getting around to asking her for details. When she arrived, I was pre-occupied with figuring out where to put all her stuff. And since she didn't immediately tell me, I wondered if I should ask.

I'm not very good at this friendship stuff. I don't have as much practice as I ought to have by the age of thirty-two. I mean, thirty-three.

"Wellll," she says, "we were eating breakfast this morning, and he said something along the lines of, 'When will you start planning the wedding? My mom's been asking about it.'"

"The planning was all supposed to be *your* job?"

"Apparently. So I said, 'You know, I don't think there's going to be a wedding,' before calmly taking off my ring. He was very confused, and then he turned a disturbing shade of red and asked if I was ending the engagement, to which I replied, 'You bet your ass I am.' He told me that I should rethink what I was saying. Because if I didn't, I would die alone, with only cats to keep me company, and I said, 'Cats are better company than you are.' I was very mature about the whole thing." She pauses. "If we find the dumpling lady, maybe she can send me back in time so I can prevent my former self from going on a first date with Joe."

"Don't even joke about that," I say before I can stop myself.

"I know, I know, I have no interest in screwing with time any further, but it's nice to imagine I never met him. Never wasted years of my life on him."

"Yeah, I can understand."

"I mean, I know that I was shaped by all the experiences I had in the past, and I probably shouldn't wish any of them away because they made me into *me*, but . . ."

I think of stress-strain curves.

"I get it," I say. "Like, I think it's reasonable to wish I hadn't been sprayed by a skunk."

"Are you seriously comparing a first date with my ex to getting sprayed by a skunk?"

I wonder if I shouldn't have done that, but she's laughing.

Despite not getting any repeats in my friendship with Avery, I feel like I haven't screwed it up too badly. And at least with her, I haven't forgotten anything.

That evening, Avery and I watch two episodes of a show that debuted—and was canceled—in the months we can't remember. New TV shows and movies! How exciting. I look at what's playing at the nearest movie theater. There are a few movies whose trailers I watched and thought I'd never get a chance to see. The historical drama that piqued our interest is supposed to start streaming in Canada soon.

While Avery is washing up, I send a text to Veronica. I texted her once during the loop, and she didn't reply before the day reset. Just like last time, I don't immediately get a response, but that's okay. Maybe she'll answer tomorrow.

I set down my phone and regard Avery's plant, which now sits on my windowsill. She used to say that it never changed, even though she'd stopped watering it, but now, it looks different than it did when I was at her old apartment. Multiple leaves have unfurled, and it feels miraculous. After so long with time being stagnant for us, it's moving again.

Yet it wasn't really stagnant. Some version of us was experiencing time in the usual way. Some version of me got the news that Cecil was born. Some version of me went to work, over and over.

I don't understand it, and I hate that.

But right now, the most important thing isn't understanding the how and why of the time loop: it's sorting out my life, as well as Avery's.

When she returns to the futon, she pulls out the novel that I bought her on January 24.

"I thought you would have finished it by now," I say.

"I did—it only took me two days. I'm rereading it."

I'm glad she's finding comfort in the pages of a book.

32

Noelle

Monday morning, to put it eloquently, sucks balls.

I'm not used to having someone else in my space as I get ready for work; I'm not used to needing to wait for someone to finish in the washroom. It'll take some adjustment.

But the worst part is the unfamiliar cramping.

My period will begin at any moment, and I haven't had a period in a very long time. Fortunately, I have appropriate supplies on hand, and I remember to take some with me.

Sure enough, when I go to the washroom midmorning at work, I confirm that my period has started. How did Avery endure having hers for seven months straight?

When I return to my desk, the drawings I was waiting for are finally done. Unfortunately, there are lots of errors. I quickly explain everything to Eloise, trying not to sound as cranky as I feel. We're supposed to issue the drawings at the end of the day—hopefully, they'll be ready on time.

And then Tyler comes to me with such an incredibly basic question, I have to resist the urge to shake him.

So by the time lunch rolls around and I'm sitting in the lunchroom with Fernando and a couple of other engineers, I'm in no mood to be reminded of the fact that someone who does the same job, with the same experience, makes more money than I do.

We manage to issue the drawings just before six. Thanks to multiple transit delays, my commute takes longer than usual, and by the time I get home, I'm not interested in anything but instant noodles for dinner. Cooking is too much effort. My cramps are also worse than usual, and I pop some ibuprofen.

"Do you always get home this late?" Avery sits across from me with her own noodles.

"Not always."

I feel like I ought to say something more. Make conversation. But the first thing that comes to mind? Wondering whether our periods will sync up.

We eat in silence until I say, "Your never-ending period is finally over?"

"Yeah. Has yours started? Is that why you're grumpy?"

I nod. "Sorry."

"It's okay. I'm the one who's in your space."

I wave this away. "It's fine. I'm happy to let you stay here." Not a lie, even if today, I'm in the mood to be alone. "Was it nice to wake up without Joe next to you? Knowing you wouldn't have to break up with him again?"

"Oh my god, yes."

We share a smile. We'll be forever bonded by what we went through, something that no one else can understand.

———

Unfortunately, Tuesday isn't any better at the office.

Is work worse than it used to be?

No, I don't think so. It's just that my tolerance for it has gone way down. Before, I was going through the motions, day in, day out, hoping that if I worked hard, I'd be rewarded.

But now I know hard work won't get me anywhere. Loyalty won't get me anywhere.

I'm not sure how much I truly believed otherwise. Maybe

I was just desperate to hold on to something, but now, I can't even pretend. The time loop snapped me out of my routine, and I can't rid myself of the knowledge that my boss refused to give me an appropriate raise.

I need to start looking for a new job. I shouldn't put it off any longer.

On the transit ride home, I read about how switching jobs can help maximize your income. I also read about how to build your résumé to get past AI screening tools, which may toss your application for the most arbitrary of reasons. It all sounds like a nightmare.

I nearly throw up on the bus. I should know better than to read in stop-and-go traffic, especially when I was already feeling like shit thanks to my period.

For a moment, I wonder if I should be happy with what I have, work-wise, and simply not bother to stay late anymore.

I quickly shove that thought aside.

I can do this.

Wednesday is another crappy day at work. I'm told that Tyler has complained I'm not spending enough time mentoring him . . . or something like that. It sounds like his performance isn't up to par, and he threw me under the bus and nobody pushed back.

Well, maybe if he put in any effort, I want to say, but I bite my tongue and fiddle with the iron ring on the pinky of my right hand. I don't see any point in arguing. I'm not going to stay here long-term.

That evening, Avery isn't around. I think she's trying to give me time to decompress alone, but I feel guilty about it, even if it's my apartment. I spend an hour looking at job listings and bemoaning the state of the world.

Thursday, I leave work right at five. Fernando shoots me a surprised look as I walk out but doesn't say anything.

Before I know what I'm doing, I'm taking the TTC toward Leaside Brewing. The last time I didn't head straight home after work—other than after I quit my job—was when I went to the night market and ate those dumplings. I chuckle ruefully.

It's a cold evening, and even the five-minute walk from the bus stop is uncomfortable. After months of mid-June weather, I'm still not used to freezing temperatures or short days, but I do like that the weather each day is a little different. Sometimes it's cloudy; sometimes it's sunny. Sometimes there's light rain that changes to snow.

But today is just too damn cold.

When I step inside, I sigh in relief at finally being out of the bitter wind. A few people are drinking quietly in the corner, and Cam is nowhere to be found.

I deflate more than I should at his absence.

"Can I help you?" the woman behind the bar asks.

I could make an excuse and head back out, but I'm already here, so fuck it. I consider being reckless and getting the BBA Junction Imperial Stout—11.9 percent alcohol!—then decide to stick with the weaker Swansea Stout.

As she sets the pint in front of me, I think about the fact that this—having one drink alone after work—is something I never would have done in the *before* time. Not just because I always went straight home, but because it's an unnecessary expense, and I was careful with my money. Some might even say I was stingy.

But several months of living in a reality where money didn't matter has changed me.

There's nothing wrong with purchasing a beer or a cupcake every now and then. It's not like I'm suddenly going to buy a

BMW and take a two-week vacation at an expensive resort. My job might not be paying me as much as it should, but I can have small luxuries without worrying that I won't be able to afford my rent or contribute to my retirement fund. I'm lucky.

"Hi, Noelle."

I jolt up at that voice. My hand knocks my pint, but Cam grabs it before any beer sloshes over the rim.

"You remembered!" I say, before I realize how silly that sounds. But I'm not accustomed to him remembering my name, and I can't help smiling. When I was stuck on June 20, I was desperate for this, and now it's finally happening. The most ordinary things seem like miracles after you've been trapped in a time loop.

"Yes, of course. Do you remember mine?"

"Lake Superior, is that you?"

I want to crawl under a table after I say that. Such a terrible joke. I'm making a fool of myself, and I can't redo it tomorrow.

But he remembers!

When Cam laughs, I wonder if he does like me in this reality, even if he didn't give me his number.

"Cam," I say, nodding. "How's it going?"

"Not too bad, not too bad. What about you?"

"It's brutal out there." I tilt my head toward the door.

"It is."

"And work has . . . well, it's been a long week."

I suspect Cam, on occasion, has people talking his ear off about their problems, but I don't want to dump on him like this.

"Problems with the jet?" he asks, and that delights me.

"Mm. How did you know?"

"You've got that look on your face. A look of—horror upon horrors—having to fly first class rather than in your own carbon-emitting machine."

First class is a lot more money than, say, a single beer at the end of a workday. The rare times I fly, it's always economy. I should have splurged on our trip to Vancouver, but it didn't even occur to me.

Are there people who are appalled at the idea of flying on a commercial airline, even in the most expensive seat they can buy? Probably, but it's hard to imagine.

"Yes," I say, "it was very tough, traveling to Bora-Bora with someone beside me." I stick up my nose in a haughty manner. "But somehow, I managed."

A couple walks into the bar, and I curse them under my breath. I want Cam to have customers, but their opening the door allows the wind to enter. I can't help my full-body shiver.

"Are you okay?" he asks me.

"Just f-fine."

"I'm sorry, I can't change the weather—"

"I'm disappointed in you," I say lightly. "Surely any good bartender has the ability to turn a c-cold spell into a warm summer day."

"I can make you some tea. There's a kettle in the back."

"It's really not necessary." I don't want to be too much of a hassle.

"Or if you'd like something with alcohol, I could make you a hot toddy or blueberry tea."

"Blueberry tea?"

"It's a cocktail with Grand Marnier, amaretto, and orange pekoe."

"Why is it called blueberry tea?" I ask.

"Some people think it actually tastes a bit like blueberries."

"Okay, I'll try one of those." Out of the corner of my eye, I notice the couple who entered a few minutes ago approaching the bar. "If it's not a bother . . ."

"I'll take their order first, then get started on your blueberry tea."

I continue to sip my cold beer as Cam serves the other customers, and I look at my phone to check the temperature. It's unusually cold for Toronto, so it's reasonable for me to feel chilled to the bone.

What's less reasonable is that I felt compelled to go to a brewery rather than heading home. I could be in my apartment, wrapped in a warm blanket, yet here I am.

And I don't regret it.

Cam is wearing a long-sleeved Leaside Brewing shirt. He pulls two pints for the couple, then heads to the back. A few minutes later, he returns with a small teapot and pours a couple of things into a glass that I believe is called a brandy snifter. He adds a slice of orange and a spoon.

"Pour the tea whenever you're ready," he says.

"Thank you." I pause. "Sorry to trouble you again, but if you still have them, I'll get one of the meat pies. Whatever kind is available."

Internally, I wince. This meal and two drinks *will* be on my credit card tomorrow, but by the time I get home, it'll be late and I'll be too tired to do anything but make instant noodles again.

"Sure thing," Cam says.

I pour the tea, stir with the spoon, and inhale, my hands cupped around the glass.

I already feel better.

My first sip warms me on the way down, and it does indeed taste faintly of blueberry, with a nice bite thanks to the alcohol. There's nothing quite like a hot drink on a chilly day, and it's a small pleasure I didn't get to enjoy when I was trapped in June. While I'm regularly overwhelmed now, I also find myself appreciating things I never thought much about before.

"Just what I needed, thank you." I smile at Cam slightly longer than I'd usually smile at a server, then wonder if that was weird and duck my head.

What do I want to accomplish tonight?

I guess I'm still hoping that, unlike last time, he'll give me his number when he hands me the bill, so that we can interact in a scenario where I'm not the customer.

"Have you had this place long?" I ask.

"Six years," he says.

It's awkward to make conversation when I know him—and he barely knows me—and unlike before, he's actually going to remember this tomorrow.

Oh god. This is too much for my poor brain.

I consider downing my blueberry tea in a hurry, throwing some cash on the bar, and leaving. Then I remember the pie that I foolishly ordered because I didn't want to have instant noodles tonight.

It would be so much easier if I didn't know him from the loop, but then I wouldn't have the memories of him slipping me his number to encourage me. Plus, if it weren't for the time loop, I wouldn't be reconsidering my decision to swear off relationships, yet now, I'm feeling a need for human connection that I didn't have before.

You changed me, I think, while looking at Cam sliding a beer across the bar to a customer. *You changed me, but you don't remember.*

My phone buzzes. Veronica has texted me back. I'm about to ask if she wants to grab lunch sometime, when a small meat pie and a serving of kettle chips are set down in front of me.

"Thank you," I say.

I cut into my steaming pie, then wait a few minutes for it to cool so I don't burn myself. Once I try it, I decide it was indeed a very good idea that I came here tonight rather than going straight home.

"How is it?" Cam asks.

"Delicious," I say.

Now, *there* is the dimple I'd missed. It warms my chest as much as the blueberry tea.

"You want another?" he asks, gesturing to my empty glass.

I shake my head. "Gotta work tomorrow."

And if I drink more, I might reminisce about all the times you kissed me.

He greets three new customers, who spend a long time debating what to order. I finish my pie and watch them out of the corner of my eye, thinking about the fact that Cam is everything I'm not. Outgoing, friendly, relaxed.

I also wonder about the group he's serving. What sort of person goes to a brewery on a chilly Thursday evening, other than a woman with a crush on the brewery owner? How do they know each other?

Surreptitiously, I glance at the other people in the room; it's still rather exciting to see unfamiliar customers here. A man and a woman in the corner are holding hands under the table. Their heads are bent close together, and he's listening intently to whatever she's saying. How long have they been together? It looks like they're a few years older than me. Do they have kids? Did they get a babysitter for date night?

I was always more of an observer than a participator. Even in my own life, I felt like a side character. In elementary school, I'd sometimes spend recess watching other kids play rather than playing myself. I was a diligent student, but not the kind who sat in the front row and stuck her hand in the air to answer as many questions as she could. No, I preferred the back corner.

I did have a few friends, and as I got older, I found myself craving romantic love too. But I wondered if it wasn't for me—complicated, messy, scary. It sounded like something for other people, although my parents' stable marriage gave me some hope.

Then I met Dave, and the end was exactly what I'd feared—at least, in terms of what it did to my emotions. To him, the breakup was probably pretty simple.

After that, I put myself on autopilot. I went through the motions to give myself financial security, a sense of productivity, without really thinking about what I desired. In retrospect, it's amazing how I could just forget to think about who I was and what I wanted for so long. I guess I was afraid of disappointment if something didn't work out.

But on June 20, I couldn't just be a bit player in my own life. The actions of other people became predictable, and *I* was the thing that was different. Me and Avery. I could take risks because they weren't all that, well, risky.

Maybe it's time to take a small risk now. My yearning is—at least temporarily—greater than my fear.

"Just the bill, please," I say to Cam when he approaches.

He prints the bill, hands it to me, and asks if I need the machine.

I shake my head. "I've got cash."

I take my time pulling my wallet out of my purse, and when his attention is elsewhere, I scribble my name and a short message on the bill, then add the money. I use an empty glass to weigh everything down, just in case the door opens and the wind blows in.

Unfortunately, Cam returns before I can put on my coat.

"See you later." I hustle to the door, not wanting to see his expression when he notices that I've left my number.

It's minus a bazillion degrees outside, and I'm wearing a dress shirt and a thin sweater. As I struggle to zip up my coat, I wonder if this zipper was always such a pain. I pull on my winter hat before returning to the zipper, feeling like I'm in grade one—I regularly needed my teacher to help with my coat then—and almost punch my fist in the air when I finally get it. Success!

I hurry toward the bus stop and arrive a mere thirty seconds before the bus—perfect timing. Once I'm safely in my seat at the back of the bus, I check my phone. No new messages, and I try not to deflate.

I remind myself that Cam's working, but at eleven o'clock, I'm ready for sleep, and I still haven't heard from him. There's always tomorrow, though. Because "tomorrow" is something that properly exists now.

Still, I toss and turn in bed, afraid I might have screwed this up somehow.

No, you were brave.

Yet I can't help wishing I could slink back into the shadows.

For the first time in as long as I can remember, I'm awake after three in the morning. When I was stuck in the loop and 3 a.m. came, the next thing I knew, my alarm was going off, but that's now how things work anymore. Normally if I couldn't fall asleep, I'd go out to the living room, but Avery is there and I don't want to disturb her. Instead, I wonder, yet again, how we got out of the loop, my thoughts spinning in circles.

After getting two hours of sleep, I shuffle into work, unhappy with my choices and trying to draw even less attention to myself than usual.

But at lunchtime, I get a message.

33

Cam

Noelle isn't like the other women who have flirted with me in the taproom, although it's hard to explain why I think that. I guess I had the sense that she's not a flirtatious person. Like it was something she had to work herself up to doing, but it's not as if it was especially awkward or forced. No, it felt natural, almost like we'd done it before, but I have a hunch that it was an effort for her. When I saw that she'd left her number, I smiled.

I was worth the effort.

To be honest, I'd considered asking her out myself—the way she'd popped into my mind during karaoke had felt like a sign—but I'd never tried to give my number to a customer before. I'm glad she made the first move.

Had she returned to the brewery on the coldest day of the year just to see me? That occurred to me when she first walked in the door, and it was more or less confirmed when she scurried out and I picked up the cash she'd left.

However, I had some unexpected crises to deal with, and by the time I could look at my phone for more than three seconds, it was late. I figured I'd wait until the next day at lunch.

> ME: Hey. It's Cam. I have to work Saturday, but I can leave
> around 7. Dinner?
> NOELLE: Sure!!

I can't help wondering how often she uses double exclamation marks. Again, I figure not very often. It's just a vague feeling I have, but something inexplicable is drawing me to her, and I look forward to getting to know her better so I can have more than vague feelings.

I haven't been on a date since October. I have a lot going on, and while my grandmother was dying, I was spending my free time with her, not on apps. It's been well over a year since I had a girlfriend, who broke up with me because she couldn't deal with my hours. She would have preferred someone with a nine-to-five job.

Which is what I suspect Noelle has, all heiress jokes aside. Yesterday evening, she was wearing clothes that looked appropriate for an office.

I suggest an izakaya that I've been meaning to try for months, and she quickly agrees. When I have a free moment, I make a reservation, then send her the details.

I wonder what my brother would think of this. He's one of those guys who believes women only like rich, white men who are over six feet tall, and poor him, because he's not any of those things.

Neither am I, and I do well enough.

———

I've had many first dates over the years. I shouldn't be nervous, yet I am, even if I don't look it.

I enter the izakaya, and the employees shout their welcome. I smile back before giving my name to the hostess. She leads me toward a table, where someone is already seated, even though I'm five minutes early.

At first, I think it's a mistake. I can see the back of the person's head, and they have short hair, but once I get closer, it's clear there was no seating mix-up.

"Hey." I sit across from Noelle. "You got your hair cut. It looks good." If she'd come into the taproom with a different haircut, I wouldn't have said anything, but now, we're on a *date*. I grin.

Instinctively, she reaches up to pat her hair. "Oh. Yes. Thank you."

Her sweater looks very cozy. It's another cold day, though not quite as bad as Thursday. She's also wearing earrings that glint in the overhead lights.

I gesture to the menu. "Have you eaten here before?"

She looks momentarily bewildered by the question, then says, "Yes, but it's been a while. When I was last here, I was able to sit on the patio."

"Well, it's certainly not patio weather today."

She laughs in the way that people do when they're a little anxious. I want to put her at ease.

When the waitress comes to take our drink orders, Noelle selects something with plum wine, and I get a cocktail with yuzu and sake. For some reason, my choice makes her smile.

After that, we debate what to order from the food menu, eventually settling on roasted shishito peppers, tuna tataki, agedashi tofu, wasabi octopus, and tempura.

Then there's an awkward moment of silence. I'm acutely aware of the laughter at the table next to us, which seems louder than it should be. The acoustics in this place aren't the greatest. That's something I was concerned about when we were building the taproom: I wanted it to be a place where people could easily have conversations.

For a second, I kick myself for not choosing another restaurant, even if the food looks good, but I can make this work. I lean a little closer but don't get all up in her personal space. It's only a first date.

"What do you do for work?" I ask her.

"I'm a mechanical engineer."

"Do you like it?"

"It's . . . okay." She chuckles. "When I was deciding which engineering discipline to study, I chose mechanical in part because it's so broad. I struggled to find a decent job, though, and I ended up at a consulting firm, doing a lot of HVAC design. The work isn't too bad, but I'm not thrilled with this particular job right now. I'm looking for something new."

"What don't you like? Your coworkers?"

"Some of them, yeah. And I'm underpaid." She pauses. "I can do better." It sounds like she's trying to convince herself more than she's trying to convince me. "I feel like I'm not appreciated. They just heap more on me and expect me to get it done without a fuss because, well, that's what I always did before."

Yeah, I suspect that making a fuss would be out of character for her.

I regard her in the rather dim light. Noelle is Asian of some sort, but I'm not sure what. Her skin is a touch darker than mine. There's just something about her that makes you want to take a second look . . . and a third . . . though I restrained myself from doing that in the taproom.

Now, however, she's right in front of me. I feel like we're on the precipice of something—and also like *she's* on the precipice of something.

I would appreciate you, I want to say.

I don't always come across as a serious guy, but I'm serious about this. I suspect I'd do a lot for her, even if I don't know her well yet.

"I hope you find something soon," I say.

We talk a bit more about our work, and then our food starts arriving, beginning with the shishito peppers and tuna tataki. As I reach for a thin slice of tuna with my chopsticks, I have the feeling that I've eaten this before, with her.

It doesn't make any sense, but I try not to think much of it.

Conversation shifts to movies, and from there, we somehow end up talking about our families. I tell her that I grew up in Toronto and have a younger brother.

"What about you?" I ask.

"I have a younger brother and sister. My brother and his wife have two little kids."

More food arrives, and she eagerly digs in. I watch her eat for a few seconds, admiring her dark eyes and the smattering of freckles on her nose and cheeks, before I help myself to some tofu.

The food is all very good, and when I ask if she wants dessert, she suggests we share the matcha cheesecake.

"It wasn't on the menu the last time I came here," she says, and she seems delighted by the new addition. Her delight is quiet, understated—but it doesn't escape my notice. Just like I noticed her pleasure when she tried the blueberry tea on Thursday.

A plate and two forks are placed in the middle of the table, and we both lean forward as we help ourselves to the cheesecake. Underneath the table, my knee brushes against hers, and I don't move away.

Afterward, she insists on splitting the bill, and we leave the izakaya and wander south on Yonge Street. She tucks her gloved hand into the crook of my elbow.

"Is this okay?" she asks.

"Of course." It's more than okay.

Tonight has certainly gone better than my date with Delphine last fall.

A few flakes of snow are falling, and it's actually rather romantic. Valentine's Day is a week away, and I wonder how I should acknowledge that when we've only just started dating. Assuming Noelle wants to keep dating, that is, but I have a feeling she does.

At Mel Lastman Square, I stop and watch the skaters on the ice. "There was a night market here in the summer. It was kinda cool."

"Oh," she says faintly. "Right. Yes. I went too. I had dumplings."

There's something odd in her tone, but before I can process that, her arms are around my neck. She tilts her face toward me, snowflakes in her eyelashes. It's the cutest fucking thing.

I drop my head and kiss her.

As soon as my lips meet hers, it feels *right*, like we're meant to be here on a February night, making out under a streetlamp. It's also strangely familiar, but I think that's just because it feels so right and good. I hold her as close as I can with our giant winter jackets and sink everything I have into coaxing soft little moans from her. She tastes of winter and matcha and something undefinable. Honestly, I'm tempted to say she tastes like magic.

"Hey," I say afterward, swiping my thumb over her chin.

"Hey." She smiles at me, though the smile disappears as her teeth start chattering.

"It's too bad I can't make you a blueberry tea right now." I take her elbow. "We should head to the subway station."

"G-good idea."

She doesn't invite me to come home with her, and I don't ask.

"You know," she says, "I got sprayed by a skunk once. Near here."

That surprises a laugh out of me. "What were you doing to upset the skunk?"

"Nothing, I swear."

"What'd you use to get out the smell?"

"Hydrogen peroxide, dish soap, and baking soda."

"Was it gone by the next day?"

She hesitates. "Yeah, mostly."

"Can I take you out again?"

It's an abrupt change in conversation, but I want to ask now because we've reached the station and I don't know if she's going the same way as me.

"Of course you can," she says, pressing a kiss to my cheek.

34

Noelle

"How was your date?" Avery asks as soon as I enter the apartment. She pauses the TV. It looks like she's watching some kind of action movie, and a man is frozen midleap.

"Good." I take off my jacket. I tried to brush off as much snow as I could before I entered the building to minimize the mess. "Good, but weird."

I'd been on many first dates with Cam—including at the same izakaya—but never one in winter. It was fun, though disorienting. In fact, at the end I was so mixed up that I told him about the time I got sprayed by a skunk, which doesn't seem like great first-date conversation. But he asked if he could see me again, so it couldn't have gone too badly.

A second date. We've never had a proper second date before.

"At one point," I say, "we walked by Mel Lastman Square, and he mentioned the night market. I had to restrain myself from telling him about all the times we'd been there and all the bulgogi poutine he'd eaten."

It's not like a woman over thirty needs more problems with dating, but here I am, struggling not to talk about all the times we hung out on June 20.

"How was your evening?" I ask Avery.

"Oh, not too exciting." She gestures to the TV, then the bowl on the coffee table. There are a few chips at the bottom.

I open my mouth to ask how she's feeling about the demise of her relationship. Then I close it, not sure if she'd want to talk about this now and not sure how best to be a friend.

⸻

After Saturday comes Sunday. Such a basic idea—the end of one day and the beginning of another—yet I'm still not used to it.

Avery is running some errands, and I turn my focus to cleaning. The Lunar New Year is coming up, and I've been conditioned to start the New Year with a clean apartment. It doesn't feel right otherwise. And cleaning is more enjoyable than it was before, because it's still exciting that my apartment doesn't reset itself each night. In the loop, there was simply no point in mopping the floor, for example.

Sometimes, the Lunar New Year feels like a do-over. A chance to restart the year in late January or mid-February and actually stick to those resolutions. But this time, I missed January 1, so it's the only start to the year I have.

What did the alternate version of me do? Did I stay home and watch a movie, eating popcorn and drinking wine at midnight?

That seems most likely. There are no pictures from that night on my phone.

It occurs to me that I could look at my viewing activity on Netflix, check if I was watching something there on New Year's Eve. But it doesn't seem important compared to the other things I've missed.

As I pull down the curtains and take them to the laundry room for their twice-a-year clean, my mind turns to the dumpling woman. Where is she now? Is she still selling magic dumplings? What made her choose me and Avery?

I return to my apartment, and before I start cleaning the fridge, I do a quick search. My previous attempts to find her were unsuccessful, but maybe something has appeared online in the last several months.

However, I still don't have any great search terms, since her booth didn't have a name, and I can't find anything.

Hmph. Maybe I'll just have to accept that I'll never understand what happened, but that doesn't sit well with me. I like understanding things.

My thoughts drift to Cam, and I wonder if he experienced déjà vu yesterday. He didn't mention it to me, but that doesn't mean he didn't feel it.

After taking the curtains out of the washing machine, I look at my phone. There's a text, and I feel like I summoned Cam by thinking about him.

> CAM: Again, just wanted to let you know that I had a great
> time last night. I won't be able to do next Saturday,
> but I'm free on Sunday, if you're interested.

Telling me that he had a good time last night? It's not something he used to be able to do. I read the words again and again, feeling almost giddy.

Then the worries set in.

I have no experience navigating our relationship once it gets to this point. And before Cam, I hadn't dated in years. I met Dave in university, and dating was different then.

I set my phone on the TV stand and continue cleaning, my thoughts whirring.

This feels *real* in a way that it didn't before. It's scary, but I don't want to completely hide from life, like I did for years. It's worth it, right?

Maybe I should make that one of my resolutions: *Don't hide from life and strong emotions*. I'm not sure it's a great resolution—it's rather vague—but it feels important.

Another important resolution: *Get a new job*.

———

To be honest, I'm rather glad that Cam is busy on Valentine's Day. The holiday has always seemed a touch too corny for me. Though maybe I came to feel that way because in high school, I got precisely zero Valentine-grams. It was better to say I didn't care than to be hurt.

Besides, what do you do on Valentine's Day when you only officially started dating the weekend before?

So, yeah, I don't mind.

The afternoon of February 14, Avery is cleaning the washroom and I'm taking a break after mopping when I get a text.

CAM: What do heiresses like to do for Valentine's Day?
ME: Drink bottles of Dom Pérignon from all our admirers.
ME: Or mop our kitchen floors. One of the two.

He sends a selection of emojis that I ought to find cheesy, but instead, they delight me.

———

On February 15, I take a while getting ready, beginning with a shower. I shave things that I usually only bother to shave in the summer, even if I don't intend to sleep with Cam tonight. I also wash my hair, managing not to absently pour too much shampoo. It took several days to adjust to my pixie cut. Though I'd gotten this haircut before, it had never actually stuck around, but now, my hair stays short and I love it.

At Avery's suggestion, I wear one of her dark blouses. It's lower-cut than anything I own, and it's certainly not something

I'd wear to the office, but I like the way it looks, and I also appreciate her help with my makeup.

Cam made reservations at a restaurant we've never been to together, and when I looked it up, it was obvious why: the grand opening was only three months ago. I order chicken with a pomegranate-walnut sauce, and we split an appetizer. When he tells me that he likes karaoke, I refrain from making any comments about what I've heard him sing in the past—or the Matchbox Twenty tribute band. He does, however, tell me about it during our post-dinner chai, and I force myself to look surprised, while on the inside, I add this to the collection of stuff I know about him that I'm supposed to know about him. Not to be confused with the stuff I know that he's not aware I know. I don't want him to think that I was stalking him, nor do I want to use my extra knowledge to convince him of our connection; I want the relationship to unfold naturally.

But, god, this is messy.

"Is something wrong?" he asks.

I school my face into a smile. I really am happy to be with him, on our second date—I yearned for one of these for so long, and now it's finally here. I'm on bench seating, a couple of colorful pillows behind me. There's a cozy warmth to this restaurant. It's a nice place for a date.

Except I used to be trapped in a time loop, and I can't tell you about it.

Or could I? I told him before, and he believed me.

But it's different now. I can no longer "prove" the time loop by predicting the future, and if he doesn't believe me, it's not like he'll forget overnight. Best to keep my mouth shut.

Still, it bothers me, our secret past sitting like a lump in my stomach.

I shake my head. "I was just thinking of all the things I have to do before the Lunar New Year."

"Will you see your family tomorrow night?"

I nod. "You?"

"Yeah. We'll go to my aunt's. It'll be weird, though, without my grandma. She passed away at the beginning of January."

"I'm so sorry, Cam," I say immediately.

His smile slips. "Lots of people lose all their grandparents before their midthirties. She lived a long life and witnessed a dizzying number of changes . . ."

"That doesn't mean you shouldn't be sad, and I know holidays can be tough. The first big holiday after someone dies—yes, I remember." I reach across the table and squeeze his hand.

"She wasn't at Christmas either," he says. "I went to see her the next day at the hospital. She was very sick. At the last Lunar New Year, she insisted I bring some of our beer so she could try it."

His grandma would have died just over a month ago, while I was living another June 20. Maybe that's why he didn't give me his number—it had something to do with his grief. He hadn't been in the mood to put himself out there, which I can understand.

"What did she think?" I ask.

"She didn't like it, but she said the can looked nice."

I laugh but sober quickly; I can tell he's preparing to say something serious.

"I got along better with her than my mom and dad." He looks down. "My parents favored my brother—his grades were always a little better than mine—and they weren't thrilled with the whole brewery thing, of course. I used to try to please them, but I've mostly managed to let it go. I'll never fully get their approval, and that's okay. I can live with it."

"Cam . . ."

"My grandma wasn't disappointed in me. It felt like she understood me better than anyone else in my family. I'm not sure why." He wipes his eyes and chuckles. "Sorry. This is a little heavy for a second date."

"No, no," I say quickly. "It's fine." He's never told me any of this before. I guess it wasn't something he felt the need to talk about on June 20. I'm glad he's opening up to me, even if I'm annoyed with his parents for not appreciating him.

I squeeze his hand, and he holds on for a moment before withdrawing.

"What about you?" he asks. "Do you have any grandparents left?"

"No, and I never knew my mother's parents. They weren't good people, so I was told, and she didn't talk to them anymore. When I was little, I didn't understand, but later, I trusted her judgment. My father's parents—we saw them regularly, and they lived with us for a while. The language barrier was a bit awkward, though. My dad was always playing translator because my grandparents weren't fluent in English."

Even then, he didn't translate everything. I think there were things he didn't fully understand himself. His Chinese isn't perfect; though it was his first language, he's more comfortable speaking English. As a child, there were years when he refused to speak Chinese. A few white kids at school had made fun of him, and the mother of a friend from Hong Kong had criticized how he spoke—she considered his Chinese low-class.

In addition to my dad's issues with the language, I suspect there was a little censoring going on too. Perhaps he didn't approve of everything his mom and dad wanted to say to us.

But I knew my paternal grandparents and loved them.

Most people in my family gravitated to the humanities, but

I was the one who'd rather write a math test than an essay, and my grandfather seemed more like me. He was quick with numbers. He wanted his children and grandchildren to get an education because he'd never had the chance himself.

"Where did your father grow up?" Cam asks.

"Here. My grandparents were from southern China. They left . . ." I make some vague gesture that's supposed to mean "Communist Revolution." The specifics of why they came to Canada were never discussed with me. I'm not sure how much my father even knows. "What about your family?" I know the answer to this question, but I ask it anyway.

"They left Taiwan in the eighties."

"Have you been?"

"A couple of times, but not in a while."

I look around and suddenly realize that there aren't many people left. The restaurant is supposed to close in five minutes.

"We should get the bill," I say.

This time, when he tries to pay, I let him.

Once again, we kiss before we get on the subway. The kiss is achingly familiar, and I wonder if it's familiar to him too. There's a part of me that thinks it must be, however foolish that seems, and I can't help longing for him to recall our past.

My feelings are a complicated mess of joy, sadness, and confusion.

A new year, a new start, is exactly what I need.

35

Noelle

I call my father while I'm waiting for the bus, but I don't mention my date with Cam. It's been so long since I dated someone, and I'm unsure of when I should bring it up. Once I consider him my "boyfriend," whenever that is? Once we've been seeing each other for a month? Three months? Only when I'm ready for everyone to meet?

I decide to wait at least a few weeks, in part because, even if I've been on numerous dates with Cam in the past, I don't know if I'll be able to make it last. And I can't casually mention a guy and expect the conversation to move on to another topic shortly thereafter; no, if I bring up something like that—with either of my parents—I need to be prepared for questions.

Although I don't say anything about Cam, I do ask, "Will Madison be there tomorrow?"

"Yes," Dad says.

"She's okay with me coming?"

"Yes, but please don't . . ." He sighs. It's not a video call, so I can't see him, but I imagine him rubbing a hand over his face. "Don't antagonize her. Don't ask too many questions."

"Don't ask too many questions?" I repeat. What on earth?

"Because anything you ask her . . . she'll be prepared for an attack."

"An *attack*?"

"About her life choices—and things that aren't actually choices."

What the hell happened between us? If only I could call the other version of myself in for questioning.

"Noelle," he says. "Certain things have always been easy for you. Following instructions. Finishing your homework on time. Getting out of bed in the morning. But many things that seem trivial to you . . . aren't simple for other people. Or they go through phases when they're not. You seem to think that if someone has a legitimate problem, as you like to call it, there will be a straightforward solution, but that isn't always the case."

This is the most my dad has lectured me as an adult, and I'm momentarily taken aback. But it provides some clues as to what might be going on.

My little sister is struggling with life. This isn't the first time; no, her mental health problems started in high school, and she's never managed to find a career that she can tolerate for long.

I cringe at the thought of what I might have said to her. How did I become so rigid? So lacking in compassion?

"When she moved back home . . ." Dad begins, and I try to pay attention to what he says next, but I'm stuck on that fact. She was living with her boyfriend. Did they break up?

And she wasn't at my parents' house when I visited last time, even though she apparently lives there now. Did she leave just because she knew I'd be coming over?

I blow out a breath. "Okay. I understand."

I'm still not sure exactly what I said to Madison, but at least I have some sense of what happened, and I understand her better now than I did before the loop.

As I board the bus, I consider some of the ways in which that bizarre experience has changed me. It's now easy for me to imagine that my sister has gone through something that I can't comprehend. Probably not as bizarre as a time loop—but I think about how I kept trying to solve that problem and got nowhere, and I'm better able to empathize.

I also recall my brief interaction with the healthcare system. I imagine doing that year after year, not just on a couple of June 20s, without success. It sounds frustrating and demoralizing.

—

Madison isn't downstairs when I arrive on Monday after work, but everyone else is already here. Dalton holds Lenora back from trying to scribble with a crayon on Cecil.

I pull the red envelopes out of my bag and give one to my niece. She doesn't fully understand what it is, but that's okay; her parents can save the ten-dollar bill for her. Cecil has zero interest in a red envelope, but I thought it was only right to give one to him too.

With infinite patience, Dalton explains over and over that you should only draw on paper, not on babies; Lenora tries to draw on her father instead. Eventually, she's redirected to the coffee table, where blank paper and crayons are set out for her. I sit on the floor next to her and help myself to a piece of cantaloupe from the fruit tray that my father has prepared.

"How's work?" Dalton asks, while simultaneously preventing all the fruit from being dumped on the floor by a toddler.

"It's fine." I stick with my standard response for now, but I'll tell my family once I start looking seriously for jobs. So far, I've just polished my résumé and done a little searching.

I hear some noise from the hallway, and a moment later, Madison appears. She's wearing jeans and a large sweater, and she looks like her typical self, to my relief. But then she glances around the room, and I swear her eyes narrow slightly when she notices me.

"Hey, Madison," I say.

She doesn't reply.

If she wants to ignore me today, that's fine—I'm just glad to see her. I think of the day we had dumplings together; I think of the fact that she was the first person I told about my strange reality who believed me.

It doesn't feel like the best time to try to apologize and make things right—I'd rather talk to her when it's just the two of us—but I'll do it soon.

As Lenora attempts to feed Cecil a slice of kiwi, I can't help wondering what their relationship will be like as they grow up.

———

The next day, I'm on the bus after work when I get a message from Cam.

> CAM: Happy new year! How was your family dinner?
> ME: Pretty good. Tired today though.
> CAM: Too much food?
> ME: of course
> CAM: So is it a bad time to ask if you want to eat some more?
> CAM: Maybe Saturday? My roommate's out of town and I thought you could come over for dinner. Or we could go out.

I've never been to Cam's apartment before, though he's been to mine.

It's nice that we don't have to rush to get everything done in one day; it feels like we have all the time in the world now. And he invited me over, which makes me suspect he has something other than food on his mind.

———

Saturday, I have a late lunch with Veronica. We meet at a congee restaurant, and she gives me a big hug. In some ways, as we reminisce about our university years, it feels like no time has passed.

Veronica, who's also Asian, has always been louder, brasher, and more chaotic than me. She's wearing a chunky necklace that I love but would never wear myself. To be honest, in different circumstances, we might not have become friends, but in our engineering discipline, there weren't a ton of women in our year, and she made a point of talking to me.

There were a few other classmates from university that I spoke to after graduation. However, they felt more like Dave's friends than mine, and I didn't try to stay in touch after the breakup. None of them reached out.

"What about you?" Veronica asks after updating me on her life, her voice carrying better in the crowded restaurant than mine does. "Are you at the same company?"

Veronica, naturally, isn't. She's just started her third job since graduation.

A part of me wants to ask if she knows a place that's hiring, but then it would feel like I texted her just to ask for career advice, and that's far from the truth. Instead, after confirming that yes, I'm still at Woods & Olson, I tell her that I've started seeing someone.

"Is this the first guy you've dated since Dave?" she asks.

"Yeah."

"Oh my god!" She slaps my arm. "Tell me everything. How did you meet?"

"He owns a brewery with a couple of friends. He was behind the bar in the taproom when I walked in. I didn't say much, but I returned the next week and flirted with him. I wrote my number on the bill."

Veronica's mouth drops open. "You, Noelle Tom, *flirted* with a bartender?" She's not saying it in a mean way. But she knows me, even if we haven't seen each other in a while.

"Uh, yeah." I don't, of course, mention all the practice I'd had.

"Can I see a picture?"

I haven't taken one, but I bring up the brewery's website and show her a photo.

"He's cuuute," she says, dragging it out in a way that offends my eardrums.

"So, yeah." I slip my phone into my purse. "That's what's new with me."

"When are you seeing him next?"

"Tonight. I'm going to his place. He's supposed to cook for me."

"Ooo-ooh."

I laugh. "Stop it."

She does not. She waggles her eyebrows, and I kinda like being teased by an old friend.

"Have you done it yet?" she asks.

"No," I say, and I feel like I'm rewriting history.

"But maybe tonight?" She shimmies in her seat.

"Veronica!"

"I'll take that as a yes."

I don't confirm, but I don't deny it either.

I've been thinking about it quite a bit. Our first time—but not actually our first time—seems like a good way to begin the year, though I still feel a bit mixed-up about the whole thing, the fact that he doesn't know the whole truth.

Veronica leans forward and drops her voice. "Is something wrong? You don't need to put out just because it's the third date and you're going to his place. *I* would, but that doesn't mean you have to. If you'd feel more comfortable—"

"No, no. It's not that." I eat some congee. "I want to. I'm just a bit nervous because . . ."

"It's been a while."

"Yeah."

She nods and pats my arm. "We should do this more often." I'm grateful for the change in topic.

"We should." I mean it. After my breakup, I retreated from the world, but I wish I hadn't. In a way, it was like I put my head in the sand and never took it back out.

I can't change what I did then, but going forward, I can do things differently. Though I doubt I will be as close to Veronica as I am to Avery, I still want her in my life.

It's exciting to be able to make plans for the future, now that I've gotten past June 20.

36

Cam

This isn't how today was supposed to go. I was supposed to get home by six o'clock, which would give me plenty of time to make the curry that I had planned.

Unfortunately, when you run a small business, there are always new problems that you never imagined, and you're the one who has to deal with them—especially since Justin is out of town this weekend, visiting his family.

By the time I get back to the apartment, it's after seven. I won't have time to cook. In fact, I only have three minutes to consider what kind of takeout we should order before Noelle's in the lobby, waiting to be buzzed in.

Punctual, as always.

Last-minute changes to plans don't usually bother me, but I'm a little annoyed that we won't be doing exactly what I told her we'd do. I put on some music and open the door as soon as she knocks.

"Welcome," I say with a bow.

I take her jacket. It's not the parka I've seen her wear before; it's an unseasonably warm day for February, so she's gone with something lighter. Underneath, she's wearing a sweater with little buttons down the front. I try not to think too much about those buttons as I hang up her jacket.

"There was a bit of an incident at Casa Cam," I say.

Her eyebrows draw together in concern.

"Nothing to worry about," I assure her. "A bear broke in and stole all my food, so we'll have to order something for dinner. It's on me, of course. My fault for not bear-proofing the apartment."

"That sounds serious to me," she says. "Bear invasions are no joke."

I beckon her into the kitchen. "I had to work late and didn't have time to cook. Would you like anything to drink while we figure out dinner?"

She declines alcohol, so I decide I won't drink either. Instead, we pore over the menus of nearby restaurants, eventually settling on some souvlaki meals from a Greek place. Then I give her the grand tour of the apartment, which really isn't all that grand; it was chosen mainly for its proximity to the brewery.

I try to see it through her eyes. Framed band posters on the walls, the same ones I've had for years—a record of who I used to be. A few nonfiction books on an end table—I forgot to put them back. The middle shelf of the bookcase, which is next to the TV, contains no books; instead, there's a row of beer bottles with cool labels.

I suspect Noelle's place is neater than mine, though it's not like I'm a complete slob, and I did make some effort to clean before the Lunar New Year began.

I gesture toward my bedroom without stepping inside. I admit I do hope we'll be making use of that later, but I have no expectations.

Once I've shown her around, I pour her some water, and she sips it daintily as we sit on the couch and wait for our dinner.

"Have you lived here for long?" she asks.

"A few years."

This is followed by a conversation about the extortionate rents in the city. It's an unsexy conversation, but when she leans over to put her glass on a coaster, her arm brushes mine, and I don't think it was an accident.

That's the thing about Noelle: she's a *deliberate* person, certainly more than I am. Even when she flirted with me in the taproom, it felt that way. Every time I see her, I can't help wanting to muss her up, just a little. I think it would be immensely satisfying.

When our food arrives—lamb for me, chicken for her—we eat at the small dining room table, and whenever some sauce clings to her lip, she immediately wipes it away with her paper napkin, not letting it linger.

I clean up, then ask if she wants dessert.

"The bear didn't eat whatever you have planned?" she asks.

"No, it didn't make it into the freezer, fortunately." With a flourish, I gesture to the ice cream selection. I couldn't cook the curry, but I can still do this. "I can make you a sundae. Which ice cream would you like?"

"Vanilla," she says, which is what I expected.

I might not have known Noelle for long, but I figured she'd be a fan of the classics, rather than, say, chocolate hazelnut brownie. Well, perhaps she'd have a scoop by itself, but not in a sundae. I'm pleased to have predicted her ice cream choice correctly.

"Okay," I say. "Now sit at the table and face the wall."

"Face the wall?"

"So you can be surprised by my creation."

She looks dubious, but she does as directed.

I set about making her sundae in a glass bowl. Two scoops of vanilla ice cream, fresh berries—very curious that the bear didn't eat those—a drizzle of chocolate sauce, a chocolate wafer roll, and chocolate sprinkles.

Then I make mine.

"Can I look now?" Noelle asks, just as I'm about to bring our bowls over.

Rather than speaking, I set down our sundaes, then gently spin her around.

"If you don't like it," I say, "you can switch with me." I point to my bowl, which is filled with chocolate hazelnut brownie ice cream and rainbow sprinkles and multiple broken wafer cookies.

"No, I think I prefer mine. Thank you."

She digs into her ice cream, and as I watch her slide a spoonful of vanilla ice cream, topped with chocolate sauce and a raspberry, into her mouth, I feel like I've seen her eat ice cream before.

Except I know I haven't. We've only had two dates before this, and I remember them well. There also wasn't any consumption of ice cream the times she came into the taproom.

How bizarre.

Setting that thought aside, I begin eating my own ice cream. It's better than plain vanilla, though I don't tell her that, even if it would be cute to see her scrunch up her nose.

Once we've finished dessert, I ask if she wants blueberry tea, and she says regular, nonalcoholic tea is fine with her, so I make a mug for each of us and we retire to the couch. As the tea cools, I pull her legs onto my lap. She releases the softest of gasps, and I'm acutely aware of the fact that we're inside. And we're not in public.

An Olivia Rodrigo song begins playing, and I ask if she wants to dance.

She shakes her head. "I'm not much of a dancer."

"All right, you can stay seated." I cup her ass and move her so she's straddling me. I sway to the music, and then I pull her closer and press my lips to hers.

She makes another of those delightful little gasps.

Kissing her, as always, feels strangely familiar, but no less exciting for it. The romantic part of my brain believes it's a good sign, a sign this is meant to be.

I set my hand on the top button of her sweater. As soon as she nods, I start fumbling with the button—and "fumbling" is the right word, but I do manage to undo it eventually. The next button goes slightly faster, and there's a fascinating hitch in her breathing when I reach the third one. Once it's been unfastened, I give up on the buttons for the time being and slide my hand under her sweater and bra; her nipple tightens beneath my hand. When her hips jerk against mine, I hiss out a breath as my erection settles between her thighs.

I really did mean to undo every single one of those buttons, but I decide that's too much effort. I pull the sweater over her head, followed by her bra.

The great thing about my roommate being away for the weekend? I can do this in the living room, though I do intend to move to the bedroom soon.

Before I can set my hands on her breasts, my shirt is tugged off, and I love that she's eager to remove my clothes. I grin dopily at her before I pull her naked chest against mine and plant my mouth on hers again.

"You feel so good," I murmur, and she responds by pressing herself more firmly against my cock.

Okay, that's it.

In one smooth motion—sort of—I stand up with her in my arms and walk us toward my bedroom. She laughs. As I set her on my bed and crawl up her body, I can't stop myself from smiling.

I fumble, once again, with the button on her jeans and slide down the zipper. I watch her expression as I slip my middle finger inside her. She goes taut, then relaxes into my touch with a groan.

Yeah, getting this woman undone is a gift.

She reaches into my pants and circles her hand around my erection, and now I'm the one groaning. In part because she's humping my hand; she's always put together in public, but now, she's half-naked and desperate for me, and I feel powerful.

"I need . . ." she begins.

I slide down her body, pulling her jeans and panties with me, and set my mouth between her legs as she squirms. Somehow, I already know what she likes—and this is confirmed when she grips my hair and comes against my lips in no time at all.

"Good?" I say smugly as I crawl up her body.

"Condom?"

I'm perfectly happy with that response.

I shed the rest of my clothes before reaching into my bedside table. It takes a lot longer than it should to find the box of condoms because she starts stroking my cock. Once I tear open the packet, she slides down and takes me in her mouth. I close my eyes and growl . . . and then I open them so I can see her suck on me.

"You have to stop that," I say.

"Why?" she asks saucily—a tone she'd never, ever deploy in public, but here, in my bed, it's different.

"Because . . ." It's too hard to find the words to finish that sentence, so I shuffle down the bed, away from her mouth, and roll on the condom.

She turns onto her back and spreads her legs wide.

I thought she'd be a little shyer in bed; I thought I'd have to coax her with compliments. Not, of course, that I would have tried to make her do anything she didn't want to, and not that I won't compliment her now anyway.

"You're so fucking gorgeous," I say, punctuating my words with a kiss.

Then I notch my cock at her entrance and slide inside.

Once I'm seated within her, I still, giving her a moment to get used to me, but when she presses her hips toward mine, I start moving.

"Yes," I breathe. "Yes."

Being inside her is pure joy and achingly familiar all at once.

I slow my pace so this isn't over too quickly and kiss her lips, swallowing her need for me, feeling like the luckiest guy in the world.

Why did she walk into my brewery?

I don't know, and I don't care.

I slip a hand under her ass and roll us over so she's on top. Her surprised laughter turns to a cry as I tug one of her nipples into my mouth, using the barest hint of teeth before soothing it with my tongue. I can tell she likes that, so I do it again, but with the other nipple.

She adjusts her position—to get friction on her clit, I think—and then her arms go limp. She collapses on top of me, and it only takes a few more strokes to find my own release.

And somehow, it feels like much more than the culmination of three dates.

———

Noelle has a dreamy, languid look on her face. She mumbles something about "before" that I don't quite catch.

"You want to stay the night?" I ask. Casually, trying not to betray just how much I want her to do so.

"I do," she says.

We're both lying on our sides, still naked. Distantly, I register that the music I put on before she arrived is still playing. I'll have to turn it off later.

But right now, I don't want to go anywhere.

As I trail my hand over her skin, I'm hit with the strangest sense of déjà vu, stronger than any I've ever felt in the past.

"Sometimes, when I'm with you," I say, "I have the feeling that I've done this before, in a previous life or something."

She stiffens. If I weren't touching her, I might not have noticed, but I can feel it.

I manage a self-deprecating chuckle. "That's not a line. I've never said it to anyone else. And yes, maybe that sounds like another line, but I'm serious."

"I know," she whispers. "What do you think it means?"

I shrug, as well as I can when I'm lying in bed. "Just that we work well together. We . . . fit." I open my mouth to say more, but I haven't known her all that long, and I think it's best to stop there, for now.

I mean, I really *shouldn't* feel anything more, yet a part of me feels like . . . I just know.

And yes, I might have felt that way a time or two before, but I was young and foolish then. Not that I'm a fount of wisdom now, but I'm not twenty-two anymore.

"Yeah," she says. "I think you're right."

There's an odd melancholy to her words, but then she rolls on top of me and kisses me, and I think I must have imagined it.

———

When I wake up in the middle of the night, Noelle isn't in my bed.

I pad out of the bedroom in my boxers. She's standing by the window in the living room, my bathrobe pulled around her.

"Hey," I say, wrapping her in my arms. "You couldn't sleep? Is something wrong?"

She steps away from me, and my heart drops. I probably screwed up, did something without thinking—

"It's my sister," she says, and that's not what I was expecting.

A little drowsy, it takes me a moment to form a response. "Is she unwell?"

"She won't speak to me, and I'm not entirely sure why. I don't know what I said, though I can guess."

It's strange that Noelle wouldn't remember, unless she was drunk or similar. But she doesn't seem like the sort to get that drunk.

"What do you think you said?" I ask.

"My sister has always had trouble sticking with something. She switched her major a bunch of times, and it took her an extra year to finish undergrad. She started a PhD in history but quit after a year. She waited tables as she tried to figure out what to do with her life . . . then quit. I forget what she did next. At some point, she'd planned to go into social work, but she got disillusioned with that. She tried doing some freelance stuff, but that didn't work out either. It feels like she can't quite figure out her life, and that stresses me out. I never switched my major. I've had the same job since I graduated."

"I haven't."

"I know, and that's fine. Not everyone needs to be like me, and she genuinely seems to struggle more with working full-time than I do. And it's not like she expects me to financially support her. I mean, I had to give her money once, four years ago, but stuff happens. I was happy to help. In fact, that's part of the reason I've always been careful about saving money: so I can help my family if they need it. I'm not very good at knowing how to help in other ways, but at least I can do that." She sighs. "But even though Madison doesn't try to make it my problem, I've always been bothered by how she jumps around. I must have snapped at her. It's unfair of me. After some things that have happened recently . . ."

She trails off and looks out the window. There's a look of anguish on her face, and I wish I could take it all away.

"I understand her much better than I did before," Noelle says at last. "I know she's doing the best she can. I want to make things right. I have to apologize to her."

I'm not sure what to say, but I appreciate that she wants to apologize. Not everyone will admit when they're wrong. My parents, for example, are rather terrible at it.

I nod and wrap my arms around her again. It's the middle of the night, and words aren't coming to me as quickly as usual.

She leans back against me. "I'm sorry. It's our first night together, and here I am, talking about my family problems."

"I don't mind," I say, and I mean it. But I think there's something she's not telling me. "Are you ready to come back to bed?"

"Yes."

I pick her up in my arms and carry her to my bedroom, just like I did earlier, in rather different circumstances. She giggles, and it's music to my ears. There's a rush of longing in my chest. I want to spend all the time that I can with her.

"Good night," I say, pressing a kiss to the back of her neck.

I can tell by her breathing that she falls asleep right away, but I don't.

On the night of Darrell's wedding, I wondered if I'd missed her, the woman for me. Now, I know I didn't—I just had to wait a little longer—but I still have to keep her.

37

Noelle

I wake up in Cam's bed, and it feels like a miracle, even though I've been out of the time loop for a while. Before I realize what I'm doing, I reach out and put a hand on his shoulder, as if testing that he's not a mirage.

Yep, he's real.

And last night was fantastic—and he'll actually remember it.

It puts a drowsy smile on my face, but then I feel a pang of guilt. He doesn't know that it wasn't really our first time together. That's what made me restless in the middle of the night, the reason I got out of bed at three thirty. But when he found me, I couldn't tell him the truth, so I told him about my sister instead.

Because how can I tell him that I was trapped in a time loop? And that while I was there, the rest of the world kept going . . . and I don't remember it. That's why I don't recall what I told my sister, rather than whatever he assumes.

It feels wrong to start a relationship with this kind of secret. I curse the time loop, but it's the reason we got together in the first place.

And yes, he believed me fairly easily in the loop, but I suspect that in our current reality it won't be the same, and if I'm unable to convince him . . .

I can't bear the thought of failure; I can't brush it off when he won't forget overnight. If I fail, I'll forever be the wacky date who claimed she'd been stuck in a single day, and I'm not sure he'd ever forget.

Memory can be both a blessing and a curse.

"Morning," Cam says, jolting me out of my thoughts. As his eyes drift open, he smiles and pulls me close.

How does this sweet man like me so much? He made a fucking ice cream sundae for me last night, and that doesn't require much in the way of skill, but it was thoughtful nonetheless.

He doesn't deserve all my complicated feelings right now, so I smile at him and say, "Good morning."

As he starts kissing my neck, that smile doesn't seem quite so forced.

"How are you doing?" he murmurs, as though he really does want to know the answer.

"Good," I say, and it's not a lie. I slept well after I returned to bed, and with his body around mine, my doubts seem far away. I marvel at having a real morning-after with him, so unlike the time I woke up alone and desperately tried to find his scent on my sheets.

He lifts his head and grins as though my well-being and happiness is the greatest news, then rests his forehead against mine.

Before I can say another word, he sets about making me feel even better.

When I step out of the shower, I pull on one of Cam's Leaside Brewing T-shirts and my underwear. Having anticipated that I might stay the night, I brought a fresh pair with me. Since his roommate won't be back for hours, I don't put on anything else.

Cam isn't around when I head into the kitchen, but coffee

is ready, and I pour myself a mug. He said he was going to get something for breakfast and would be back soon. I sit down at the table and inhale deeply. It smells even better than coffee usually does, almost like all my senses are heightened after last night.

He returns a few minutes later with a package that smells even more incredible.

"Are those cinnamon buns?" I ask.

"You bet." He leans down and kisses me, as though he just can't help it, as though it's his natural reaction to seeing me now. "The best ones in the city."

"That's a bold claim."

He sets one cinnamon bun on a plate for me. The aroma is heavenly, and the icing looks perfect—not too heavy or too light. I practically drool. This morning feels like pure decadence, and when I break off a piece and take a bite, that feeling is affirmed.

"Wow," I say.

"Right?" He pours himself some coffee, then adds milk and a tiny bit of sugar. "We served them at the brewery one weekend in January, as a pairing with our barrel-aged imperial stout. I'd open one for you now if it weren't ten in the morning."

"I've never really thought about beer and food pairings." Though I am intrigued.

"It's also good with chocolate. Or you can pour it over vanilla ice cream—a grown-up float."

"That all sounds amazing."

I lick some cream-cheese icing off my fingers. I can't care about being polite when I'm not wearing pants. Besides, it's fun to hold Cam's gaze as I slide my finger into my mouth. His eyes narrow, and his breathing hitches.

I'm a little different when I'm with him. Better at truly enjoying myself and living in the moment—especially now that my earlier guilt has dissipated after more sex, a shower, and a gooey cinnamon bun. I also feel like Cam never wants me to be anyone but who I am, and I realize, with a start, that this wasn't quite true of Dave.

I put those thoughts aside for later reflection.

"Have you done any other kinds of pairings?" I ask.

As I polish off my breakfast, Cam tells me about an event they did in November, a collaboration with a restaurant downtown. I wouldn't want to do his job, but I like hearing about it. All the care he puts into getting things right. It's fun to listen to people talk about what they love.

Once I wash the remnants of the cinnamon bun off my hands, I pour myself more coffee and return to my chair. I move it closer to his so I can rest my hand on his leg, feeling the need to touch him. I want all the leisurely Sunday mornings we can have together.

I remember one of the questions Cam asked me, the day I told him about the loop. *What's the very best thing you've eaten?* If someone asked me that now, I might choose that cinnamon bun. Yes, it was objectively a well-crafted baked good, but it's partly because of the association I'll now have: the breakfast that he picked out for our first morning-after.

I know I'll think of him whenever I smell fresh cinnamon buns.

38

Cam

I find myself whistling as I clean the kitchen and vacuum the apartment, even though vacuuming is my least favorite chore. It's not just because I had sex three times in the last twenty-four hours, though it had been a very long time since that happened. But spending so much time with Noelle Tom is just a lot of fun, and I can't help but be in a great mood afterward.

Noelle doesn't have what you'd call a bold personality. She's not the sort of person who commands attention the moment she walks into the room. In fact, I think she'd hate it if that happened. She's milder—but with a lot of depth.

And watching her enjoy herself is my new favorite thing.

When she goes out, she favors crisp dress shirts and nice sweaters, but the image of her with damp hair, wearing one of my T-shirts and enjoying a cinnamon bun at my kitchen table . . .

I don't know why that was so erotic, but it was. I love seeing her when she's relaxed. It felt like a treat, just for me.

And since it's my day off, I decide to have another treat in the afternoon. I open a can of the Junction—our imperial stout, named after the last dry neighborhood in Toronto—and enjoy it with some dark chocolate as I watch a movie. It's a good winter beer, as is the Retaliator Doppelbock, a collaboration we did with another brewery. They're both seasonal offerings.

By the time Justin gets home, the movie is almost over and I'm slightly tipsy. When a beer is over 10 percent ABV, a tall can is a good amount.

"How was it?" he asks. "Have a good night?"

"Couldn't make the curry, but yeah, it was fun."

The credits are starting, so I pick up my phone to see if she's texted. Justin knows exactly what I'm doing, and he rolls his eyes as he sits down on a recliner. I toss a pillow at him, careful to ensure there's no danger of it hitting my nearly empty snifter. I don't really care about his reaction, though. I'm in a great mood, and he can roll his eyes all he wants; it doesn't bother me.

"*Very* good, I see." He smirks. "When did she leave?"

"Around one."

"And you're ready to text her and say that you miss her?"

"Hm. Good idea."

I say that mainly to make him laugh—and it works—but I might as well message her. I do miss Noelle, even if we've only been apart for a few hours, and I wish I could watch another movie—this time, with her. There are so many things I haven't done with her yet that I'm looking forward to doing.

ME: When can I see you again? Tomorrow?
NOELLE: Sure!

I didn't expect her to actually agree to that—I thought she'd have a rule about being responsible on a Monday night—but I'm sure as hell not complaining.

"You are so gone for this woman." Justin shakes his head.

"Yeah, I am."

I think back to the night of Justin's first date with his boyfriend, the way he tried not to grin when he came home. Unlike him, I don't play it down, but my smile dims as I think of finding her in the middle of the night. Was something else up, other than what she told me?

Sometimes, I have the oddest feelings when it comes to Noelle. Like a prickle at the edge of my consciousness, but I can't quite get there.

Perhaps there's something she's not telling me, or perhaps it's just my imagination. We had a good morning together, after all.

I decide I won't worry about it.

———

On Monday, Noelle comes over after work while the curry—the one I was supposed to make on Saturday—is simmering on the stove. Justin won't be back for a few hours, so it's just the two of us.

"It smells great in here," she says as I hang up her jacket. "No bear incidents today?"

"Nope, nothing to interfere with my cooking plans."

I pull her in for a kiss, eventually dragging myself away to tend to the food.

"Dinner will be ready in a few minutes," I say. "Do you want a beer? We could split a can if you don't want to drink a lot, or I could make you some tea."

"Beer sounds good." She smiles at me, and for a moment, I think it really is too bad that we need to have dinner, even if I enjoy watching her eat.

Some people would serve an IPA with this meal, but I have a hunch she doesn't like those, so I select a crisp lager instead. It's not one of ours; it's from a different Toronto brewery.

"What's the difference between a lager and an ale?" she asks. "I know I read about it once, but I forget." She's blushing a little, and I have no idea why. When I don't immediately answer, she says, "I, uh, did some research about beer before we went on our first date."

"You wanted to impress me?"

"No! I mean . . . well, I just wanted to know more about you, that's all." She sips the lager. She's still blushing, and I take the glass out of her hand and kiss her again, because I can't seem to do otherwise.

———

After dinner, she insists on helping me clean up before we retreat to the bedroom, where I coax more moans out of her. While she did seem to enjoy my food, I think she enjoys this even more.

And after, I get to lazily hold her. I feel like my mouth is hurting from smiling, yet I don't want to stop. I trace the freckles on her cheeks with my finger, then dip my hand to her chest—she's still naked.

My phone rings on my bedside table.

"Crap," I mutter, looking at the screen. "It's my mom."

"You can get it," she says.

I do, but I'm determined to make it fast.

"Hello," I say into the phone.

Mom clucks her tongue. "Why did it take you so long to answer?"

"Sorry, I was cleaning up after dinner, and my phone was in the other room."

Beside me, Noelle covers her mouth, failing at hiding her laughter. She pulls the sheet over her chest, as though being naked while I'm on the phone is a faux pas.

"You're still coming for dinner on Saturday, yes?" Mom says. "I'm calling early in the week to make sure there won't be any *brewing emergencies* to prevent you from coming."

The thing about emergencies is that you don't know about them in advance, but . . .

"Don't worry, I'll be there."

"You know, it has been a long time since you brought a girlfriend to meet us. I was thinking about that the other day. Are you seeing anyone? Tell her to come on Saturday."

Good thing she can't see my face right now.

Since I intend to keep Noelle in my life for a long, long time, I say, "I am, but it's too early for you to meet her." I speak this as firmly as possible, but I know that won't matter.

Beside me, Noelle's eyes widen slightly.

Over the phone, my mom starts asking a barrage of questions. She doesn't give me a chance to answer before insisting that I bring Noelle to dinner, and I do my best to get her off the phone as quickly as possible, which isn't quite as quickly as I'd like.

Then I set my phone aside and take Noelle into my arms again.

"I can't believe you told her about me," she says.

"She asked if I was seeing someone, and I didn't want to lie. Is that okay? I promise, you don't need to meet my family anytime soon. I can deal with . . . that." I gesture to my phone to encompass all the questions I will receive in the near future. In fact, I half expect my phone to start ringing again a minute later, but fortunately, it doesn't.

"It's fine," she says, smiling to reassure me.

And before I can ask if she's sure, she pounces on me.

39

Noelle

Once again, I struggle to sleep at Cam's, but this time, I don't get out of bed when I'm still awake at three in the morning. Am I doomed to have insomnia whenever I stay over at his place?

Tonight was good. Great.

But in the middle of the night, the worries flood back. Why couldn't I have met Cam Huang in a normal way? Like on eHarmony or Hinge, or whatever dating sites exist these days. I don't even know, because before I ate those magical dumplings, I didn't date.

Dating seemed too risky. I just had to think of how I felt after Dave dumped me out of nowhere, how I sobbed on my kitchen floor and wished I could carve my heart out of my chest with a spoon—because surely that would be easier than dealing with my emotions. Yeah, dating hadn't held much appeal after that relationship ended.

But in the loop, the lack of consequences made me freer. I started to feel like I'd been missing out on so much. Banter over mini-golf. Laughter over poutine. Lips against lips. Skin against skin. I'd forgotten how *vivid* life can be.

Big emotions are part of it. You can't completely avoid them, even if you keep reliving the same day.

I've just never been good at such things.

And I'm not dealing with them well now. I watch Cam, his lips curling up like he's having a happy dream. I feel a strong urge to be honest, like how he was honest when his mom asked if he was seeing someone. You ought to be honest about the big things in a relationship.

But I'm also convinced that Cam, as easygoing and under-standing as he is, would not be understanding about the time loop now. I can't blame him; I sure as hell wouldn't be. If I hadn't had personal experience with it, and the person I'd re-cently started dating told me that they'd repeated the same day over a hundred times, I might ghost them.

The idea of him ghosting me is agonizing.

The thought of not being able to tell other people—like my parents or Veronica—the truth doesn't bother me as much. Ve-ronica never responded to my text in any version of June 20; there's no gap in our relationship. As for my parents, yes, I talked to them in the loop, even saw them a few times, but it doesn't fundamentally change anything.

Cam, however, is a whole different matter.

I scrub my hands over my face and try not to let out a frus-trated sigh.

Tell him. Take a risk, a part of me says.

But although the time loop made me more comfortable tak-ing risks, I'm not in the loop anymore, and this seems like a step too far.

When I was a kid, I watched a movie whose main message was that you should seize the day and face your fears. The main character upgraded to a first-class plane ticket when he couldn't afford it, and this was supposed to be a good thing? *Carpe diem* seemed like an excuse to defend bad choices.

There's nothing wrong with the fact that I've always been a

little cautious. I shouldn't feel the need to become a completely different person.

I won't tell Cam.

Except how can we stay together if I'm keeping a big secret from him, the secret of dozens of first dates? It seems like too much, and I know it will continue to eat away at me. I can't do that long-term. With my extra knowledge about him, I feel like I have the ability to manipulate him, perhaps even unintentionally, and I don't want that.

If only I'd bothered, back on a June 20 when I'd told him the truth, to ask what I should say once I got out of the time loop—what I should say to get him to believe me. But I didn't have the forethought to do that, since it was hard to think beyond June 20 when I wasn't sure I'd ever escape it.

I roll away from the man next to me with a sigh, my heart heavy. He's sleeping peacefully, while I'm doing anything but. Time is advancing normally now, but I feel trapped by what happened to me, trapped by the past.

I don't check the mail every day. I get most of my important stuff electronically, and I stopped checking it entirely when I was in the loop. But after work on Tuesday, I give my mailbox a look. To my surprise, there's a pale pink envelope. I don't pay attention to the return address, just tear it open as I wait for the elevator. My eyes widen.

Dave is getting *married*?

It's one of those invitations with the year written out in words, in an intricate font. I skim the details as I ride the elevator. *Why didn't I know about this?*

After unlocking the door to my apartment, I set down my bag and take a seat on the futon. Avery is in the shower. I read the invitation over and over, then pull out my phone and scroll to my text history with Dave. The last one is dated five months ago. I'm not sure why I didn't notice it earlier. Maybe because it's in between a couple of two-factor authentication messages?

> DAVE: I'm engaged, and we're getting married next year.
> DAVE: Just wanted you to hear it from me, instead of someone else.
> ME: Oh, congrats!!
> DAVE: No hard feelings, right?
> ME: Of course not! I'm happy for you.

As I read what I apparently wrote months ago, I wonder how this news affected me. It doesn't hurt now, not in the way it once would have. I'm more frustrated that I'm was caught off guard because I don't remember half of last year. Also, why the hell did he send me an invitation? Is it a huge wedding, and he's inviting everyone he's ever known? That seems unlikely, but he certainly didn't invite me because we remained friends. Ha! We did not.

Or perhaps he wants to rub it in my face? Show me that he's happy without me?

No, that doesn't sound like something Dave would do.

Yet I don't really know him. I mean, I did, once upon a time. Though after he dumped me—something I didn't see coming at all—I wondered how well I really knew him, and the knowledge I had has been tinged by my former heartbreak. And over time, it feels like he's become a blank space in my mind.

I'm over him now. Truly. I just feel rather annoyed.

Avery comes out of the washroom in a bathrobe, a towel wrapped around her hair. "Hey, you're home! How was your night?" She waggles her eyebrows, then frowns. "What's wrong?"

I hand over the invitation. "My ex invited me to his wedding. I didn't even know he was getting married because . . . you know."

She nods sympathetically. "That asshole."

I manage a watery chuckle and show her my texting history with Dave.

She reads it out loud. "'No hard feelings, right?' He just phrased it like that so you'd agree with him—it would be awkward to contradict him afterward."

Avery is frustrated with men in general at the moment, so maybe I shouldn't put much stock in her words, but still, it's good to hear her say that.

"I also . . ." I swallow. "Last night was good, but I don't know if I can stay with Cam." Saying it out loud . . . it makes me want to crumple. It makes the uncertainty of our future feel more real, but what does "real" even mean?

"Why not?"

I do my best to explain everything that's been going through my head, but I'm making a muddle of it. Avery keeps nodding as if I'm making perfect sense, even though I know I'm not, bless her.

"What do you think I should do?" I ask.

"Well, it *is* tricky," she says, "but . . ."

I wait for her to finish the sentence.

She doesn't.

———

That night, I find myself thinking about Dave. About what our actual relationship was like, not the end. For so long, I tried not to think about it because it was too painful—and now it's painful in a different way.

Sure, Dave wasn't like Joe. He wouldn't do things like, say, forget my birthday, and he did know how to do basic chores. But there were little digs.

Why are you wearing that?

Upon reflection, I don't think I performed femininity quite in the way he wanted. I'd forgotten all about it, but now, a dozen examples come to me.

Was that part of why he broke up with me? I'm not sure.

Memory is, indeed, a strange thing.

———

For the next couple of days, I lose myself in my routine.

I wake up at the same time every day. Have coffee. Eat breakfast. Avery and I have figured out how to coordinate our mornings by now, so we don't get in each other's way.

Then I go to the office. Check my email. Do my work. Wish I could swear at Lee again. Get annoyed at Tyler but seethe in silence.

At five thirty or so, I take the TTC home. Eat a quick dinner. Clean up. Watch TV while Avery looks for apartments.

My days aren't identical—there are slightly different tasks at work, for example—but I lose myself in the familiarity of them, which is, ironically enough, something I couldn't do when I was literally reliving the same day.

I wonder what I should do about Cam, but I'm unable to think about it too much without my heart aching, so I don't. It's like I'm putting my head in the sand once more, despite the resolution I made for the Lunar New Year.

I recall what he told me on the weekend. *Sometimes, when I'm with you, I have the feeling that I've done this before, in a previous life or something.*

I replay that in my mind, wondering if there's a way to retrieve those memories. Then I remind myself that I never figured out why the hell I got stuck in the loop—other than that it had something to do with the dumplings—and I have no idea how I got out of it. How on earth could I figure out how to unlock those memories?

At the same time, I wish I could unlock my memories of the seven months when the world kept moving without me, memories created by a different version of me. I make the occasional mistake or weird comment at work that I wouldn't make if only I could remember those damn months.

I don't know what kind of amnesia this is, but I hate it.

40

Cam

On Thursday, we're organizing some things in the back when Justin starts singing "Drunken Sailor," clearly expecting me to join in, as I always do.

Darrell, of course, isn't expected to sing. However, maybe if he'd sing right now, there would be less attention on the fact that I'm not.

Justin moves on to "The Last Saskatchewan Pirate," a blatant attempt to lift my spirits. I crack the tiniest of smiles, but that's it.

"Okay, time out." He uses his hands to make a T.

I roll my eyes and stand still, hands on hips, by Tank 2.

"What happened, man?" he asks. "You were in a good mood—a *great* mood, I might say—when I got home on Sunday, and everything seemed fine on Monday . . ."

Darrell looks at me in concern, and the fact that he's actually stopped doing the task at hand speaks volumes.

I pinch my brow. "Something's up with Noelle, but I don't know what."

We've barely texted in the past few days. She leaves me on read for hours. It wasn't like this before we slept together.

I think of the weekend, when I found her in the middle of

the night and she told me about her sister. Maybe that's part of it, though I'm convinced it's not everything.

I consider what I might have said or done to fuck this up, but I'm drawing a blank. I'm sure there are things I could have done a little differently—I'm not perfect—but even after so little time, I know Noelle, and this is odd.

Although . . .

I groan at the recollection.

"What is it?" Darrell asks.

"I said that when we're together, I sometimes feel as if I've done this before. Like, in a previous life."

Justin shakes his head. "That sounds like such a line."

"I know," I say. "But it's not."

"I know you don't usually say thing like that, yes."

"I just had this weird feeling. The words came out of me, and she stiffened afterward."

Darrell has a sympathetic *you're an idiot* expression on his face.

"Is it really that bad?" I ask. "She said she understood. I told her that I just meant . . . we fit together. Nothing more. Everything seemed okay, but maybe it wasn't."

Yeah, maybe she thinks I'm some kind of charming playboy, but that's not the case. It's not like I'm always trying to get a woman in my bed.

Justin slaps me on the back but doesn't say anything more.

"I also told my mom that I'm seeing someone," I say, "and Noelle, uh, heard that conversation. I didn't want to lie and treat her like a secret, but it might have been too much?" Though she said she was fine with it, perhaps she wasn't.

But I have a feeling it's something else.

———

Here's the thing about beer.

A lot of people who drink it—whether at a kegger in university, or in the backyard alone after a long week, or at a gastropub with friends—know little about how it's made. They might have some hazy notion of yeast and hops, but they don't talk about the mash and the wort and all the steps that go into creating it; they simply enjoy the finished product.

Yet there's so much behind that pint glass. So much science goes into it—and knowing it doesn't dim my enjoyment of beer but makes me appreciate it more.

Still, my knowledge about the beverage itself pales next to that of Darrell, who's the brewmaster. He has multiple books just about foam. Foam is serious business. And even he is forever learning.

We can't all be experts in everything, from archeology to zymurgy. There isn't enough time in the day, for starters.

But I do want to be an expert in Noelle Tom, and no matter how much I learn, there will always be more. I want to devote all the time that I can to her.

———

Later, when I'm in the office organizing some files, I take a break and text Noelle.

ME: Hey, just thinking about you.

Hm. Maybe that was too much, but it's honest.

ME: You want to do something on the weekend? We have an event on Saturday, so I'll have to work all day, but I'm free on Sunday. I'm yours, if you're interested.

I wonder what she's doing right now. I suppose she's at work, so I shouldn't expect her to answer right away, but when I haven't heard from her ten minutes later, I'm tempted to send her another text and ask what's wrong. I restrain myself from doing that, but I can't stop thinking about Noelle. I don't like feeling off-balance. I'm usually a pretty even-keeled guy, yet the thought that something's wrong between us makes me feel anything but.

Because, like I told her, I believe we fit together. We *belong*.

I know it's early to feel that way, but I can't help it.

I picture her sitting at her desk, brows lightly furrowed in concentration, in that cute way she has when she's studying a menu, for example. To be honest, I don't know exactly what engineers *do*—as in, their daily tasks—but she said something about a recycling plant. Of course, she was mostly naked at the time, so it's possible I misheard, but I don't think I did.

At last, I get an answer.

NOELLE: Yes, let's do something on Sunday. I'll make time to talk to you tomorrow too.

That makes me feel better temporarily, but then I worry it'll be some kind of serious talk. Though why would she have agreed to see me on Sunday if she plans to end things?

It's unlike me to worry so much, but I continue to wonder if something's wrong. I wish I could relive this past weekend—and Monday night—so I could fix it, whatever it is.

I also wish we'd started dating last year, so she had the chance to meet my grandmother, who could have told her about the bootlegged dramas on VHS that we used to watch together . . . and how they made me cry. The timing of everything seems horribly unfair.

When it comes to Noelle, I have endless wishes, yet I have no idea what she wishes when it comes to *me*. I thought I understood her, but now, I'm positive I'm missing something. I just can't figure it out.

41

Noelle

When I get home from work on Thursday, I change into some more comfortable clothes and debate what to have for dinner. I'm usually—as in, pre–June 20—the sort of person who plans most of her meals the weekend before, but I didn't do that last Sunday, and I haven't been in the mood to cook all week. So once again, I open up the cupboard where I keep my instant noodles. I needed to shop at two different Asian grocery stores to build this collection, and I've been going through it faster than usual.

"No," Avery says, suddenly appearing at my side as I start the kettle. "You're not having ramen again like a broke university student."

I'm offended. "These aren't the kind of instant noodles that broke students eat. They're expensive ones." Not too expensive, of course. Still cheap enough that my frugal self didn't feel guilty for buying them.

Avery rolls her eyes as she puts the noodles back into the cupboard. She knows where everything goes now.

"Hey!" I say. It's nice to feel outraged, to have an outlet for my negative emotions.

She gestures to the oven. "I'm making you dinner."

"You don't need to feed me."

"Noelle." She says my name sharply, and it makes me stand up straight. "You've let me stay here for weeks without complaint, even though I know you don't like having people in your space, and when I tried to pay you, you refused. The least you can do is let me cook you dinner every now and then."

"Fine," I grumble. Whatever she has in the oven does smell good.

Fifteen minutes later, we're seated at my small dining room table. We each have a plate of baked ziti and green salad. I start with the salad because the pasta looks a little hot.

Avery, rather than eating, says, "You've been mopey lately."

"Have not." I'm doing a good job of sounding like a sullen teenager today.

"What happened with Cam? Have you spoken to him since Tuesday morning?"

"We texted," I reply. "I agreed to see him on Sunday."

"You don't sound very excited, considering you're in love with him and all."

"But he's not in love with me! He doesn't know me well enough for that."

"Look," she says, "you're an honest person, unlike some people I know. I get why you feel the need to tell Cam about the things he doesn't remember. I think you should. Yes, it's scary, but you won't know until you try. Did the wedding invitation bother you that much?"

I pick up a forkful of pasta, watch the steam rise from it, and set it back down with a sigh. "I'm convinced it won't go well, and unlike before, I won't have a chance to try again. I don't like putting myself out there."

"Yet you did it anyway. Many, many times."

"Like I said, it was different then."

"But Cam believed you every time you told him, didn't he?"

That's true, but I don't have the "proof" that I had back then. It's just my word—and Avery's. Plus his slight feeling of déjà vu.

I look at the person sitting across from me. Before the time loop, most of my day-to-day interactions were surface-level conversations with coworkers. I'm not used to someone talking to me like this, not used to speaking so openly with a friend.

A friend who's here even when I try to retreat into myself. A friend who will continue to be here even if things don't go well with Cam.

I try a bite of baked ziti and nearly groan aloud at the cheesy goodness.

"This is amazing," I say.

"Hard to go wrong when you use that much cheese." She pauses. "I don't expect you to act exactly like you did when we were trying to figure out what was going on and spending money carelessly because it didn't matter. I know you're looking for a new job, but I think you could be more like time-loop Noelle in other ways too. Just a little."

"Yeah. Maybe." I look down at my plate. "Though before I talk to Cam, I need to talk to my sister." I've been preoccupied with my love life lately, but I'll feel better if I make some progress with Madison.

On Friday, I email my boss to say that I'm sick. Then I spend a few hours looking for a new job, and I even send out my first application.

But that wasn't the reason I pretended to be sick.

At 11 a.m., I take a deep breath and text Madison.

ME: hey. I know you don't want to talk to me, so I'm texting

you, and you can read it and reply . . . or not. But I
hope you'll at least read it.

ME: The truth is, I don't remember exactly what I said to
you and why we're not on speaking terms. I know it'll
be hard to believe, but I have amnesia. I lost 7 months
of my memory. While everyone else was living life like
usual, I was stuck in a time loop, repeating the same day.
I think it was caused by magical dumplings.

ME: I KNOW. But I'm serious.

ME: While I don't have memories of your reality, you also
don't have memories of mine. When I was inside the
loop, I told you what was happening to me, and you
believed me. We got along better than we had in a
while, maybe because having my world upended made
me see things differently. I think I understand you better
than I did before.

ME: I'm sorry that this is what it took, and I'm sorry we
haven't been close in a long time. I want to get to
know you as an adult, without being so judgmental
because you're not like me. It came from a place of
concern . . . you're my little sister, and I only wanted
the best for you, but I know that's not how it felt.
I promise to do better in the future.

ME: If you want to meet up today, I took the day off
work.

I've never sent so many texts in a row without a response, but
knowing how Madison feels about email, I think this is the way
to go. If she wants to call me, she can.

I wait, and I wait. After five minutes of staring at my screen,
I get a response.

MADISON: You're taking a day off????

I chuckle. I know that's difficult to believe, but is it really more unbelievable than everything else?

I don't dwell on that for long. The most important thing is that she's texting me back.

ME: yes, really.
MADISON: In this alternate reality, where did we meet up? Let's go there.

———

I've read through the menu twice, and I keep checking my phone, half expecting a message from Madison that says she's not coming or only just left home. She's ten minutes late now.

A moment later, she sits down across from me, and I nearly sigh in relief.

"This place doesn't seem familiar," she says.

Unlike Cam, she doesn't get déjà vu with me.

She peers at me curiously. "Why did we go here?"

"Because I was trying all the dumplings in Toronto in the hopes that—"

"You'd eat some that would get you out of the time loop?"

I nod. Then I smile at the face that's so much like my own before my gaze falls to one of the physical differences between us: the tattoo on her wrist. She also has a row of piercings on her right ear; I only have one in each ear.

"What did we get last time?" She doesn't wait for an answer, just insists we order exactly the same thing.

The server brings us our tea, and I place the order.

Once again, Madison looks at me curiously. She makes me tell her what happened, like she wants to hear it in person even after all the text messages. She's not skeptical about my story, though. Or, at least, she's significantly less skeptical than most people would be.

"Why do you believe me?" I ask.

By now, we have our dumplings. She reaches for one with her chopsticks, shrugging at the same time.

"Because you don't make shit up," she says simply. "Even when we were kids, you might 'lie by omission' on occasion, but that's it. So if you're telling me this, you have to be serious."

To my sister, the idea of me making up a fantastical story is so unbelievable that she simply . . . believes me. It's similar to what she said in the time loop.

I feel a smidge of annoyance that Madison sees me as so straight and narrow, but mostly, I'm relieved.

"Now tell me," I say, "what happened between us."

She sighs. "I cut back my hours because I couldn't handle it anymore. Not so much the kids, but the parents."

Madison, unlike me, has our father's gift for teaching. For the past year, she's been doing one-on-one tutoring and after-school English classes as her main source of income.

"You rarely disapprove of my choices out loud," she says. "But that time, when I told you—and when I told you that I was moving back home—you flipped out. Told me I was taking advantage of our parents, even though I'm contributing toward the bills. Even though living with your parents beyond graduation is common in many places. I don't know why it's so much easier for most people to have full-time jobs than it is for me, but it is. I get overwhelmed so easily. And my periods are getting worse too."

Madison has always had killer periods. She suspects she has endometriosis, but she's never gotten a diagnosis. The last time she attempted to get one, the doctor told her to lose weight. I don't think I fully appreciated how that affects other aspects of her life.

I was just so focused on wanting her to have security—that's what our grandparents hoped for when they moved to this country—but the way I treated her pushed her away, and you can't have total security in this world anyway. Things can change in an instant, despite your best intentions.

She mumbles something about productivity and value and late-stage capitalism, then says, "And Mom had a breakdown."

"Mom *what*?"

My sister chuckles. "You see? This is how I know you're not lying. You're a terrible actor. You wouldn't be able to fake that kind of reaction. Anyway, Mom was distraught that we weren't on speaking terms, and she felt like she'd failed us as a parent. I think it affected her so strongly because of her own trauma."

My parents aren't perfect, but when I was younger, stories from classmates would regularly make me thankful for the parents I had. I could appreciate how hard it had been for Mom to figure out motherhood when the examples in her own life had been horribly lacking. She did her best to make sure our childhood was nothing like her own.

Mom stopped talking to her parents before she married my father; they weren't at the wedding. She continued to have a relationship with her sister, though it was always fraught. As children, my aunt had been the favorite and my mother had been blamed for everything. It colored their relationship as adults.

"Shit," I say quietly.

Usually, when I hear stories about myself that I don't remember, they're told by my parents, about one childhood antic or another. Like the time I got a tricycle for my birthday and threw a tantrum because it wasn't allowed in bed with me. Or the time I tried to give my baby brother away to Santa Claus at the mall.

But these stories, they're about me as an adult. My sister isn't telling me things that I dimly remember but don't recall in detail; nope, I have no memory of them whatsoever.

"I shouldn't have said that," I tell her. "I don't remember, but it's entirely believable to me, and I'm sorry I was that person. I . . ." I don't know how to put into words everything that I feel. I look down at my dumplings, as if they could have the answer. Ha. Looking for answers in dumplings hasn't gotten me anywhere lately. I glance at the tattoo on her wrist instead. "I want you to be happy and healthy, and I admire that you've never been afraid to try new things."

She snorts. "I've always been afraid."

"Okay, yes—but you did it."

"Sometimes it's pure desperation."

I hesitate. "I never try anything, except when I was stuck in that stupid loop. Like, I asked my coworker what his salary is."

"And?"

"It's higher than mine, even though I figure we should make about the same. So the next day, I asked my boss for a raise."

Her eyes widen. I'm not insulted that she's surprised.

"How did that go?" she asks.

"Not well."

"Have you tried to change jobs, since coming back to the so-called real world?"

"I applied for something this morning, and I'm going to look harder this weekend."

I tell her a little more about what happened in the loop, and I tell her about Avery, but I don't mention Cam. I'll tell her eventually, no matter the outcome, but I don't feel like talking about that just yet.

"What about you?" I ask. "Tell me more, other than our fight. Christmas. Cecil."

"Right. You don't remember when he was born."

I shake my head. "I knew Mona was pregnant, though. Dalton told me in some of the iterations of June twentieth."

"She had a better pregnancy than last time, so that was good."

We spend the next half hour catching up.

"You know," Madison says, "it often felt as if you were in survival mode when you didn't need to be. Like our grandparents, at times."

I think she has a point, especially after my breakup. Parts of me shut down, and I forgot to start them back up . . . until recently. My little sister has always been very smart.

"But you're doing okay after your breakup?" I ask.

"Yeah." She chuckles. "Don't worry, that's the least of my problems." Her expression sobers. "The other thing that bothered me? I worried you thought I was like Uncle Matthew. Someone who constantly needed help because he made every terrible decision possible and took advantage of people's kindness."

Like my mother's relationship with her sister, my father's relationship with his brother was always complicated. It felt like my uncle didn't understand consequences.

"Don't worry, I know you're very different from him." I set my hand on top of hers.

Outside the restaurant, she gives me a long hug, and I smile against her hair. As I head to the TTC, I feel lighter than I did before, but then a faint aroma hits me, becoming stronger as I pass a bakery.

Cinnamon buns.

Not just any cinnamon buns. I swear they're exactly the same ones I had for breakfast the other day, and suddenly, I can barely get enough air into my lungs.

The first time I stumbled into Leaside Brewing, it was after eating dumplings at that same restaurant with Madison, which is also not far from Cam's, and I knew the cinnamon buns came from somewhere nearby. Still, the coincidence of that scent is nearly enough to knock me to the ground, and I ache at the memory of our morning together.

Once I put myself back together, I consider running to the brewery, but I don't. I'll see him on Sunday, as we planned.

———

It's weird being home at 4 p.m. on a Friday. Sometimes, I was home at this hour during the loop, but I've quickly acclimated to working again.

I feel better than I did before I left. I've patched things up with my sister, and having one person believe me makes me feel more hopeful about telling Cam, though it's a very different situation. Madison has known me her whole life; Cam, not so much. He has no reason to think I'm the kind of person who'd be incapable of lying about such things.

After starting a load of laundry—might as well get that out of the way—I work on my current crochet project: a scarf. My thoughts turn to what I should say to Cam and where I should suggest we meet on Sunday. Unlike with my sister, I don't want to do it in public. I'm sure Avery would be happy to make herself scarce for a few hours if I had him over, but I'll suggest his place when we speak tonight.

I hope we can figure it out, but if he doesn't believe me, I don't see how we can be together. I try not to obsess about that now, though, when there's nothing I can do.

Feeling like I've made enough progress in changing my life for one day, I settle down in front of the TV with a snack.

Cheese and crackers, even if I ate multiple days' worth of cheese in the ziti yesterday. Whatever. I'm going to enjoy myself. I've realized that's an important part of life, even if it's something I neglected for a long time.

However, a text message soon disrupts me.

AVERY: I found the dumpling stand

42

Noelle

In her subsequent texts, Avery gives me more details.

After work, she decided to go to a new food hall downtown for dinner. There are several permanent vendors, plus a rotating selection of guest vendors each weekend. The dumpling stand is one of the latter. She knows it's the same one because it has the same handwritten sign, even though the woman working there is younger. Her name is Judith, and apparently, the older woman was her mother, who has since passed away. Judith has agreed to speak to us—I'm not sure what Avery told her—once she closes up at 9 p.m.

Since I don't have to leave quite yet, I decide to finish the episode I'm on, but I'm distracted, and I have to pause and rewind twice because I miss something important.

Then, even though it's a little early, I head out.

The food hall is nothing like the mall food courts of yore, where you might eat frozen yogurt or fries during a break in your shopping trip. No, it's much swankier. Many of the seats look like fancy picnic tables, with polished wood tops and benches. Near the entrance, some men dig into delicious-smelling noodles and curries.

It takes me a minute to find Avery. She's seated in a corner, nursing a bubble tea, which is now mostly ice and tapioca pearls.

"Does this place close at nine?" I ask. "Will we have to leave in a couple of minutes?"

Avery shakes her head. "No, some of the vendors are open until eleven, so we can stay."

I get my own bubble tea and sit across from her. Though it's not quiet in here, I swear I can hear the beating of my own heart. I've wanted answers for months, and now I'll get them . . . maybe?

Avery and I don't talk much at first. I suspect she's also deep in thought about what we're going to find out, what it all means. Then I remember that I didn't tell her about my day.

"Lunch with my sister went well," I say.

She perks up. "Madison believed your story?"

"She did, and she caught me up on some of the stuff I don't remember."

Avery reaches across the table and squeezes my hand. "I'm glad it worked out."

We lapse into silence again, and I glance around at the clientele. There are a few businesspeople who look like they just left the office. A group of women in their thirties, dressed a little nicer than I am, a couple of them with cocktails in their hands. A middle-aged couple.

My gaze then wanders to the businesses. The ones with permanent storefronts sell things like Thai street food, Korean hot dogs, shawarma, and fried chicken. Next, my eyes land on the small cart in the corner. Like at the night market, I don't see a clear sign. A young couple is ordering, and as soon as they walk away, I look back at Avery, not wanting anyone to catch me staring.

But a few minutes later, I venture another look, and I see

a woman in an apron. As Avery said, she's definitely not the woman who served us dumplings on June 20.

I return my attention to my bubble tea and phone, scrolling through social media without really seeing anything. Wondering if what I'm about to learn will make it easier to tell Cam, easier for him to believe me.

Shit! Cam! I was supposed to call him.

ME: I'm so sorry. Something came up. I can't talk tonight,
     but I'll see you on Sunday? Your place?
CAM: Sounds good. Want to come over around 2?
ME: That works

Eventually, the woman from the dumpling stand approaches us.

"Come with me," she says by way of greeting. "Too loud here. I will show you where it's quieter." She waits for us to get up, and we follow her behind a pillar, where there's a small table with three chairs. She's right: it's quieter here. Better for a conversation.

I don't know where to start, especially since I'm not sure what Avery told her, but I introduce myself. "I'm Noelle."

"Judith." She nods, businesslike. "I don't understand why you want to talk to me. If you had some problems with the dumplings last year, I apologize. My mother . . . she was old, operating this business without a license, and I didn't even know about it until months later. She was living with my brother—why did it take so long for him to notice?"

"I'm sorry for your loss," I say, feeling a little awkward. Such insufficient words for the death of a parent.

Judith nods briskly again.

"The dumplings were very good," Avery says. "We didn't get

food poisoning, don't worry, but after we ate them, something strange happened to both of us. We started reliving June twentieth over and over."

Judith doesn't nod this time. No, she's very, very still. While there's an expression of surprise on her face, she doesn't seem nearly as surprised as she ought to be.

This, I think, is a good sign for us getting some kind of answer.

Avery continues, "We were stuck in a time loop. Every day, June twentieth repeated as though it had never happened before, and we were the only people who could remember the previous versions of it. When we returned to the night market, everything was exactly the same as before, except the dumpling cart wasn't there. There was no sign of your mother."

"How did you get out?" Judith asks.

"We don't know," I say. "One day, the loop just ended, and it was January. We don't have any memory of what happened in the regular world during those seven months, but apparently, we existed in it."

Judith nods once more, as if this all makes some kind of sense. "I did not know my mother was doing . . . that."

"She told us that the dumplings would give us what we needed most."

Judith is silent for a long time. Finally, she says, "My mother could manipulate time."

I let that sink in. I'd suspected something along those lines, but it's still a shock to actually hear it out loud.

"Have *you* been stuck in a time loop before?" I ask.

"No, but a few times when I was a kid, she'd let me relive a good day."

"Did the rest of the world move on without you? Did you lose the memory of a day that everyone else remembered?"

"Yes. She called it . . . ah, I don't know. Conservation of time, or something like that."

"Were these incidents caused by food?"

"I'm not sure how she made them happen." Judith sighs. "I'm sorry, I don't have all the answers you seek, but I believe your story, and I believe my mother was capable of causing it. Also, June twentieth was the summer solstice last year, yes? Her abilities were stronger around the winter and summer solstices—and a few other dates—but I'm not sure of the reason. She could make herself invisible then, which is why you couldn't find her again."

It had occurred to me before that it might have something to do with the summer solstice. But I didn't see how that would help me get out of the loop, so I didn't think about it much.

"Do you have any idea why she chose us?" Avery asks. "What did she think we'd need most, and how would a time loop have helped us get it?"

"Well, what *did* the time loop do for you?"

"It allowed me to take risks I never would have taken otherwise," I answer. "It also helped me better appreciate certain things in life, now that time is moving normally." I pause. "Was she aware that would happen? What could she have possibly known about me? She'd never seen me before."

"I'm not sure," Judith says, "but she did have very strong hunches, and sometimes she knew a lot about a person without being told. One time, she told me not to date a certain man, told me bad things would happen if I did, and then I found her hiding in the bushes on a date. He was furious, and he never called me again. I was mad at her, of course, but I thought she was just an interfering, overprotective mother who wouldn't let me live my own life." She chuckles wryly. "A year later, he was in the news. He would scam the women he dated and leave them with nothing. I doubt she had the power to know the details of your lives, but she probably had . . . a feeling."

I absorb her words. "You don't know much about her abilities?"

"No. When I was little, I thought it was something all mothers could do."

At first, that sounds unbelievable. But when I was a small child, my parents were like all-powerful beings, and it took a while to understand that they were fallible too. I suppose I can see it.

"What day was it when you came out of the loop?" Judith asks.

"January twenty-fourth. Was that the day she died?"

Judith shakes her head. "No. She died on the fifteenth."

So much for that theory.

"But January twenty-fourth was her wedding anniversary."

Huh. Interesting.

"I really don't know why everything happened as it did for you two," she says. "She got sick in the fall. Even before then . . . she was ninety. I don't think she could control her powers as well as she thought she could anymore, and maybe that's why you were there for so long. My best guess is that January twenty-fourth was a date she preset. A fail-safe, so you wouldn't repeat the same day forever."

I think of the strange night when I saw 3:01 a.m. on my alarm clock. Did Judith's mother try to get us out of the loop that night, but she wasn't strong enough to do it?

"I doubt she had any ill intent, even if it felt that way. I suspect she only wanted to help you." Judith pauses. "Though I've never been stuck in a time loop, my brother was. I don't know the details because he won't talk about it. But I do know that she was able to see what was going on in his reality, and she brought him out when she thought he'd done what he needed to do. He grudgingly admitted that it changed him for the better, but he still resented her for it, and when she came to Canada, he made her promise that she wouldn't do such things here. Until now, I thought she hadn't."

"So you really have no idea," Avery says, "how she was able to do it? You never asked? If my mother performed magic—"

"Of course I asked. She just wouldn't tell me, and I knew better than to keep pestering her with questions that might be related to her past." She looks away. "She lost both of her brothers before I was born. There was a lot of tragedy in her early life, and by not telling us much about it, she felt like she was protecting us. Though, based on something she said once, I believe her mother had similar powers. But if I can do magic, I have no knowledge of it, and no children of my own. I'm not sure how it's passed down."

Avery looks like she's struggling to understand the gaps in Judith's knowledge. However, it's not hard for me to wrap my mind around it, based on my experience with my own family. Sometimes, you know that half-truths are all the answers you'll ever get, and you hold on to them as tightly as you can. I never knew much about my grandparents' lives in China—and it wasn't because of the language barrier.

"Thank you for what you've told us," I say.

"I'm sorry I couldn't be of more help." Judith sounds warmer than she did at the beginning. "Now I know why Ma started this." She gestures at the cart. "It wasn't just about the food. Aiya! My brother was so mad when he found out."

"Why did you continue it?" I ask.

"I don't know. Something to do, I guess. I'm retired, no adult children to fuss over." She smiles at us. "A way of feeling connected to her once she was gone. It's only a few days a month."

I can understand using food like that. When I was a teen-ager, my grandfather taught me how to make beef and broccoli the way it was served at the restaurant where he'd worked. Two years later, he passed away, and there was something comforting in the fact that I could make it exactly like he had.

So I don't know Judith well, but I feel like I understand her on some level.

"Your lives, they turned out okay?" she asks. "You said you took extra risks?"

I'll never be a big risk-taker, and that's fine. But I'd become so afraid of taking any risk, so afraid that one small misstep would be catastrophic, and that wasn't healthy.

I think back to my conversation with Madison and what she said about our grandparents. For them, at one point in time, a small mistake may well have ended in catastrophe. It might have even been fatal—I don't know. They didn't share those memories with us. I'm lucky not to be in that situation, and I don't have to live like that, but perhaps some tiny part of me carried on the trauma of the generations before me.

In the loop, I was able to let go and try some things I wouldn't have otherwise done, and I'm happy with the results, except . . .

"I met a guy while I was in the time loop," I say. "Every day, my life reset, so he didn't remember me—aside from his strong feelings of déjà vu. After the loop, I found him again, and we're together, but . . . I have to tell him the truth. That I know him from another timeline. I'm not sure he'll believe me."

"Hm." Judith taps her chin. "Maybe Ma's goal had some-thing to do with romance." She looks at Avery.

"I broke up with my boyfriend," Avery says. "Over and over and over."

Judith turns back to me. "If he's right for you, he will believe you."

That's a starry-eyed notion, one that makes me want to snort, but I hold it in. It also seems at odds with the woman who sounded wary and businesslike at the beginning of our conversation.

But what do I know? I first spoke to her twenty minutes ago, and even people you've known for years can surprise you.

"I should head home," Judith says. "I'm not used to being on my feet for so much of the day. If there's something else you want to know, you can call me." She hands us each a business card. "Or come to one of the markets. They're listed on the website."

"Thank you," I say, though I have no intention of eating any of her dumplings, even if she claims to not have her mother's powers. There are countless other dumpling places in Toronto, and it's not worth the risk.

When I look over at Avery, I can tell she's having the same thought.

————

The next morning, I tell my temporary roommate that I'm cooking dinner for her.

"In exchange for the ziti," I say as we're drinking coffee together.

"You don't need to," Avery says. "Like I said, you're letting me stay for free."

"Just this once, don't worry. Besides, you're the one who found the dumpling cart. I owe you for that. I might never have come across it myself."

She huffs. "We're friends. We don't need to keep score."

True. I frown, worrying that I'm screwing up this friendship thanks to my lack of practice. I don't want to keep a running tally of who's done what for whom; I just want Avery to accept that I'll cook dinner tonight.

When she pats my hand, I take it as a yes.

"Joe's the last person who cooked for me," she says. "Except I got food poisoning because he cut raw meat on the same cutting board as the vegetables for the salad."

"Oh dear. I promise I won't do that."

That afternoon, I go to the grocery store and buy ingredients for a recipe I've never written down, never tried to change. At home, I begin preparations for my grandfather's beef and broccoli. It's the only way I'd eat broccoli as a kid—even when it was loaded down with cheese, I'd decline it. We struggled to communicate with each other at times, but food was a form of connection.

When everything is ready, I serve us each a bowl of jasmine rice, then put the wok in the center of the table and tell Avery to help herself.

"Wow," she says after a bite. "You've been eating ramen when you can cook like this?"

I shrug. I'm uncomfortable with the compliment because I feel like it should be for my grandfather, not me. "I don't want to cook like this every day."

"I get it. I don't want to cook dinner every day either. That's why I can't understand people who don't like leftovers. Leftovers are the best."

"Agreed."

We eat in contented silence for a few minutes before we discuss what to do for the evening, eventually deciding to get a trial of a different streaming service for variety. Avery insists on cleaning up afterward, and I retreat to the futon and look at my phone. There's a text from Madison, telling me that a restaurant we used to like when we were young has closed. I smile. Not because the restaurant has closed—that's a bummer—but because she's texting me.

I'm about to put my phone aside, when I get a text from Veronica.

> VERONICA: I know this is a long shot, but do you know anyone who's looking for a place to live? I have a friend who needs a roommate.

"Avery!" I say, and she turns off the tap. "I might have an apartment for you."

———

That night, I struggle to sleep. There's a lot on my mind. Things that have happened . . . and things that have yet to happen. Tomorrow, I'll tell Cam the truth, and I'm not sure how it'll go. I'm glad I have some explanation for him now, but it's not much of one. I don't like that I'll never have all the answers.

I eat leftovers for lunch, and then I head outside, my new scarf wrapped around my neck. It was nice to make something with my hands—and not have it disappear overnight.

Before going to Cam's, I make a stop at the Filipino restaurant that sold the halo-halo at the night market, and I buy some leche flan. I don't want to show up empty-handed, and the flan was delicious. I also can't help thinking of how strongly the scent of cinnamon rolls reminded me of our morning-after. Maybe seeing or tasting the flan will jog Cam's memory. Doubtful, but it's worth a shot.

I dawdle from the transit stop to his apartment. I normally have a determined, quick pace, but not today; I'm delaying the inevitable. The hard conversations.

When Cam opens the door for me, I smile. I can't help it. He looks happy to see me—as always—and his relaxed posture is a contrast to my own. As soon as I take off my winter boots, he kisses me, and the kiss makes me ache with longing.

I wonder if I'll ever get to do this again.

"You weren't replying to my texts early in the week," he says. "I worried that something was wrong, but I'm glad you're here now."

"Yes, well, about that." I pause. "I'm sorry about blowing you off on Friday. Something important came up, which is related to what I have to tell you. Would you mind making some coffee?"

Cam's mouth briefly turns down, but then he's smiling again. "Sure thing."

I'm delaying the inevitable just a little longer. Waiting until I have a mug to hide behind. I think of all the exchanges, all the touches, that have led us to this point, so many things he doesn't remember.

Once we're seated on the couch, leche flan on a plate in front of us, coffee on Leaside Brewing coasters, I say, "Okay. Here's what happened."

43

Cam

"We've actually met before this year," Noelle says. "I was stuck reliving the same day over and over, and in many of those repeats, I saw you."

"You're saying you were trapped in a time loop?"

"Yes."

I'm not sure what I expected her to tell me, but it certainly wasn't that. It usually takes quite a bit to shock me into silence, but she's succeeded.

"On June twentieth, I was working late, and I didn't feel like cooking, so I went to a night market that was happening at Mel Lastman—the one you mentioned when we walked by. I ate some dumplings, and the next day, it was June twentieth again. But nobody had any knowledge of the previous June twentieths except me—and Avery, as I later learned. She was also repeating the day."

"How do I fit into this?" I ask.

"The first time I saw you was at the market. I was having a bit of a breakdown, owing to the whole trapped-in-a-time-loop thing, and you asked if I was okay. Another time, I saw you at a bubble tea shop. You were kind and good-looking and I thought maybe if you kissed me, it would break the curse. Like a fairy tale."

Speechless, I gesture with my mug for her to continue.

"So I kept trying to talk to you," she says. "I knocked into you with my bubble tea for a cute-yet-disastrous meeting. We never kissed any of those times, but one day, I randomly walked into Leaside Brewing, and there you were. I flirted with you, and you gave me your number. We went on a date. Every morning, though, I had to start over because you didn't know who I was, although I did give you a strong sense of déjà vu, and on a few occasions, you got close to guessing my name. You could also remember minor things about me, like my preferred beer, even if you weren't aware of having met me before."

"And you were doing that all in the hopes that I'd kiss you and send you back to your usual reality."

"Well, at first, but I did like you, and even once I discovered that the kiss didn't work, I kept returning. We went on dozens of first dates." She describes many of them.

"Where was our first kiss?" I ask.

"Behind a building . . . near the market . . . after I had halo-halo." She points to the untouched leche flan on the coffee table.

I shut my eyes and try to picture the kiss. I can conjure up an image, but it's not a memory. Yet at the same time, there's something familiar about it.

"I'd sworn off relationships after what happened with my ex," Noelle says, "but I thought it was safe with you. You couldn't remember, so it couldn't be a real relationship. Except I began to care for you."

"Okay," I say slowly. "How did you get out of the loop?"

"One day, it just ended, and rather than being June twenty-first, it was January. The real world had moved on while I was in the loop, but I didn't remember it. It's like there was a different version of me that was living that life, and I can't access the memories." She pauses. "Anyway, I found you again, and we had a conversation similar to one we'd had many times before . . . and it was a novelty to have you actually remember my name."

"Did we ever sleep together when you were in the time loop?"

She nods. "I didn't want to do it until you knew about the loop—it felt dishonest—so I told you. The fact that I could 'predict the future,' such as it was, seemed to convince you."

"Then the next day—in your reality—I didn't remember that conversation. I didn't even remember your name."

"Correct."

I sip my coffee and run a hand through my hair. It's pretty obvious why Noelle was nervous about telling me this. It's one ridiculous story.

"Did you like living in the loop?" I ask.

"Ha. Well, I enjoyed the lack of consequences at times—money didn't matter—but I wanted to find a way out. I wanted to live real life again."

"You're sure the dumplings are what caused it?"

"Yes. We found the woman's daughter. She said her mom could manipulate time. We met with her on Friday—that's why I couldn't talk to you."

"Sorry, I, um, need a moment to process all this."

"That's fine. I know it's a lot." Noelle's trying to be calm, but her voice is shaking.

It all sounds impossible. I'd be a fool to believe it, wouldn't I? And yet . . .

I'm struggling to doubt the sincerity in her voice. Besides, why would she make up something like this? It must be true, yet how can it be?

But in some ways, it fits. There are the odd feelings I occasionally have with Noelle, for example, which is why I said that I feel like I knew in her in a previous life. Maybe my subconscious is aware of this alternate reality, even if I have no clear memory of it. She had a strange reaction when I said those words, and now, that slots into place.

"If you'd never been in the time loop," I say, "we never would have spoken to each other."

"That's right. Flirting isn't something that comes naturally to me, but in the loop, I had the opportunity to mess up without you remembering." She takes my hands in hers. "Trust me. I wouldn't be telling you this if it weren't true, and I didn't hallucinate it, I swear. You can talk to Avery. Ask her anything you want. She experienced the same thing as me—we both ate the dumplings that night."

I shake my head, and her expression—her whole body—drops.

"No, no," I rush to say. "It's not that I don't believe you. It's just . . . I don't think there's anything I need to ask your friend."

"You really believe me?" Her words are tentative, hopeful.

"Yeah." Even if I can't fully explain why. In my world, we might not have been on many dates, but I feel, in my bones, like I know her—and I know she wouldn't tell fantastical tales. I have to believe her, especially with those feelings of déjà vu.

And if I go back to last year, there were a few instances when I felt like I was missing someone without knowing who she was. That must have been Noelle, who would have been stuck in the loop then. Some other version of me would have already met her.

"Does it bother you," she says, "that you can't remember what I remember?"

"I wish it were otherwise, but I can manage."

"I wouldn't believe it if I hadn't lived through it myself, and I still don't like that I can't fully understand how it happened."

"That's okay. Some things you can't fully explain." Like when a note in a song makes you cry, and it feels like magic. "That's just the way it is. I think love often has some element of that."

While I didn't say that I love her, I still used the L-word. It's a scary word for some people. Perhaps I shouldn't even be thinking it when we've only been on a handful of dates. Except it's actually dozens of dates, even if I can't remember them, and maybe that explains my feelings.

"Anything else you want to tell me?" I set my coffee down and pull her into my lap. "Are you actually an alien princess from another galaxy?"

"You really believe me." It's not a question this time, but there's wonder in her voice.

I don't have any more words to assure her, so I tighten my arms around her and nuzzle the crook of her neck. More than ever before, it feels like a miracle that she's *here*. With me.

She's the one who begins the kiss, her lips moving urgently over mine.

"Cam," she says.

Nothing more, just my name, and I think of all the times I must have introduced myself to her, unaware that she already knew who I was. It's remarkable and ridiculous, all at the same time.

But the fact that I was still able to subconsciously recall things like her taste in beer? It's like some part of me was trying, desperately, to hold on to the memory of her.

Maybe because, as I thought before, we really do just fit.

I take her to the bedroom, where I strip off her shirt and her bra. I grin when I look down at her, topless below me.

"Cam," she says again, with more desperation in her voice.

She didn't have to tell me, but I'm glad she did. I know sharing something like that takes a lot of guts, and she might not see herself as gutsy, but I do.

I dip my head and take one of her nipples in my mouth, and then I begin working at the button and zipper on her jeans.

"I need you," she says.

"I know, sweetheart." As I say those words, I feel like I know it in more than the here and now; I know it deep in my bones.

When I slide two fingers inside her, she arches against me and moans. I tug off the rest of her clothes, and then I set my mouth on her. I've been dreaming of tasting her again since Monday; I've thought about it far too much when I was in my office at work.

I lift my head. "Did we ever have sex in my office?"

"Once. The first time."

I grin. "Was it hot?"

"Yeah. It was . . . ahhhh." She groans as I lick her clit.

I love that her noises aren't shy and tentative. I smile against her before I cup her ass and get down to business. Within a few minutes, she's gripping and twisting the sheets, and I know she's getting close.

I shuck off my clothes and roll on a condom. She pushes me onto my back, then lowers herself onto me in one smooth move. I hiss out a breath and look up at her, gorgeous and riding my cock.

I still don't understand how I could ever forget this. Even if it was some other version of me who experienced it, I don't understand.

But it doesn't matter. I have her now.

As she rides me, I try to tell her that. In the way I move with her. In the way I admire her in the late afternoon light, then pull her against me because I need to kiss her. I put everything I can into it, and she finds her release as her lips and chest are pressed against my own.

I don't have complete knowledge of what happened in our relationship, but being together like this . . . I feel complete.

Pressure builds inside me, and I whisper her name as I come.

"Noelle."

I know I'll never forget it again.

———

Afterward, we lounge in bed. I'm content to laze here with Noelle as long as I can . . . until my stomach grumbles.

"Oops." I look at the clock. "Just realized I forgot to eat lunch today." I was so focused on her impending visit that I couldn't think about food. "You hungry?"

"After all the work I just did? You bet." She's playful and relaxed, unlike when she arrived here an hour ago.

We take our time putting on our clothes, then venture to the kitchen. Justin isn't home yet—he'll be at the brewery for at least another hour.

"We still have the leche flan," she says, "but I'd like something with less sugar first."

"Dumplings?" Thanks to her story, dumplings are on my mind.

"Sure."

I open my freezer. I have the regular dumplings that I buy at the Asian supermarket, and I also have two bags of homemade dumplings from the fall. A part of me wants to save them, but if I wait much longer, they'll get freezer burn. Besides, it feels right to eat them with Noelle.

I take them out. "My grandma and I made these together, just before she got sick. This is the closest you can come to meeting her now—eating something she made." Despite my smile, my voice wavers, and Noelle squeezes my shoulder.

I put some oil in a frying pan and cook the dumplings until they start to brown. Then I add some water and cover the pan with a lid. As I wait for the dumplings to finish cooking, I wrap my arms around Noelle's waist.

"Did I ever make you dumplings before?" I ask.

She shakes her head.

"I apologize for my sins," I say with a laugh.

I can't seem to stop touching her. I lift the lid to check how the dumplings are doing, then replace it and return my hand to her waist. I went almost a week without being able to touch her, and that was far too long. I'm tempted to kiss her, but I'm worried if I do, I'll burn the dumplings, and that seems sacrilegious.

After all, I can't get more of these.

Eventually, the water has evaporated and they're the perfect color. I deposit six in a shallow bowl for Noelle, the other six in a bowl for me, then get out the condiments.

We sit down at the table where we ate takeout last weekend, and I smile at her before reaching for a dumpling with my chopsticks and blowing on it. Noelle hasn't picked up any of her dumplings yet, but she could be afraid of burning her mouth.

I bite into the dumpling, the juicy meat-and-vegetable filling taking me back to when I last ate dumplings with my grandmother, right after we made them. Back when I didn't know how little time she had left.

Then the strangest thing happens. There's a sharp pain in my head, and I choke down the rest of the dumpling and put a hand to my forehead.

"What's wrong?" Noelle's voice seems far away.

"I . . . I don't know."

It feels like someone's zapping my brain. I drop my chopsticks, squeeze my eyes shut, and curl up on the chair.

"Cam?"

And then, as quickly as it appeared, the pain vanishes. It's like the sun appearing after a storm, and I feel different.

"Holy shit," I whisper.

New memories fill my mind. Some of them are things Noelle told me about earlier, but now I know details that weren't in my imagination before.

The taste of her mouth after eating halo-halo.

The breeze on my face as we ate and drank on the patio at the izakaya.

Her ass on my desk at work as I knelt between her legs.

"What is it?" she asks. Not in my memory, but in person.

"Holy shit," I repeat, opening my eyes and looking at her. I can't piece together the order in which everything happened, but it's all gloriously vivid. "I *remember*."

44

Noelle

When Cam set the dumplings in front of me, I had a hunch. These dumplings were different from all the ones I'd eaten in my quest to figure out what happened on June 20 . . . and Cam's grandmother died in January. Judith's mother died in January. They could be the same person, right? His grandmother could be the one who served me dumplings at the night market, in what feels like another lifetime.

As I sat there, contemplating that possibility, Cam started eating, then doubled over.

"You remember," I repeat. "You remember all those iterations of June twentieth?"

"Well, I remember all the time I spent with you. I remember introducing myself to you over and over. I remember you spilling bubble tea on my crotch. I remember beating you at bowling and losing to you at mini-golf after I got my ball stuck under a kraken."

I cover my face with my hands.

"What's wrong?" he asks. "I'm glad I have all these memories of you."

"I'm glad too," I say. He already believed me, but if he had any doubts, this should erase them. Except . . . "Some of the early things . . . I only felt free to act the way I did because there were no consequences. I knew you wouldn't remember anything the next day, other than maybe a vague feeling. I can't believe I tried to trip myself in front of you. Spilled bubble tea on you."

He shrugs. "It's all good."

That's one of the things I learned about him in the loop: he's better at shrugging things off than I am.

"But what I don't understand," he says, "is why these dumplings did that. I—"

"Your grandmother was the woman at the market. Her daughter, Judith, must be your aunt." She said she didn't have kids, so she can't be his mother.

He nods slowly. "Yes, I have an Auntie Judith. But I didn't know that my grandmother ever sold dumplings. Or that she could manipulate time."

"Your aunt said her brother—your father, I assume?—made her promise not to do it when she came to Canada. Apparently, she put him in a time loop once."

Cam seems to have reached his threshold of shrugging things off. He sits there in silence, absorbing it all, and I take his hand and squeeze it. With his other hand, he picks up his chopsticks and eats another dumpling. This time, he doesn't look like he got a sudden migraine.

I can't help wondering what this all means.

"Your grandmother said the dumplings would give me what I needed most," I say. "I can't help thinking it was related to you."

"You think she was trying to set us up?" Cam asks.

"It *is* quite a coincidence that I fell in love with her grandson."

Did she somehow arrange it? I'm not sure I like the idea that this was fated to happen, thanks to some matchmaking grandma. When she went to the market, was she looking for someone for Cam?

"She didn't force us to fall in love," he says.

"Are you positive? What if something in the dumplings acted as a love potion?"

"I can't imagine it. We watched a drama together once, and she disapproved—strongly—when someone used what was essentially a love potion." He pauses. "Sure, maybe she had a feeling when she saw you, and by giving you the dumplings, you had the opportunity to encounter me over and over. But it was you who made the effort to talk to me, to ask if Canmore is where I was conceived."

"Oh my god." I cover my face with my hands. "You remember that now."

"Seems you asked it more than once." A smile plays on his lips.

"Because the first time we had that conversation, we started flirting. It was like following a script. It got me where I wanted to go."

Does that make sense? Does *anything* in the world make sense?

"It doesn't matter," he says. "However this happened"—he gestures between us—"I'm just glad that it did."

Same. Still, I'd like to have answers. I'd resigned myself, after the conversation with Judith, to never having all of them, but this is a curveball I wasn't expecting, and I'm struggling to wrap my mind around it.

"I guess your grandma had the ability to imbue food with some kind of magic. Could she choose when to put a person in a time loop versus make a person remember someone else's time loop? Could they have different effects, depending on who eats them?"

I'm just thinking aloud here. Cam doesn't have the answers, and I have to be comfortable with the unknown sometimes.

"I wonder what else I didn't know about her," he says faintly, "but I'm glad you met her, however briefly."

"Me too."

He pops another dumpling into his mouth, but I eye mine with suspicion.

"I'm worried that if I eat them, I'll get stuck in a time loop again," I say. "I don't want that to happen. I like the way things are going for me now."

On the other hand, maybe they'd make me remember, like they did for Cam. I might recall all the things that happened to the alternate version of me. It would certainly be easier if I remembered.

"I'll eat them if you don't want to," he says. "I don't think anything else is going to happen to me, beyond what already did."

"Maybe that would be best." I should take more risks in life, but this one doesn't feel right. "I do remember the taste of your grandma's dumplings, though. They were really good."

"I'll get something else for you as soon as I finish."

And that's how I end up eating a grilled cheese sandwich, followed by the flan.

Much as I want to spend the night at Cam's, I didn't bring all my work stuff, so it's easier for me to head home. Otherwise, I'd have to wake up super early tomorrow morning to return to my apartment.

When I arrive, Avery is furiously typing something on her laptop, but she pauses as soon as I enter. I think she started writing fanfic for her favorite series a few days ago.

"Based on how long you were out," she says, "I assume it went well? He believed you?"

"He did." I sit down beside her. "You'll never guess what happened next."

Avery's eyes widen as I explain what I discovered this afternoon.

"Wow," she says. "That's . . . wow. I don't blame you for not eating the dumplings. I wouldn't have either. I mean, in hindsight, maybe that time loop was what I needed, but it's certainly not an experience I need to repeat. I wouldn't take even a small risk of that happening." She pauses. "In less exciting news, I got an apartment."

"That's not less exciting news! It's a big deal. The place Veronica suggested?"

She nods. "I went to see it today, and it's really nice. Hard to know for sure how the roommate situation will work out until I actually live there, but I thought we clicked."

"That's good."

"You'll have your apartment to yourself again soon."

"I've been happy to have you here, but you must be looking forward to having your own room."

"I can't deny that," she says, "but thank you. For giving me a place to stay when I needed one, and for making the time loop much more bearable."

I chuckle. "I wonder if anyone has ever said that sentence before." But I need to acknowledge her words as something other than an unlikely phrase. "Having you there made it much better for me too. I didn't have any close friends before. I was rather isolated, and now . . ."

I can't quite find the words, so instead, I lean forward and give her a hug.

That evening, Avery and I finally get around to watching the historical drama whose trailer we saw countless times while in the loop.

Unfortunately, it wasn't worth the wait. Everything good about it was clearly crammed into the trailer. But we enjoy ourselves nonetheless, making comments through much of the two-hour movie and sharing microwaveable popcorn that will not reappear in my cupboard tomorrow.

As the credits start rolling, I turn to Avery. "I assume I was put into the loop to fix the interpersonal relationships in my life. To fall in love with Cam—because if it weren't for the loop, we wouldn't have met. Possibly to fix my relationship with my sister too. But I think part of it had to do with you. When I celebrated your birthday—candles and a gift—that was some kind of "proof" of our friendship. I'm not sure exactly what Cam's grandmother could see of our reality, but I'm convinced she tried to get us both out of the loop that night but failed because she was sick."

"And me . . . I was in the loop to break up with Joe and become your friend?"

"That's my guess." As I say the words, it feels right.

Neither of us had a close friend before . . . and now we do. I'm grateful that Avery is part of my life. Grateful Cam's grandmother could tell this would happen—I assume she had an intuition about the two of us.

On Monday, I find myself leaving the office at the same time as Fernando. I think back to that first June 20, when he commented on me working late again.

I rarely work beyond five thirty now. Yes, it happened once—there was an error that needed to be corrected at the last minute—but I've also been saying no to some of the extra tasks my boss tries to thrust upon me, while glaring at the back of his head when he's not looking.

The job market isn't ideal, but hopefully, I'll find something else in the next few months, and in the meantime, I can manage. When I'm not with my new boyfriend, I spend my free time crocheting and reading. I barely let myself relax for years, but that's changed now. I've let myself relax a little when it comes to spending too—I should be able to enjoy some of my money. Being obsessive about saving was causing me to stress unnecessarily over finances, and that stress was, in fact, what I'd hoped to avoid.

This morning, I packed an overnight bag, and I smile now as I head to Cam's apartment. While I'm waiting for the subway, a melody pops into my head. It takes a moment for me to figure out what it is: the sea shanty that Cam and Justin were singing the first time I walked into the taproom. I text him and ask if he remembers.

He does.

It's such a simple thing, sharing a memory with him—but I don't take it for granted.

Plus, it's not as simple as it might initially seem. The fact that we're very different people will color how we remember events and how we move through life. That's part of the splendor of this strange world in which we find ourselves.

Cam and I are going to make so many great memories together, and I can't wait.

I also know that the experiences we have, both good and bad, will change who we are. The placeholder versions of us—the Cam I met over and over on June 20, and the me who moved forward in time while I was in the loop—couldn't change, from what I can tell, because they weren't the real versions of us. I once wished that my ex hadn't changed and moved on, but there is beauty in being able to transform, even if it's frequently in ways that are small and not terribly dramatic.

Though I don't know exactly who Cam and I will become, after everything that has happened, I have faith that we can change and grow together.

45

Cam

Taste and smell are ancient senses. They're processed differently from sight and sound. When we smell something, signals go to the parts of the brain involved in memory and emotion. A subtle aroma in a beer, for example, may conjure up pleasant memories from years gone by, contributing to the drinker's enjoyment of it, even if they're not entirely conscious of that. I once had a cinnamon bun stout, and I know if I drank one of those now, it would evoke different memories than it did before.

Because of Noelle.

Neither of us will ever fully understand the details of what happened. How were there two different versions of me, one stuck on June 20 and one experiencing time as normal?

But it seems logical that food was a trigger, that taste and smell were involved.

The main thing that drew me to beer wasn't the science, but the way it could bring people together, yet that degree of mine did make some things easier to understand.

Looking back, I think I might have even felt something change in my brain before I tasted the dumpling, just from the aroma, but perhaps I'm mistaken. The whole experience was just so odd.

I wish my grandmother were here so I could ask her questions. I'm not convinced I'd get many answers, but I wish I could see her reaction to my words. Maybe get some hint of whether she knew Noelle was right for me from the moment she saw her. I assume that was the case, and my grandma simply did what she could to ensure we didn't miss each other.

Most of all, I just wish she were *here*.

Unfortunately, that's not something I can change, but her bringing Noelle and me together was a beautiful final gift. I will hold on to what I do have—and my many memories—with everything I can.

I remember sitting with my grandma at the hospital on Boxing Day. She was asleep much of the time, but at one point, she woke up and mumbled in a language I don't speak. Then she bounced between Mandarin and English. Her voice was weak, and I still couldn't follow what she was saying. It was something about time, and she was upset. I tried to soothe her, but I didn't know what to say.

I now assume her words were related to Noelle and the time loop, as were some things she said back in September.

I hope, somewhere, she knows that it all worked out in the end.

Epilogue

Noelle

It's June 20 again, and I'm throwing a birthday dinner for Avery. Just us and a few other friends, including Avery's new roommate and Veronica. I reserved a table for six at a new restaurant downtown, and we've also pooled some money to buy the designer purse that Avery has been coveting.

This is, sadly, a lot more than Joe ever did for her birthday.

After we finish our meals, the waitress brings out the cake that I arranged to be served: a salted caramel chocolate cake from a nearby bakery. On top of the cake is a single candle.

I admit I was a bit nervous as this date approached. It's not like I truly expect it to trigger another time loop, but still.

June 20 will always have extra significance for me.

Avery squeals with delight when she opens her gift. She thanks us effusively; I'm just glad my friend got a proper celebration in her honor without having to relive the day.

After leaving the restaurant, we all head to the subway together, and as Avery hugs me goodbye, she whispers, "Text me first thing in the morning, okay?"

"I will," I promise.

Because I've never lived this particular June 20 before, I'm unable to predict the downpour that happens as soon as I exit the bus near Cam's apartment. By the time I arrive at his place, I'm soaked.

"Oh no," Cam says as he opens the door. "I knew it was supposed to rain, but I didn't realize it would be that heavy."

"Neither did I." And I'm rather miserable about it, but I remind myself that once upon a time, rain on June 20 was a novelty.

Besides, I still get to spend the rest of the evening with Cam. We've been together for more than four months now. Well, it depends on how you count things, but that's what we tell everyone when they ask.

Giving your heart to someone is always a risk. It means being vulnerable—and I certainly felt very vulnerable when I told him the truth about what had happened to me.

But completely avoiding anything that makes you vulnerable? It's a difficult way to live. In fact, I'd say it makes you vulnerable in a different way, if that makes sense.

"Let's get you warmed up," Cam says.

He grabs the extra clothes I keep at his place while I head to the washroom and jump into the shower. Once I'm dressed, I walk to the kitchen, where I discover that he's made blueberry tea.

I smile as I reach for the mug. "How did you know this was just what I needed?"

"Lucky guess."

I sigh in contentment as I sip the spiked tea, and we head to the living room. When we sit down on the couch, he puts his arm around me. This casual intimacy is so natural now.

I met his parents last weekend. I felt like I didn't quite meet their standards, but I think that's just the way they are, and he assured me it went reasonably well. Tomorrow, he's going to meet my parents. I also called Judith to tell her what happened, and she laughed. She believes it's entirely possible her mother had a strong sense that Cam and I were right for each other, just from seeing me briefly. When I meet her one day with the rest of Cam's family, I'll pretend I'm meeting her for the first time—we have no plans to tell Cam's mom and dad exactly what happened.

At least, not yet, though Cam might ask his father about his time-loop experience one day. He thinks it explains the tension between his father and grandma. According to Judith, Cam's father also worried that his eldest son had inherited some of his grandmother's powers, especially when Cam strayed from what was expected of him. But Cam—so far as he knows—is unable to manipulate time. However, we do wonder if his déjà vu is evidence of some unusual abilities, though we figure it's more likely a sign of our connection.

Whether or not I'd told him the truth first, I assume he would have uncovered the memories when he ate the dumplings, but I can't say for sure. When I was stuck on June 20, I could try different things under the same conditions, like it was a science experiment, but I can't do that now, and that's okay.

I'm glad I told him, and I'm glad he believed me.

"Are you worried about Monday?" Cam asks.

"A little, but I still feel good about it."

Monday is when I start my new job, which I'm happy to say pays me more than the last one. Trying something new is scary; sticking with what I know is more comfortable. But despite my nerves, I'm excited. I hope this will be a better fit for me. After months of looking and a few interviews, I practically squealed when I got the offer.

I finish the blueberry tea and set the mug down on the coffee table. When I turn back to Cam, he has two wrapped gifts in his lap.

"Where did those come from?" I ask.

"Magic," he says, and I laugh.

I think there's more magic in the world than I believed before, but in this case, I suspect he had them stashed beside the couch and I just didn't notice.

"It's sort of our anniversary," he explains.

"That's true."

He hands me the larger package first. It's a bit bigger than my hand. I tear open the floral paper to reveal a framed photo of the two of us. I think it's one that Justin took last month.

"I thought you could put it on your desk when you start your new job," he says. "Or leave it at home. Whatever you like."

I run my finger over the edge of the frame and think about the fact that we have no photos of all the times we saw each other last June 20, even though we share the memories.

The next box contains a pair of delicate gold earrings.

"If you don't like them—"

"No, no, they're perfect," I assure him, and it's true: they're exactly my style. "I'll wear them on Monday. Thank you so much." I press my lips to his.

And then he takes me to bed and does some things that make it a very, *very* good June 20.

———

I wake up without an alarm at 7:55 a.m., Cam asleep next to me.

My phone is on the bedside table. When I pick it up, I see a text.

AVERY: It's June 21!
ME: It is!!

After all this time, I've finally made it to June 21, and I couldn't be happier.

There's something amazing about the passage of time. When I first saw my parents after the loop, I thought my mother's hair had more gray in it, and that tiny difference caused some complicated feelings. I don't like thinking about my parents' mortality, but I appreciate that each day is different from the one before it. The most ordinary experiences feel miraculous now.

I don't feel as if I'm held together by duct tape anymore. I know things won't always be easy; I know bad times will happen. But I have an inner strength I didn't have before, and with that—as well as the great people around me—I can make the most of my life.

I never expected a fairy tale of my own, but I feel like I got one nonetheless.

Acknowledgments

Thank you to my amazing editor, Lara Jones, for all of her hard work on this manuscript, and the rest of the team at Atria, including Camila Araujo and Holly Rice-Baturin (publicity), Aleaha Reneé and Morgan Pager (marketing), and Annette Pagliaro Sweeney (production editor). I'm also grateful for the support I've gotten from Cayley Brightside and others at Simon & Schuster Canada. And thank you to Marcos Chin for the wonderful cover.

My agent, Courtney Miller-Callihan, has been an incredible cheerleader for my writing, and I couldn't have done this without her.

Lily Chu read an early draft of the novel (when it was much more confusing!) and provided invaluable feedback.

My husband and my father might not always know the details of what I'm working on, but they are supportive nonetheless, and they both understand the magic of a good book.

I would also like to thank my author friends at Atria and Berkley, as well as Toronto Romance Writers. Having a great community is such a necessary part of publishing, and I appreciate all of you.